JADE ROOSTER

R. L. Crossland

ID0901770

Broadsides Press

Copyright © 2006 by R.L. Crossland

ISBN 0-9779977-0-7

All Rights Reserved

Dedication

To the officers and men
of the Republic of Korea Underwater Demolition Team,
and of the Naval Reconnaissance Unit,
especially those
who shared raw octopus,
canned rations,
and meckju with me

*****

Acknowledgements

The author gratefully acknowledges the assistance and cooperation in the writing of this work of: Paul Stillwell, editor of Naval History magazine, R. Richard Liverine, CAPT Terence McGinnis USNR (Ret.), CDR Byron King USNR and the staff of the Navy Historical Center at the Washington Navy Yard under the leadership of Dr. William S. Dudley.

They share in any of its perceived strengths. Any of its flaws are mine alone.

The Regular Navy Man

"He wears no wrist-watch, nor gold braid
Ter sparkle in the sun;
He don't parade with gay cockade
And posies in his gun;
He aint' no pretty sailor boy
So lovely, spick and span;
He wars a crust of real sea dust
The Regular Navy Man;
The perchin', lurchin'
Seagoing urchin
Regular Navy Man.

"He ain't at home in Sunday School,
Nor yet at social tea
And on the day he gets his pay
He's apt ter spend it free,
He ain't no temperance advocate,
He likes it now and then,
He's kinder rough and may be tough,
This Regular Navy Man,
The rarin', tearin',
Sometimes swearin',
Regular Navy Man."
-C. E. Graff

CHAPTER ONE

The whaleboat bobbed in the waves drifting sideways to the wind, nearly broaching. The currents of the West Sea, as it was known locally, carried it through the dissipating fog. Two two-fold blocks, constituting the lower half of the launching falls, were fouled in unraveling lengths of line and rattled across the flemished painters in the fore and stern sheets. No oars were visible; in fact no oarsmen were visible. The crutch clattered in the bottom boards. It was just a boat adrift, with its mother ship, a Yankee-built barque, nowhere to be seen. Painted on both sheerstrakes in pale green letters were the words "Jade Rooster." Hastily tied to the thwarts were four flat bamboo baskets.

Nestled in each bamboo basket lay a cleanly severed, and very pale, human head.

It was a statement. The originators had chosen to make their communication in a manner underscored with grisly menace. A message in a bottle would have been the time-honored method for casting a communication adrift—to be read by the random discoverer—but to the cold-hearted originators a more dramatic form of message had seemed more appropriate. It was after all "make see pidgin."

* * * * *

It was mid-morning in Yokosuka, and the harbor waters were as still as those of a millpond.

Sabatelli leaned against the landing's railing and watched the famous *Mikasa* glide to its mooring, spewing great billowing clouds of cindered smoke. Japanese coal was notoriously dirty and some years had passed since *Mikasa's* great victory over the Russian Fleet at the Straits of Tsushima.

Military ships always struck him as overturned anthills, with their swirling dots clad in white cotton. Those massed dots represented extremely large crews by merchant marine standards. Those dots now hustled to "man the rail" of the famed flagship of the Battle of Tsushima as it came into its homeport. As a ship entered port, manning the rail or standing at attention near the rail that rimmed a naval ship and on its yards, was a longstanding naval tradition.

Mikasa and its fleet had turned the world upside down. It had been centuries since a non-European navy had beaten a European navy. The steamboat was America's first world-class invention and now where that invention's ramifications would end, Providence only knew. As a merchant shipping agent, Sabatelli knew navies were necessary, but tried to keep a good distance from their power, arrogance, and asceticism. He didn't care for navies, nor did he care much for Spartan Yokosuka, an imperial Japanese naval base. He was glad his office was in the merchant shipping port of Yokohama which only a decade or so earlier had been exclusively a settlement for foreigners. For the word "ascetic" did not fit well with Sabatelli's view of what was good and important and he found Yokohama far more relaxed and more accommodating to civilized western diversions.

On the road that paralleled the harbor Sabatelli could see a few aristocratic Japanese women in broad belted robes and large paper and bamboo parasols, who were followed by their maids. Their skin was like porcelain and they carried their belongings in carefully folded silk scarves. The men bustled by in broad conical hats and sandals carrying baskets, buckets, and sacks—sometimes on poles. Sabatelli had a theory that the longer the robe or kimono, the higher the station of the wearer. Laborers wore little more than tights, sandals, and a shirt length robe-like jacket. Yokosuka was a gritty little naval base and fishing town and the short jackets were prevalent. The predominant colors were peach, plum, and faded crimson.

This morning his duties had necessitated the train ride down to Yokosuka. The presence of an American naval collier, which was moored on the other side of the harbor, and the expected arrival of the American naval attaché, had left him no choice.

In the distance two Japanese crews were racing double-banked pulling boats and doing so with a great deal of clamor, far too much clamor for a nationality known for its enigmatic reserve. Several Imperial Navy coxswains waited in their gigs on the lee side of the landing and provided commentary on the race in a language Sabatelli had only recently begun to study.

An American officer, rowed by two bluejackets in a single-banked wherry, tied off crisply at the base of the landing and the officer strode ashore full of purpose. "Bluejackets" they might have been called, but it was late summer and they were not wearing jackets at all. What they did wear was predominately white. One of the bluejackets lifted a white seabag, lashed hammock, and enameled bucket out of the wherry and placed it carefully on the dock. The other man began to row the wherry back out to the collier.

The sailor who remained waited and looked back out to sea thoughtfully. He wore dress whites with dark blue cuffs, a matching dark blue collar with three white stripes, and the now-popular Fighting Bob Evans whitehat. While rowing he had rolled up his cuffs to display embroidered Chinese dragons on the reverse and his cuffs remained unbuttoned.

He had extremely well developed forearms and had what was known as the bent-at-the-elbows look, which Sabatelli noted, was not as common as it had been among seafarers only decades earlier. Once sailors had been distinguished by the abnormal development of their arms, the product of daily handling of lines to raise and adjust sails. The advent of steam had made this singularity of physique less common, but navies still had sailing launches and cutters with lines to haul and sails to raise. Presumably he was from the collier. That meant the unending shifting of coal, which too developed the forearms.

If former President Roosevelt's physical fitness initiatives had not completely eliminated the sailor's hips (and those of his fellow sailors), naval fashion worldwide had eliminated the presence of pockets to hang on those hips. In this case, the style had a svelte and favorable effect.

He wore his rating badge on his right arm. Sabatelli vaguely remembered that this had significance. Most sailors had specialties, he remembered. The strictly seagoing naval ratings wore their badges on the right arm. The wearers of right arm ratings possessed skills that could not easily be converted into civilian professions ashore. Occasionally the right arm rates found their way into the merchant marine. Carpenters, sailmakers, machinists, painters, and ironworkers wore their badges on the left arm. They had learned skills that could earn them a living out of the Navy. They could find work ashore.

Farther down his sleeve the sailor wore a figure-eight knot. Sabatelli had a vague recollection this symbol had minor significance.

The bluejacket's hair was nearly black, his cheekbones high, his cheeks hollow, and his lean build set off the flared billow in his bellbottom trousers.

He reached down and pulled a corncob pipe out of his sock. As he did, Sabatelli noted a small tattoo of a rooster. A pig no doubt was tattooed on the other leg. Sailors were a superstitious lot and naval sailors had their own particular superstitions. Tattoos of a rooster and a pig, one on each leg, ensured a sailor would not drown.

The sailor took a puff on his corncob and said something to the gathered Japanese coxswains, which elicited a laugh. It was Japanese, a language very similar in its phonetics to Italian. Italian and his Italian heritage were one of the reasons Sabatelli had been posted in Yokohama. Unfortunately, Sabatelli was a third-generation Italian-American and spoke neither language. The other reason that Sabatelli was in Japan was that he had never been able to forego the comforts of society. This had led to his being caught in the wrong bedroom and formed the second reason he had been assigned to Yokohama.

Sabatelli wasn't sure whom he was meeting and settled in to wait.

* * * * *

A half-hour later, another American bluejacket with a thick neck, and a girth suggestive of heavy armor plate stormed down the dock with his hat in his hand and his neckerchief askew. He, too, wore his rating on the right arm.

"Goddam *Baltimore*, where's the goddam *Baltimore*."

There wasn't a protected cruiser in sight. He muttered, kicked pilings and threw his hat down onto the dock. His words were slurred and he had trouble keeping his balance.

The sailor with the corncob said something to a nearby Japanese coxswain.

The Baltimore turned and squared on the collier sailor. "Hey, you got something to say, auxili-airy-fairy, you say it in goddam American, not Nip sing-song."

The collier sailor said, "Chum, I said 'Rocks and Shoals: Missing ship after absence with or without leave,'" and spat. He did not back away or change his casual posture.

This seemed to enrage the Baltimore further. "Yeah, well what do you know. Gunboat Gunnarson got the skipper the gold football and the gold rooster – *Baltimore's* cock o' the station -- and Gunboat Gunnarson ain't gonna git no Summary."

Sabatelli started on hearing the words, "gold rooster" and pondered its significance.

"No how, no way, not from my skipper. Only thing I'll get is maybe a pat on the back. Naw, not Gunboat Gunnarson, he ain't gonna get no loss of pay, get no confinement, get no nothing. Won every smoker for the ship I ever fought in. Say, sleeve, maybe you're some kind of wiseacre? Lemme give ya a little pat, either end'll do."

This speech he said all in one breath, with the words accelerating to near flank speed at the end. The heavier man had raised both fists in the posture of a prizefighter in a rotogravure, and he'd begun to bob and weave unsteadily. A right cross for emphasis provided punctuation. The collier sailor skipped sideways to his seabag, hammock, and bucket without crossing his feet, and the punch swung wide.

The Baltimore feigned another right and then let loose with a very practiced left jab.

The corncob sailor must have anticipated the blow because he stepped inside, and grabbed material inside the Baltimore's cuff with his well-developed hand and forearm. He twisted, put the bottom of his brogan against the Baltimore's shin and seemed to sweep him up off his feet. The Baltimore seemed to levitate for just a moment, like the crest of a wave about to break.

The Baltimore, Gunnarson, fell on this side with a great exhalation. He looked confused and rose to one knee. He didn't know what had just happened, but sensed Asian treachery.

"Careful there, Gunner's Mate, these decks are some sloppery in the morning with the fog and dew and all," the corncob sailor said, tapping his pipe against the bollard and looking thoughtful. "Wicked sloppery and slicker than a smelt. Well, got to go, got an appointment."

"Next time, you smart-mouthed, coal shuttle Ferris wheel..." the thickset cruiser sailor snarled holding his side, "...you're gonna be spitting salvos of teeth."

"I guess," the lean sailor replied vaguely. "Hobson, Quartermaster Third, glad to make your acquaintance while your were staving around. By the by, we of the Ferris wheel rate," he looked down at the ship's wheel on his Quartermaster's rating badge, " . . .are who navigated your ship here."

He puffed a moment on his pipe thoughtfully. "Could be that we'd be the ones who left you here, too."

The rawboned Quartermaster standing over the burly Gunner's Mate called to mind the pictures of Remington, the popular magazine illustrator. The scene was awash with the same whites, blues, buffs, and craggy faces. Remington was known for painting Westerners. Why, wondered Sabatelli, had he overlooked Easterners?

An early Monday morning in Yokosuka could be every bit as entertaining as a morning in Yokohama, Sabatelli mused to himself, running his finger along the fabric of his vest lapel. Sabatelli looked landward to see two American officers, in high-collared white uniforms and white hats that looked like pills with visors, walking with noticeable determination in his direction. Ah, he thought, my meeting with naval management is at hand.

CHAPTER TWO

Sabatelli left his place at the rail and his path converged with the naval officers in the shade of an outdoor noodle shed in the lee of a red brick warehouse.

Sabatelli assessed the two officers. The taller one had a strong jaw and the chiseled features of a young Captain Sims, the well-known naval gunnery innovator. The shorter one wore thick glasses and the rumpled look of an old laundry bag. Sabatelli noticed he wore anchors everywhere the taller one wore stars.

"Lieutenant Commander Coley Wheelwright, USN" the taller one with the firm jaw said extending his hand.

"Lieutenant Junior Grade Stuyvesant Draper, Naval Militia," the other said without actually looking at Sabatelli.

"What's that last part mean?"

"Naval Militia? Kind of a new category, the states have been running naval militias, similar to army militias, for a couple decades now. The Navy Department has started to get involved. He's a part timer, but full time now, he's going to do something else in a year or two outside the Navy I guess, " interjected Wheelwright diplomatically. "I'm the Commanding Officer of the collier, *Pluto*. Draper works for the…er…Bureau of Navigation, at the Embassy in Tokio. Colliers are under the Bureau of Navigation, too."

"You going to help me?"

"The cargo was partially naval. That sailor over there is going to help you." He pointed to the sailor with the corncob pipe who was leaning against a warehouse across the street and stirring his noodles with chopsticks. Wheelwright waved him over.

Sabatelli recognized him from the landing. Mondays in Yokosuka could be both interesting and disappointing.

* * * * *

"This is Petty Officer Third Class Hobson of *Pluto.*"

The sailor stood at attention.

"Hobson? The Deuce, you say. Any relation to the Hobson, the Hobson of Havana Harbor?"

"Naw, that just a cut above zero slip knot never even blocked the channel...," the petty officer stated firmly after a moment of reflection.

The officers stiffened.

"Ah yes, but a very brave and resourceful slip knot. Mighty heroic," Hobson said, adjusting his neckerchief.

"Thank Providence, no relation 't all." He thought a moment more. "He was an officer, a naval constructor."

"Yes, not an officer of the line," Wheelwright felt compelled to interject. "A man of resource and imagination, but not an officer of the line."

"I need a man with an education, knowledge of navigation and seamanship, and a grasp of the local language," Sabatelli said petulantly. He had the feeling he'd been short-changed and had wasted both a day and a train trip. "I'm sure this very-well-turned-out young seaman is quite invaluable aboard ship, but I need someone who can make educated guesses about shipping, speak something more than bargirl Japanese, and can, to borrow from Kipling, maybe hustle the goddam East."

The Quartermaster studied the tips of his shoes. He was an item for barter at this point and, from a class standpoint, not really there.

"He's the best we can come up with on short notice," Draper said peering out of the side of his glasses and with a sort of a sigh. "This is, after all, only an insurance investigation, not a matter directly related to national interests or the defense of the Asiatic Fleet."

13

Sabatelli flattened down the edge of his vest and rubbed the inside of his high celluloid collar. He was what people might describe as "stout" and enjoyed the pleasures of a good meal and life ashore. In his youth, he had gone to sea, and there was still the hint of physical power in his deportment. He might enjoy life ashore, but he had learned his trade at sea.

Sabatelli was not to be consoled. He seemed to harden and grow in size, "Petty Officer, how many years have you got out here in the Far East, I mean, among Oriental people?"

"'Bout a score and five."

Two skylarking Japanese boys ran by in dark blue school uniforms that made them look like steamboat skippers. A group of schoolgirls of the same age in middy blouses hugged their schoolbooks and studiously ignored them.

Sabatelli examined him and then examined him again, confused. "You are near the required thirty years for retirement?"

Sabatelli knew the number of years for retirement because that was the point when many naval veterans crossed over into the merchant marine.

"Thirty years gets you three-quarters pay. Except you asked how long I'd been in Asia, among the people, that is. I'm only starting my second hitch in the Navy," he said, tapping the single hash mark on his sleeve.

"So I assume you were out here before you joined the Navy?"

"Born in Yokohama, grew up mostly here in Japan. Spent my last four years out here in Chosun."

"Korea," Draper clarified.

"Your parents foreign service?"

"Lay missionaries, er…sir."

There was a harshness to Hobson's delivery, a certain broadness to his 'A's' that reminded Sabatelli of a few Downeast merchant skippers he had known. It was difficult to believe the sailor had been raised this side of the dateline.

"Your parents approve of their son's service with the Department of War?" Sabatelli said skeptically.

"They don't say much of anything anymore. Passed on to their reward."

Sabatelli paused, and made a bobbing motion of his hand to dismiss his indelicacy.

"Well, how well d'you speak the lingo?"

"Pretty well, sir. Can't make out many Japanese kanji, like those what you might call pictograms over there . . ." He said pointing to some signs on the street, "but there are a lot of Japanese who can't do much better. I can read both their phonetic alphabets though. I can do about the same in Hangugo, Korean, and can read a few hundred hanja – that's their pictograms -- and can read their single phonetic alphabet. There is a whole pile of levels of Japanese; I can understand most o' them. Not elegant, understand, but I can understand 'em. Can't begin to speak them all."

"Hmmm. Alphabets and pictograms, well, better than I can do." Sabatelli observed with a sense of resolution. "I picked up a little in Hawaii, but spent most of my time there trying to learn Cantonese. Looking for a posting to Shanghai, but got sent to this backwater instead."

Draper, who had seemed nearly asleep, straightened up and looked at Wheelwright. "Not your first choice? Wouldn't call Yokohama a backwater, no. Wouldn't very well do that."

"You speak from a naval point of view. You know how it is; office politics was my undoing. Shanghai is a plum. Far more trade flows through Shanghai, for that matter more trade flows through Kobe and Osaka. Well, Hobson, we'll see. Maybe you will be some help. Your namesake has surely been a success."

Hobson looked at Lieutenant Commander Wheelwright. "Sir, how long am I ashore for?"

"Depends on the shipping agent here . . . until the job's done. He will cover the cost of your messing and berthing. There's a written understanding with the Paymaster."

Hobson's eyes took on the gleam of promise.

"In keeping with that of a day laborer," Sabatelli interjected, looking at Draper. Sabatelli did not trust Draper, sensing something was amiss. There should be more tension between a ramrod like Wheelwright and a ragbag like Draper. Sabatelli might have been wrapped in self-importance, but he had survived as a shipping agent using a well-developed sense of social dynamics. These men were naval. Why would a member of an organization that's purpose was to project an image and deter enemies, assume an appearance that was less than impressive, he thought?

"Not quite, sir. More in keeping with that of a translator, non-commissioned officer, and a skilled labor," Wheelwright said stiffly and rising. "It's a new Navy and the times are changing. The Great White Fleet sent that message. I'm surprised a man in your position isn't aware of that. Roosevelt may be out, but Congress wants its Navy to match our country's rightful position in the World. This new president, Wilson, will have difficulty slowing that momentum, if that's his inclination."

Sabatelli said no more and Draper and Wheelwright made their departure.

As they walked away Hobson called out, "Be back in time for the jade rooster, Mr. Wheelwright. Count on it, sir."

Wheelwright turned and smiled.

Sabatelli started again on hearing the words, "rooster." It was the second time that day. This time "rooster" was linked to "jade" and it disturbed him. He quickly excused himself, broke away from Hobson, crossed the alley, and pursued the officers.

* * * * *

"Gentlemen...Mr. Wheelwright, a word," Sabatelli whisked the executive officer to one side. "Dash it, really this is truly vexatious. The loss of this barque has been extremely costly. Lighthouse Insurance may not be able to cover it and survive as an underwriter. We made that clear to the Senator. I was given to understand that I was to be assisted by an officer."

Wheelwright made a mollifying gesture. "Petty officer. How many Japanese-speaking American naval officers do you think there are? I think Draper does -- probably not as well as Hobson -- and that's about it. And he's occupied at the Embassy in Tokio. Japan is a rising naval power. Knocked the Russians on their backsides. First time in several centuries an Asian country has ever taken on a European country and won. You may not have noticed, but relations between our countries haven't been that good since the Western States began legislating against Japanese immigration."

"Well this Hobson...is he really up to it?" Sabatelli said struggling to find an opening. "This comes on a string of losses to typhoons, and well, it has the greatest financial significance. We wouldn't have gone to Senator..."

At the second mention of "the Senator" Sabatelli noticed Wheelwright and Draper exchange glances and concluded that Congressional intercession had indeed brought results, albeit at a level below his expectations.

17

"He will surprise you. He has navigational skills and is one of *Pluto*'s back-up coxswains for the sailing cutter. His judgments are going to be as reliable as most junior naval officers on seafaring matters."

"Not really good enough. No, sir. May I assume Lightship Insurance has been given a low priority?"

"If you chose to look on it that way."

CHAPTER THREE

Sabatelli re-crossed the alley and returned to Hobson with a very evident look of exasperation. "Okay, Mr. Hobson, we'll talk on our way over to the train."

"Just plain Hobson, mind. You don't know much about the Navy, do you sir?"

"Merchant shipping, yes. The Navy, no. Just bits and pieces that have been useful to know in merchant shipping."

"Look, not so sure I enjoy feeling like the last gal picked at the dance, but Uncle Sam thinks I am what you rate right now, an' I am willing going along with it." Hobson had his kit up on his shoulder and seemed resigned. "Haven't been ashore much and well I kind of feel a need to use my Japanese and Korean every now and again. A chance to exercise my linguistories."

Sabatelli wondered how he would survive on his shipping agent's salary alone. He saw little future in the Lighthouse Insurance sideline. He could do ship surveys...

The streets were muddy and coolies with carts were everywhere. Imperial Navy sailors swaggered individually or marched by in groups. Shop girls giggled behind their hands. Women in kimonos of russets, faded reds, and peaches reminded Hobson that fall was approaching and his blues were still on *Pluto*.

"So who went and lost something? Something insured and of naval interest."

Sabatelli smiled. Hobson was quick enough. "Well, not much naval interest from what I can see. The Royster Line is who has lost something and that something is the barque, *Jade Rooster*. *Jade Rooster* is overdue and may be lost. She set out from California for Yokohama,

Shanghai, and back. She never showed up in Yokohama. One of her boats was salvaged by a British mailship off Tsushima."

"Wrong end of the Japanese Islands, for that series of port visits."

"Here's what they found in the boat. The second mate on the mailship was an amateur photographer. They found four heads in four bamboo baskets. Here's a picture of the lifeboat and of each of the heads."

Hobson studied the pictures. Four heads, three Caucasian and one Asian. Hard to guess their ages. One was bald; several had mustaches or beards. Their eyes were closed. He wondered if that was the way they were found or the photographer had done that. The baskets were to protect the heads. Was that out of compassion or so they would survive to be identified?

"Well the heads aren't on pikes outside the town gate. This is all 'make see pidgin.' Do we know who these fellows were? Where are the their chums?"

What a luxury to be asking others batteries of questions which did not require cut-and-dried answers, Hobson mused. Questions whose answers did not need to start with either "yes," "no," or "no, excuse." Perhaps that wasn't really accurate. He asked his shipmates on *Pluto* questions by the score, but the answers had been lighthearted and of no consequence. He had always been able to generate questions. More questions than anyone ever wanted to answer.

"What's 'make see pidgin'?" Sabatelli asked.

"Pidgin means business. It's Chinese, I believe. Pidgin English is sufficient English to conduct business. "Make see" in pidgin is putting on a show or demonstration. This is demonstration business; it is a demonstration of something. Sometimes people refer to 'make see pidgin' as maintaining "face".

"Where are the rest? We don't know yet. We have a crew list and passenger manifest. The Imperial Japanese Navy says they have picked up the crew of an American sailing ship northeast of Tsushima, adrift in small boats. A torpedo boat destroyer will be bringing them into Yokohama this afternoon. They decided to bring them to Yokohama instead of Sasebo since there was a greater European presence. Also, it will be easier to wash their hands of the crew and the whole situation. It has a bad odor."

"Outbound cargo?"

"Whale products loaded in Hawaii, U. S. manufacturing equipment, and supplies for the Asiatic Fleet."

"Whale products? I thought whale oil had gone the way of the stovepipe hat. What did you expect the return cargo might be?"

"Ceramics from China and silks, jute, and tea, from Yokohama."

"Y'know exactly what naval supplies?"

"The bill of lading says sugar, condensed milk, nutmeg, and alcohol. A few sundries, shoes, shoe polish, brass polish, and chemicals for Navy painters to mix paint"

"What kind of alcohol?"

"I can't say."

"Seems all they needed were eggs and hot water for a Man-o'-War cocktail," Hobson chuckled and then flickered the boat photograph. "It's all worth money to someone. No one deadheads cargo on a Pacific crossing, I suspect. What a waste."

"The loss of life?"

"Well, sure, that's a waste, too. But more wasteful than that, you can see whoever did it probably weren't a sailor. See this . . ."Hobson pointed to the blocks in the bow and stern of the boat. " . . . They cut a fall. No sailor's a mind to do that. There would have been two blocks and connecting line at either end of this boat when it was up in the davits — with the line most likely spliced into the becket of one block in each tackle. Someone deliberately cut through each fall. All they needed to lower the boat was to let run the falls. Instead, someone cut them like Alexander the Great and that infernal knot of his."

Hobson thought of his missionary father who had taught him about Alexander the Great and a great many things that did not have much use in his present situation. For the life of him, he could not remember the name of that knot and he knew dozens of them. His father had been a well-read, self-educated man. Hobson had several books stuffed in his seabag. Hobson's fondness for books was considered eccentric, but Asiatic Fleet sailors had a reputation for eccentricity. When Hobson said the tackle, it had sounded more like "take-ul."

"Four severed heads, that's got more theatrics than a medicine show. Two severed tackles, that was out of haste, jus' gawmed ignorance. A tackle has value, can save a lot of work, and once reeved, is designed to be used over and over again. Depending on the number of folds in a block, one man can lift a ton with block and tackle, no steam needed. Cutting rope needlessly is near sacrilege at sea. Cutting spliced line is eternal damnation. No, whoever did this had little respect for that barque's thrift and little concern for her future. No seaman did this and another thing . . ."

Sabatelli nodded, nothing more.

"They were at sea when this happened."

Sabatelli looked again at the picture. He was becoming irritated with this young crackerjack. He was an experienced shipping agent and knew every part of the business of seafaring. He couldn't argue, but he had not drawn these conclusions himself. "Now, what makes you say that?"

"See that rowlock crutch and that single steering oar? There's no rudder about. Whaleboats like this use a rudder in port and a steering oar and rowlock crutch at sea. She was fitted out to be lowered at sea."

"That's according to naval discipline."

"That's abiding common practice and good seamanship and commonsense. I was a sailor before I ever set foot on a naval ship. One other thing, one of the heads is Asian."

"Yes, I noticed that myself."

"He's got a Western haircut and clean shaven and he has gray, nearly white hair."

"What's that mean?"

"Don't know yet. Except for in Japan, one of the privileges of age in most of the Far East is to grow a beard. This fellow seems to have gone totally Western. He may or may not be Japanese."

"Hobson, you mentioned a jade rooster, before to Mr. Wheelwright. Do you know this barque?"

"No, we were talking about a different jade rooster. There are different Navy sports trophies for rowing. Different trophies for different sports, depending on crew size. Gold for the big ships, silver for smaller crews, and then bronze for the smallest. A football for football, crossed broadswords for fencing, a banner for baseball, a model cutter for sailing. Rowing's always the top team event and it's always been a rooster Navy-wide. Well, this one's kind of special and it's jade. We want it bad aboard *Pluto*. Colliers are dirty ships and they spread dirt to others. In the Navy cleanliness is set well above godliness. We get a lot of resentment, not much respect. We are, what my dad would have called, 'a pariah.'

"Well, anyway this trophy's a little different. Asiatic, I guess. Special to *Pluto*."

"Ah yes, a competition. Anything else, my young crackerjack?" Sabatelli concluded, resigned to his bad bargain. Rooster tattoos, rooster trophies, rooster barques…his head was swimming.

"Well, yes. Why are you and me doin' this? Sure you have to figure out what to tell the insurance company, but shouldn't there be some sort of constable or sheriff or policeman or Pinkerton or someone do this?"

"Ah, but there isn't. At least, at this point, there isn't. It is a United States vessel, but we are beyond the waters of any individual state, so state authorities are unconcerned and there aren't many federal officials out here who will actively get involved in a criminal investigation. Often the nearest country disposes of those matters related to the incident, whatever they may be. Right now we don't even know where the barque is or who took her. Someone is going to have to get angry before any country is going to get actively involved here. We need to find something to make someone, or rather some country, angry enough to take an interest. Or we have to find a nice business resolution of some kind.

Hobson wondered what he meant by a business resolution.

"In any event, that's not what I am interested in. It is my business to salvage as much of the barque and its cargo as I can to defray the cost of the claim that is going to be made to its owners and the owners of the cargo. Of course, for you, it's different. Your charge is 'to protect U. S. seaborne commerce from all enemies foreign and domestic.'"

"Well, your insurance company is taking some strange steps to locate a mess of whale oil, odd hardware, and Navy geedunks." Hobson smiled and looked thoughtful. "Can't see for the life of me why the Navy's even involved in this, but I'll take on a little shore leave from time to time. I think the cost of messing and berthing for Quartermaster Third Hobson is going to be more than you had thought, but still a bargain."

CHAPTER FOUR

The unlikely pair continued on to the railway station that was nestled in the midst of a warren of small booths and eateries poised to serve the weary rail traveler. As they waited for the train, a young woman and her maid floated to the platform. She wore a hat like a helmet with a veil, but her face could be seen and it was heavily powdered. Her kimono, obi, and coat were very elaborate and clearly very expensive. She acted as if Hobson and Sabatelli weren't there.

"Meiko," Hobson whispered and maneuvered to stand back to back with her at a reasonable distance. There was no one else at their end of the platform.

Hobson began talking in Japanese and the woman let out a short yelp. She twirled and looked all around her, but could not seem to tell where the voice was coming from. She chattered with her maid who gestured toward the sailor whose back was to them both. Then the young woman began to talk, turning her back to him, opening her fan and fluttering it rapidly. To Sabatelli, it was like a conversation between ventriloquists. The voices were there, but no one could tell where they were coming from. There was occasional laughter and the words were rapid and intense.

At no time did they ever face each other.

Eventually the train came and the woman, her attendant, Sabatelli, and Hobson boarded without acknowledging each other's existence.

*****

"What was that all about?" Sabatelli asked as they took a compartment.

"Mental drill. A drill. 'A sailor ashore must be in the constant state of vigilance' is the gist of the Landing Party Manual."

"Yes, yes, and who was she?"

"A meiko, an apprentice geisha."

"A prostitute?"

"Not really -- American misconception -- but not a fancy Victorian lady either. She's an entertainer in a profession where getting romantically involved has become sort of a tradition. She's just a youngster. Some of the best-known geishas are old enough to be your mother. She's something like our stage actresses who are always scandalously in love with someone or other. Like Lily Langtry."

Hobson continued, "She's from an okiya in Tokio. An okiya is a sort of geisha stable. She leads a very stylized life with its glory and comforts, but not like you'd wish on someone you liked. "

"So what were you saying to her?"

"Flirting, word games. I told her it seemed terrible for a such a bright flower as she to be consumed by a huffing dark beast of a locomotive."

"Her response?"

"She said, 'Bright flowers had been submitting to beasts from the beginning of time. The future of mankind demanded it.'"

"Yet, you never looked at her and she never looked at you."

"It would have been unseemly. I am a foreign barbarian, and a low caste swabbie to boot."

*****

The train meandered through the rice paddies pursued by a sinuous dragon of smoke. Sabatelli noted it was narrower and smaller than American trains. Everything here was on 7/8's scale. The train puffed and rumbled over stone bridges, and passed the Buddhist temples until the skyline suddenly changed. It was Yokohama, what Sabatelli often thought of as Japan in Western Dress. Hobson pulled out his corncob and somewhere behind them his smoke and the trains intertwined.

*****

To Hobson, the ryokan was a luxury. Hobson hadn't had a room of his own in five years and a room in a little Japanese inn, a ryokan, just inside Yokohama's newly enlarged borders was something approaching paradise. On *Pluto* he slung his hammock with dozens of others every night and took it down every morning. Absent was the orchestra of snores, coughs, moans, sighs, and wheezes. No one muttered or cried out in the night. In good weather on warm evenings, he might put a caulking mat down and sleep on deck. His futon was sort of like a caulking mat, but the quilt was far nicer, and the tatami mats had more give to them than haze gray steel. On *Pluto*, he washed out of a bucket. Here in the ryokan, he could walk to the end of the hall and reserve the ofuro, the hot bath, for a half-hour and use more water than he was allowed in a fortnight on *Pluto*. The ofuro was like a giant's oak bucket, a hogshead with no tumblehome that was about a yard in diameter. He had taken rooms ashore before, but they had always been shared with shipmates, bargirls . . .

Sabatelli had given him a set of the photographs. He studied them and tried to read character into their frozen startled expressions without success. He wondered if he should have said something about the flat bamboo baskets. No, he wasn't sure, and would not say anything until he had figured where all this was leading. That double interwoven blue reed along the edge seemed so familiar… Yet five years of naval service had taught him circumspection. Until he had some sense of why the men were killed, he would hold back. "Don't win one tiny candyass battle, and lose the whole goddam war," Phipps was always saying. Phipps, a first class petty officer on *Pluto*, was the source of countless, colorful maxims and descriptions. Gems like, "Seniority among ensigns is like virtue among hookers -- ain't none... Cold as a brass brassiere... Walking around like he had a busted rudder, totally useless..." Sometimes they contradicted each other, often they were funny, and occasionally they were useful. Phipps looked like five miles of bad road and was as ugly as a tarbucket – to apply his own expressions, but he was always thinking and trying to discern useful patterns in the naval experience.

Sabatelli would be impressed if he suggested where the baskets had come from, but who would gain and who would suffer? What if he was wrong? It would be better to be sure.

The fourth head looked Korean. That bothered Hobson, too. Trouble was you could never be one hundred percent sure. There were Japanese who could only be Japanese and there were Koreans who could only be Korean. Then there was an overlap of about 25% who could be either. The Koreans had overrun Japan several centuries back and some had settled. Now that Japan had Korea under its thumb, the situation was going to get even more confusing. The Koreans were being forced to learn Japanese and some were taking Japanese names to get along and before long no one would know who was who. Maybe he was just losing his touch.

His first tour of duty had taught him that the Navy went out of its way to make things direct and clear. That he had concluded within the first month of his first cruise. It had to do with the Navy's mission as the last option of what Mr. Wheeler called "diplomacy." It was the Navy's job to apply destructive force with heavy floating equipment. The best way to bring diverse men together and moving in one direction was to keep things simple, straightforward, and clear. In no other way that he could think of could a large group of men remain focused in one direction and be capable of responding quickly in war.

On the other hand, the Orient, it seemed, made things indirect and unclear -- even when those things did not have to be -- and somehow the element of time carried less importance here than elsewhere. It had to do with the Orient's overriding theme of harmony. A little confusion and a little indirectness allowed the wiggle room to avoid disharmony. Confrontation and accusations of error or wrongdoing, were disharmonious, and very un-Oriental.

Cultures in conflict, so far, seemed to be the strand interwoven through his personal lifeline. For some reason or other, he understood the points of conflict between East and West better than most. If a Third Class Quartermaster buried deep in the bilges of the naval organization could be useful -- useful at all -- it was probably where he could be most useful.

* * * * *

The Imperial Japanese Navy brought the survivors to the Naval Hospital at Yokohama. Sabatelli made sure to be there as soon as they walked down the brow of the Japanese torpedo boat destroyer onto Shinko Pier. Hobson studied the torpedo boat destroyer with keen professional interest.

The survivors were sunburned and many were hatless, coatless, and some shoeless, confirming that they had left *Jade Rooster* in a great hurry. Across the fantail was an overturned whaleboat much like the one in Sabatelli's photograph. Several U. S. Navy hospital corpsmen and a naval doctor were there to meet them with motorcars rigged to take a

29

reclining passenger behind the driver. They were calling these vehicles "ambulances."

Sabatelli and Hobson hailed a ginricksha and wended their way through a maze of brick warehouses. Waiting in the hospital, Sabatelli and Hobson decided on the three or four survivors they would interview first after talking to the senior doctor. The first mate, MacLeod, was on the second floor and Reeves, the supercargo, was waiting to be examined down the hall. Among the passengers, Mr. Atticaris was nowhere to be seen, and the Korean couple, the Kims had already left.

*****

The naval hospital was a study in white. Everything had been cleaned and inspected and then cleaned and inspected again. Its designers had studied the modern treatises on sanitation and determined that if cleanliness were next to godliness, then polished brass and simplicity must be, too. Nine out of every ten deaths in the last war had been attributed to disease. The Navy, a combative organization, sought to engage all enemies.

MacLeod stayed aloof. This was a naval hospital and he did not hold the same authority here, nor command the same degree of respect that he might expect on a merchant deck. Then too, he'd lost his ship. Merchant officers' careers were built on reputations for competence and luck. Luck meant a lot in the Trans-Pacific trade. In this instance, his luck had run out.

Several inches over six feet, he was massive and tanned with red muttonchop whiskers. Each hand was the size of tinned ham. His nose was flat with an undecided curve. There was a belligerent air to the way he carried himself. There was little doubt he had risen to first mate with

30

a bullying style of leadership. Hobson had heard the stories of merchant bucko mates, hard captains, and hell ships. The Navy had its own variations on these themes.

"Captain," Sabatelli whipped a small flask from his vest pocket. MacLeod probably did have a master's certificate, many mates did. "Would a bluenose deepwater sailor join us for a little conversation and…"

MacLeod gave a smirking grin and wiped his upper lip with a clenched fist. Sabatelli knew his trade.

Hobson looked around the room. The Navy had recently gone dry under a Quaker Secretary of the Navy and Hobson hoped this little excursion wouldn't turn into anything embarrassingly naval.

MacLeod eyes flashed. He was in the professional habit of controlling situations. "And who might you be?

"Eduardo Sabatelli, Shipping Agent representing Lighthouse Insurance. Petty Officer Hobson here is helping me."

"What's the Navy's interest here?" He said with a dark look.

"Not that much really. Some of the sundries in your hold were naval supplies, and you will notice looking around you that this is a naval hospital and it is always good to have a guide," Sabatelli said with dazzling brightness. "If it was anything important, they'd have sent an officer, wouldn't they have?"

"Harrumph, well just so long as everyone knows who the real sailors are. Not spilling soot all over and loitering about in their white teakettles for years on end off a single coast."

Hobson eyed the overhead.

"What happened?" Sabatelli said offering MacLeod another tug on the flask. No one seemed to notice.

"Pirates, Chinese pirates. We anchored and put in for water off the coast. They came aboard at night, overpowered the watch, seized the ship, and set us adrift in boats. Killed some of my crew. Some of my passengers, too."

"How many passengers were you carrying?"

"Not many, eight. Four from 'Frisco, took on the other four in Hawaii. Can't see how they'd be important to you. The cargo and the ship, they're lost. That's what ye'll have ta pay off. No insurance on passengers."

"How many boats did you put over?"

"Three, I think. We were all set adrift at once. There were four on the barque. Never understood why the owners had her carry so many. The crew fights harder to keep a ship afloat if there ain't enough boats. Don't know where the rest of the crew has got to. I expect that's where the first and second mate are. Saw the third mate run through clean, by the after companionway."

Hobson started to take his pipe out of his sock. "What did the pirates look like?"

"Ugly yellow bastards. Swords a-waving, dirty, speaking heathen gibberish and smelling heavy of…fish, yeah of fish. Two boat loads, maybe twenty of them."

"Guns?"

MacLeod turned pale. "Excuse me?"

Hobson began again, "Did they have guns."

"Yes, oh yes. Big percussion lock things, rifles or shotguns they were. One had a revolver, a big hogleg, looked like a naval revolver. Muzzles waving all over in a heavy sea."

"Can you identify the heads in this picture?"

MacLeod shook his head, sucked at his teeth, and released a deep rumbling unpleasant laugh, "Ah-ha, the little yellow men have a sense of humor. Served up in baskets like fruit or dead fish. Yeah, there's Captain Brewer, a hard'un from Boston. First time I ever saw him silent

32

and with his mouth closed. There's the second mate from Frisco, a fellow named Carson. He owed me money. Well, that's money I'll never see. The fellow with the big waxed mustache is a passenger named Hoyt who was traveling with Mr. Atticaris, always working a percentage on somethin'. That Asian was another passenger, a Korean I think. Could have been Japanese or Chinese. Can't remember his name."

Hobson took some tobacco out, thought a minute and put the pouch back in his sock. "How were your boarders dressed?"

"They wore pyjamis, with big straw hats."

"What did the straw hats look like? Were there any women?"

MacLeod paused and his eyes really flared. "Hell, I don't remember. A straw hat is a straw hat as far as I am concerned. And naw, no women, though in those outfits might be hard to tell. Now I've told you, *Jade Rooster*'s been pirated in the Yellow Sea off the Chinese Coast and I'll sign an affi-davey to it. Anyway that's 'bout all I know, the captain and me weren't so close. He didn't take my counsel much. Kept his accounts to hisself. To my lights, that's all you need for your underwriters and insurance matters. I made my report in writing to the Japanese Navy. Go bother them."

"Oh yes, you are quite right, captain. We were just trying to picture the incident in our minds. In your hurried departure, were you able to take the log?"

"No time looking down some heathen's blunderbuss."

"How did you happen to be in the Yellow Sea when your first port call was Yokohama."

MacLeod looked impatient and thumped the flask down with finality. "Typhoon blew us off course. Excuse me, I have to get in touch with the owners."

A corpsman came into the room and asked for Sabatelli. Hobson wondered if it had to do with the liquor. Sabatelli left the room. MacLeod and Hobson were alone.

"What business you pretty boys in your white suits got with all this? Hain't you got some parade to go to rather than interviewin' honest seamen."

Hobson looked at MacLeod and seemed to think about it.

"Well, swabbie? Probably not my business, but shouldn't you be polishing brass someplace or waving flags at something?"

Hobson leaned forward and spoke softly, "Your bein' a United States citizen, I have to be polite, don't' I? Well, don't try your bucko ways on me. These ships you sail, they mount any ordnance? They mount guns, say, for killing people?"

Hobson was methodically unbuttoning his cuffs. He opened them and folded them back neatly to reveal the dragons.

"See these here white suits. Well, they just make us look just so sanitary and civilized, that's the devilment of them because it tain't necessarily true. We have to keep them clean, which makes a strong contrast with what we have to deal with sometimes. You'd be surprised the bilge slime we have to deal with sometimes. I have a lot of friends that wear these suits and I like those friends pretty well. Hadn't given it much thought, but this organ grinder's monkey suit is…well, it's hunky-dory with me and I'm not sure I take well to words making mock of my friends or my togs."

He placed his cover squarely on the table.

"Now, your merchant ships, they're just built to sail. Our ships they're made to sail, and fight. In fact every little cog in the big Navy machine's made to fight… down to the lowest sailor in a pretty organ grinder's monkey's suit. And we cogs we hang together pretty well. We can sink vessels like yours, in a large-caliber way, and heck; we little cogs

34

in our nice white togs can sink individual fellows like you, in a small-caliber way, to my way of thinking."

Hobson's eyes narrowed.

"In fact, I can reduce this to a very private engagement right here and now if you'd like, Mr. U. S. Citizen, Mr. Honest Seaman. It's all the same to me. I get this suit a little scrappy an' they'll issue me another. Now tell the truth. Am I reading you right, do you have a problem with the United States tarnal Navy?"

MacLeod put his hands up as if to gesture, "misunderstanding" and became very quiet.

CHAPTER FIVE

By the time Sabatelli had returned, the heat had left the room.

Sabatelli returned informing Hobson that not all of the passengers were still in the hospital. Sabatelli sensed something amiss as he edged in his last question, "And the last you saw, *Jade Rooster* was anchored?"

"Yes, anchored in heavy weather."

"Why anchored?"

"Well, the fog and the skipper was having problems taking sights."

Hobson coughed politely, "Did you have guns?"

MacLeod looked at Hobson with disdain. It was a practiced look. "The guns were locked up. And I, gents, is underway."

With that he rose and stalked out of the room like a brief dark storm.

Hobson twirled his tobacco-less corncob with his fingers thoughtfully. "MacLeod makes out that Brewer was a hard captain, but wasn't carrying a gun and his mates were also unarmed. Seems peculiar to me. The hard officers on the hellships normally make all crewmen break off the tips of their sea knives and always appear on deck with a revolver. Didn't think hard captains were in the habit of carrying passengers, either. With them, 'Their word is law and their whims are as good as performed.' All schedules met and crews are occasionally paid what is coming to them -- if the crews live that long. Passengers are unwelcome. They talk and might be linked to management or busybodies and they aren't under discipline."

Sabatelli nodded in agreement. "Perhaps Brewer's a reformed hard captain, or perhaps the owners made him take the passengers."

Hobson wondered if the word "reformed" had any true place in the English language, as he knew it.

*****

36

Sabatelli and Hobson found Reeves in an examining room lying on his back and looking at the ceiling. He was in his shirtsleeves, barefoot and hugging a battered carpetbag between his knees. When they entered, he muttered something unintelligible, then shifted from lying on a gurney to sitting upright in a nearby chair. He was a thin, awkward man with a bad haircut and bad teeth. Tight with a dollar, Hobson thought, the perfect supercargo.

"Mr. Reeves, I represent your underwriters. My name is Sabatelli; Petty Officer Hobson here is assisting me since a portion of *Jade Rooster*'s cargo was naval stores."

"Hobson? Not the naval Hobson." Reeves seemed more at ease, delving in details.

Hobson looked embarrassed, "'Fraid not, never served on the *Merrimac*, or in the Caribbean. He's out now, a congressman I think."

"You were the ship's purser, I believe." Sabatelli felt he knew the type. They were the bane of his existence. Clerical drones who totally immersed themselves in the nickels and dimes and were forever losing sight of the big picture.

"Supercargo, purser's more a term for passenger ships. The terms are used interchangeably I guess. The Royster Line is mostly a shipping line, only does occasional passenger trade. So the officer in charge of financial matters and the cargo is referred to as the supercargo. We're more and more into the steamship business these days, but we have a few sailing ships like the Nova Scotia-built barque, *Jade Rooster*, for the long crossings with cargos that'll wait. A rooster is on several funnels plying the Trans-Pacific trade…Amber Rooster, Ebony Rooster, Emerald Rooster…"

"Any variation from the cargo recorded as shipped out of San Francisco? Do you know of anything that will change the claim."

37

"Well, we took on some equipment in Hawaii when we picked up Mr. Atticaris, typewriters and sewing machines. Heavy stuff in crates, though not for our account. He paid the freight. His original vessel was laid up in Pearl Harbor and he had a deadline. Destined for Yokohama. If there's an insurance claim it's his, not Royster Line's."

"What was it like with the pirates?"

"Well all of a sudden mostly. I was in my stateroom, and next I knew, I was being escorted off the ship by pirates, or cannibals, or whatever they were. They didn't seem real happy. I know I wasn't. Wouldn't give us oars or a sail. Just set us adrift."

"Well, they could have left you like this." Reeves looked at Sabatelli's photo and swayed. "So they got the captain, the second mate, Hoyt, and one of the Koreans. Carson and I shared a stateroom. Hoyt kept accounts, too, for Atticaris, kind of like me."

Reeves began to shake. Sabatelli gave him several minutes to resume his composure.

"Yes, kind of like me. Were there any others ended up like this?" He would not look directly at the photograph, but blinked at it out of the sides of his eyes.

"These are the ones we know about. Where'd all this happen?" Hobson asked.

"Not quite sure. The mate, MacLeod, could tell you. It was dark and overcast and couldn't see very far 'cause of the weather, but I had the feeling we were in a group of islands. Don't like any of this. Royster Lines is not going to pay me from the minute we lost the cargo. I'll be lucky to find a ship back."

"Where do you think the barque is now?" Hobson asked casually.

"At the bottom. They didn't look like they could handle a vessel that size. I know ship's wages, and that means ship's manning. Them pirates didn't have the men, and probably not the skills for Rooster.

Well, if the rest of the crew doesn't turn up, then aboard her they stayed. Maybe they took them for a slave crew to run Rooster."

"Were you able to take anything with you?"

"A few financial records and the like."

"We'll want transcriptions later." Sabatelli said patiently.

Reeves pondered that for a moment, then nodded affirmatively.

"Here's my card. I'm sure we can find you a berth back to 'Frisco." I don't know about Royster Lines, but Lighthouse doesn't leave officers or crew stranded.

Reeves smiled an unsettling, crooked-toothed smile.

*****

They missed Atticaris at the hospital, but Sabatelli was able to trace him to the Grand Hotel. The Grand Hotel was a stately brick hotel with porches on the first two of its three stories. Sabatelli had a room there. Sabatelli sent his card up with a bellman and shortly Atticaris was down to meet them.

Atticaris was one of the Quality. Tall and well-dressed only hours from an ordeal in a lifeboat, he smiled with ease and the confidence that a certain station in life guaranteed. Somehow he'd managed to come up with a tailored suit, celluloid collar and cuffs, and a pocket watch on extremely short notice. The cufflinks and studs Hobson recognized as Japanese. He had even found himself one of those stylish new hard-straw boaters, one with a distinctive blue and white band, and a lanyard. His center of gravity seemed to be bunched up in his head, neck, and shoulders like a kingfisher, Hobson observed.

"Everett Atticaris. Ah, I see Mr. Sabatelli that you have brought along a naval Quartermaster Third Class. Is this about my father? I really have very little recollection and nothing to do with all that. It was so long ago."

There was an almost baby-fat softness to him, an aura of good living unmarred by the hard knocks that Hobson and his shipmates experienced everyday.

"Your father?"

"Captain Atticaris, surely you or the Quartermaster have heard of him?"

Sabatelli looked uncomfortable. "I have only a passing acquaintance with the Navy. That's why Hobson is here with me. Hobson, do you know a Captain Atticaris?"

Hobson shook his head and Atticaris' mouth muscles tightened. He put the fingertips of one hand to his pomaded hair.

"A naval officer," he placed great emphasis on the third word, "would remember my father's name. "He wrote the best seller, *Cruising the Antarctic*, while he was the executive officer of the *Levant*. He was with Farragut at Mobile Bay as skipper of the *Saratoga*. He retired in 1867."

Sabatelli tilted his head as if remembering something, and then smiled, "Oh yes, now I make the connection. Never really heard the name said out loud, only read it in the papers. Your father, the captain, died a few years later under unusual circumstances in a Connecticut industrial town. Bridgeport, I think. It was a well-known claim in the insurance industry. Yes, something of a mystery."

Atticaris dismissed the memory with a broad sweep of his hand, "Well simply history, simply history. Now you're here about *Jade Rooster*."

Sabatelli's eye settled upon an elegant young woman with strawberry blonde hair. She was seated across the lobby and attended by a male

40

servant. Atticaris followed his gaze just as another woman who looked much like the first glided into the sitting room.

"What happened on *Jade Rooster*?"

Nothing much. Had a terrible crossing, heavy weather throughout. Captain Brewer anchored to take on water on the coast and effect some repairs I think, and instructed all passengers to stay below."

"Take on water?"

"Yes, the crew was at the pumps constantly. When it happened, there was land nearby, though we couldn't see it. Staying below was not unusual; we had had similar instructions during the crossing. Suddenly, in the middle of the night, bandits were all over us and we were forced into open boats without oars. Never did see everyone put into the boats. Ours held a few crewmen, Reeves the purser, MacLeod the first mate, and a Korean couple, the Kims."

"What do you think of Captain Brewer?"

"A rough diamond, but necessarily so. Competent, very competent. Very strict and forceful, but very competent. Coming from a naval family, I think I can understand the reason for his strict and demanding nature. Not all the classes appreciate the necessity for good order and what less understanding persons might call harsh discipline. There are those who serve before the mast, as it were, who need a strong guiding hand."

Atticaris avoided meeting Hobson's eye. Hobson seemed not to notice, but concentrated on the facts of the incident. "Sir, off which coast was this? What did the boarders look like."

Atticaris voice seemed strangely distant. "Korean? Chinese? Don't really know. You should ask First Mate MacLeod, he would know for sure. As for the bandits they were barefoot and wore that loose muddle of clothing typical of the Orient. Swords, guns, big straw hats."

"What sort of guns?"

41

"Revolvers and rifles. Don't ask me what type, I carry a nicely engraved gentlemen's derringer which I have never fired and that's the limit of my knowledge of firearms."

Sabatelli, distracted by the brace of strawberry blondes in shirtwaists at the other end of the room, seemed impatient to get the interview over with. "If I may be so bold, Mr. Atticaris, what do you do? Or have you the good fortune to list yourself as a gentleman?"

"No sir, I must 'do' things. My father died a bankrupt. I own several small companies. I am a manufacturer of sewing machines and this new gadget called a typewriter, which I hope to introduce to the Far East. My home state, Connecticut, is famous for its manufacturing. We have a massive building full of elves tinkering away, just stamping gewgaws out."

"Bridgeport?"

"Bridgeport and New Haven."

Sabatelli indicated he was impressed and showed Atticaris the photograph.

"Grisly, so very grisly. I guess one must expect that sort of thing in this part of the world. Poor, poor Hoyt."

"Can you identify them?"

"One, my secretary, Owen Hoyt. That's him, the third one. Oh yes, this other one is Captain Brewer. I guess I got off lucky with too much sun and a terrible thirst."

He gestured to one of the staff for a cup of tea. "Chinese, make it Chinese, not that ghoulish green stuff. Would you gentlemen like some tea? A fine establishment, given the circumstances really. Out here one must take one's recreation where one finds it. Old Nakamura puts out a good breakfast. Can you imagine the natives here have soup for breakfast?"

Conversation ceased, not awkwardly, but of its own accord.

Sabatelli looked at the strawberry blondes and gave an unconscious sigh. Atticaris brightened. "Sir, it seems we may be of mutual advantage. We were planning to see the show at the Gaiety Theater tonight. Could use a second gentleman. Might I introduce you to the Sisters Rowbotham?"

Sabatelli could barely contain himself and gave Hobson a look that could not be misinterpreted.

The sisters were at the far end of the lobby draped decorously across well-stuffed chairs in languid diagonal slashes. Their resemblance to several well-known art nouveau poster girls could not have been totally unconscious. Each wore her hair in a dizzying study in swirls and eddies. Both smoked with hand gestures that assured the smoke too flowed in sinuous curves. Emancipated women.

"Excuse me, but old seadogs such as myself must be off into the evening to carve scrimshaw or tie intricate knots or construct ships in bottles." Hobson assumed a wry expression. "Actually with extended time ashore, I'd set my sights on a rather large tattoo of a barebreasted maiden from the Sandwich Islands."

Atticaris and Sabatelli pondered the image, and it seemed to inspire them.

Hobson left, but no one seemed to notice. It was not a hotel he could have stayed in without an aggressive sponsor.

CHAPTER SIX

The next morning Sabatelli was positively buoyant.

"Ah, the Sisters Rowbotham," he mused then caught himself, and his jaw setting like a steel trap.

"Learn anything more about Atticaris?"

"Not much, a charmer for sure and one great one with the ladies. A socializer and a good hand at cards. Hard to believe he's his father's son. Can't see him barking orders in smoke and sweat alongside Farragut. It all came back to me about his father."

Sabatelli adopted a thoughtful look. "The Captain was a bookwriter and with Farragut all right. He also got into a lawsuit afterwards about prize money at Mobile Bay. Left a sour and materialistic aftertaste to a famous heroic incident. He married into New England society. He then proceeded to blow everything on the stock market. In the early '70's he was found dead in a back street in Bridgeport with an old horse pistol lying nearby. Looked like a hold-up and murder. A newspaperman thought something was fishy and eventually there were allegations that the body was not Atticaris, allegations that the whole thing was staged and insurance fraud. There was a settlement, all hush-hush. It wasn't a Lighthouse Insurance matter – they don't handle life insurance -- so we'll never know the details, but I think it could be interpreted to mean something was rotten. Still for the time being I'd like to stay on his good side.

"Well sir, young Everett seems to have done all right in the world and makes friends easily." Hobson observed dryly. "Now, if he can only learn to put up with Japan's 'horrid green tea.'"

Sabatelli gave Hobson a look of pure class-inspired disdain.

*****

The fading afternoon light was not kind. This particular edge of Chinatown was dirty and rundown. Large ceramic storage jars and the pervasive aroma of garlic and charcoal burners identified it as the Korean quarter. Hobson had explained that since the Russo-Japanese War, the Japanese had abandoned all pretense that Korea was an independent country. Japanese intrigues had left Korea under Japan's iron fist and the only surviving member of the Korean royal family was under house arrest in Japan. Japanese military police in Korea numbered about a hundred thousand and the Koreans had been relegated to a servant race.

It was Hobson who found the Kims at a Korean-run ryokan in Yokohama's Chinatown. His fluency in Japanese and Korean had been the key, since the two Asians blended in physically and the Korean community was closed and circumspect.

Two Korean laborers built solid and low to the ground challenged Hobson and Sabatelli as they approached the ryokan. They were dressed in western overalls, the attire of dockworkers in Yokohama, not the traditional dress they had seen in Yokosuka. There had a certain masonry-block physique that was distinctly Korean. This community knew it was depended on itself for security and these two were the visible tip of volunteer security. Fortunately, with a few words, Hobson both mollified and mystified them. A Caucasian who could speak Korean was about as common as a talking dog. An unfortunate analogy perhaps, Hobson mused, because the few dogs in Japan that wandered into the Korean quarter ended up in stews. The larger laborer guided the two Americans to the ryokan. He gave them one last look of warning and the benefit of a few words under his breath. Even talking dogs required discipline.

The Kims seemed to have mixed emotions, pleased to have callers, but not comfortable with Western strangers. Mrs. Kim was poised, strikingly beautiful, and seemingly mismatched with Mr. Kim who was stooped and moved in awkward surges.

Hobson started in Korean, but was cut short.

"If Mr. Sabatelli does not speak Hangugo, I think it would be more polite to speak in English," responded Mr. Kim. "My wife, she understands English, but has difficulty speaking the language. I studied English with American missionaries in Korea and in Hawaii. I wish to be an English teacher some day. We would like to avoid the Japanese authorities. They are always unpleasant to Koreans who have studied in the West. We are embarrassed by the attention our sea journey has attracted. We weren't expecting Western visitors."

The room was furnished in Korean fashion, a few embroidered cushions, and no chairs. Mr. Kim studied their faces very carefully.

Hobson made note of the fact that Mr. Kim was extremely thin and looked very tired. He was sunburned, but his skin had an unhealthy pallor. There was other discoloration, perhaps old bruises, but neither Hobson nor Sabatelli could be sure. He moved very little and seemed physically uncomfortable. Sabatelli was equally uncomfortable kneeling, but that was understandable. Hobson seemed used to the posture.

Sabatelli brought out the photograph. Mr. Kim gasped and Mrs. Kim began to weep.

"Do you know them?"

"Yes, the captain, a businessman from Connect-i… an American state I cannot pronounce, one of the ship's officers, and Mr. Sato."

"Anything we should know about them, you think? Do you have any idea why they got this… this particular treatment?"

"We are confused about what happened. It happened quickly. These men came and put us into a small boat."

"What nationality were the men?"

He looked at his wife and spoke with hesitance; "They spoke to us in Hangugo, in Korean."

"Anything else that might identify them or where the ship might be?"

"They were fisherman I think, at least some of them."

"What makes y'say that?"

"The way they looked at the ship and some of the words they used. One of them looked at a cargo net and thought its weave was too large for regular fish. I thought I saw tall islands in the distance, but I cannot be sure. The captain never told us much. In the boat the ship's officer said we were in the West Sea, what you call the Yellow Sea."

"Anything more?"

"Yes, my wife thinks they were Christians."

"Why?"

"She is not sure. They put us off boat and did not kill us. Wako is the Japanese word or haejok is the Korean word...what is your word?"

"Algerines, pirates," Hobson interjected.

"Haejok, they would not leave women alone as these men did. Women they are part of..."

"Spoils."

"Yes, spoils."

"She think they have some problem and they have some principles."

"Why?"

"She just knows."

*****

"Pirates with principles, who set heads in baskets adrift in pulling boats," Sabatelli called to Hobson from his ginricksha. His ginricksha had pulled up parallel to Hobson's as they overtook a horse car.

As they passed the fountain in front of Yokohama Station, a Japanese military officer jogged to intercept them and with a wave of his hand stopped their coolies short. He wore what might have been a Prussian mustache and severely cropped hair. He was short, but burly, and had a bright, even smile. He wore his glasses low on his nose in a way that gave him a jolly professorial air.

"Gentlemen, if you will join me for a meal, I must request some assistance, if I may?" He seemed out of breath.

"With respect to...?"

"*Jade Rooster.* A Japanese national was among those murdered."

"...And the meal? Lieutenant...er....captain?"

" Major Koizumi. Western cuisine, I assume. There is an Italian restaurant where I am well known."

Sabatelli brightened, "The Venetian?"

"The same."

Hobson observed that the ginricksha coolies had caught their breath, but were standing motionless with their eyes riveted on the major.

Hobson seemed thoughtful. "Sir, you're an Army officer, a major. Why the interest in a barque, a civilian vessel? Isn't the Navy filing the report?"

"Things are never that simple. I am with the military police. Paperwork, bureaucracy, we must be correct in all matters. We are an emerging country and must always strive to do our best. We must be correct in all matters. There is an Imperial Rescript, I believe, on the matter."

"We'll meet you there."

*****

48

"You know we never asked the Kims about Sato." Hobson said thoughtfully. "We ought to go back."

"Tomorrow, tomorrow's another day. Let's get supper out of the Japanese major. So far Sato doesn't seem to have much to do with anything."

"Well at this point he's Japanese and that may be reason enough to attempt to find out where he fits in all this. Perhaps we should keep the fact that I speak passable Japanese to ourselves. At least, let's not tell this major."

"Why? Is this really necessary"

"Who knows? Might give us a negotiating edge at some point. He seems to be coming on a scrid strong. Maybe I just don't like the Army. One of the worst insults on *Pluto* is to suggest someone's guilty of 'soldiering.'"

As a shipping agent, Sabatelli had spent long hours learning the fine points of negotiation. Partial disclosure was a tactic he understood.

*****

A Japanese staff worked the restaurant dressed like gondoliers, but a beached Italian sailor ran the pasta-oriented establishment. Sabatelli's ancestors would have approved the fare.

"Did you find the Kims? I would be most interested in talking to them." Koizumi brushed his cuff, then tilted his head from side to side like an old wrestler cracking his neck. Hobson noted that his neck, arms, and shoulders were well developed.

Sabatelli nodded. "Hobson found them in the Korean section of Chinatown. You should be able to find them, too."

Koizumi smiled, "No, I am Japanese and represent authority. I doubt the inhabitants of the Chosungai will be very forthcoming, but I will try. You see we act as a sempai, as a helpful older brother, to our little brother, Korea. We watch out for the Russians – ah, the worst kind of decadent empire -- but not all look upon our help with favor."

Hobson had adopted a distant look.

"What was the nature of the naval supplies aboard *Jade Rooster*?"

"Sugar from Hawaii, condensed milk, nutmeg, and alcohol," listed Sabatelli.

"Anything else?"

"Sundries, shoes, shoe polish, brass polish, and chemicals for paint."

"Ah, little to inspire intrigue." Koizumi observed and smiled. "A very boring cargo."

"Intrigue? Has there been any mention of intrigue?"

"No," Koizumi said grasping Sabatelli's forearm with a mollifying gesture. "No, I am making a small joke. Was the cargo all naval stores?"

Koizumi's glasses rested low on his nose. Hobson noticed he never looked through them.

"No, but the naval stores were the insured portion of the cargo and I have the paperwork for that portion of the cargo."

The meal was consumed without further discussion of *Jade Rooster*.

CHAPTER SEVEN

When Sabatelli and Hobson met at the Grand Hotel for breakfast, Hobson again insisted that they ask the Kims about Mr. Sato. Sabatelli agreed, but with little enthusiasm. He could think of no immediate reason why Sato was important.

The door to the hotel dining room opened and Koizumi entered with his bright even smile.

"They have disappeared," Koizumi said shaking his head. "I was afraid this might happen." In this country, when Koreans choose to blend in, they can make themselves impossible to find. The Kims have disappeared. They haven't been in touch with you?"

Hobson looked at Koizumi, and Sabatelli thought he detected skepticism in Hobson's look. Major Koizumi seemed to struggle with what he had to say next.

"Now, my interest is a good deal more… official. Something has happened to Mr. Reeves, from *Jade Rooster*, the financial official…the treasurer…"

"The supercargo?"

""Yes, the supercargo. Have you any thoughts on where the Kims might be? I don't know what has transpired, but I am on my way over to the Four Sisters ryokan. You know the word ryokan? It is a Japanese inn very much like your boarding houses. The runner from the ryokan was so uninformative that I must conclude that something has happened to Mr. Reeves and that it involves a crime. One committed on Japanese soil."

Koizumi had difficulty pronouncing "Reeves" and showed the briefest lapse in composure.

"May we come along?" Hobson said breaking his silence. "He had shipping records that will need interpreting and concern *Jade Rooster*."

Koizumi nodded absently and raised one hand and fluttered it as if symbolizing something with little weight.

*****

Reeves' throat had been cut.

He had died soundlessly during the night. A familiar carpetbag lay open on one side of the room. A middle-aged woman, presumably one of the Four Sisters, appeared very upset. Deaths were bad business, the deaths of Westerners were worse business, and violent deaths were the worst business. If this had been a normal ryokan in any other part of Japan, she might have had to close. Fortunately, Yokohama still maintained the style of a foreign settlement and the Japanese were quick to write off foreign improprieties. Barbarians were barbarians. And everyone knew that barbarians were virtually unteachable.

There was another Japanese man present in uniform that spoke to Koizumi and reported stiffly.

"Deuce, the carpetbag's empty. No logs now," Sabatelli exclaimed.

Koizumi looked at Sabatelli. "With *Jade Rooster*'s chart and log, we might have been able to work from the master's last fix." Sabatelli proceeded to describe navigational records aboard ship. With records they would have had a more detailed place to start.

The ryokan was seedy compared to Hobson's. The tatami mats were stained by the shoe marks of careless sailors. It catered exclusively to foreign seamen, so its standards of cleanliness and shoelessness had dropped accordingly. Hobson grinned as he thought of the Sisters' possible attempts to enforce the rules of ofuro -- hot tub -- etiquette on her Western guests. One was supposed to wash before entering the tub and the water was not changed after each guest. He guessed that the rules were hard to enforce.

52

Koizumi looked at the wound. "Was nicely cut. A clean cut, no sawing, and deep almost to the neck bone. A very sharp knife."

Hobson's eyebrows raised at the word "nicely."

Hobson recalled Sabatelli's photograph. It hadn't occurred to him that those heads had also been severed "nicely." No sawing or hacking there, a single stroke per victim, no more.

"The police officer says there is a bag for luggage or documents, but it is empty. Some one with experience did this. Someone who uses a knife the way others use a tool. Perhaps a sailor or perhaps one of our own people. The use of blades of different kinds has significance in our culture. A short knife, I think, not a katana, a sword."

Koizumi wiped his glasses on his sleeve.

"But not beheaded." Hobson added thoughtfully. "Not beheaded. No high drama this time. Really hardly a matter for the military police I'd think. But for us, the log and ship's documents were very important."

"Oh, we assist the police from time to time. You see, I speak English and there are so few who do. So the different police organizations share...what is the word, "resources'." Koizumi responded.

For a brief moment, Sabatelli thought he saw Koizumi's smile slip.

The policeman spoke up suddenly in Japanese and the woman nodded.

"Ah, Mr. Reeves brought a bargirl home with him, but the proprietress never saw her, she only heard her. Paper walls. The bargirl spoke with an accent."

Koizumi looked from one to the other, "Whatever the story with *Jade Rooster*, it involves more than piracy."

Koizumi smiled and turned Reeves' lifeless head to one side. "I should know a bar girl like this."

*****

Once they had left and were out of Koizumi's hearing, Hobson added, "I figure he's right, you know."

"How so?"

Hobson hesitated, "There's a good deal more to this than random piracy. When he introduced himself to that police officer in Japanese, he said he was a major in the Kempeitai."

"What's that?"

"Imperial Japanese Secret Service. They are some truly bad actors. Poison, drugs, blackmail, sex, and assassination. The Japanese are out to build an empire with the very newest western technology and a very old-fashioned sense of skullduggery. He's a member of their intelligence service. No country's intelligence service plays by the Queensbury Rules. He's not out to find a crate of cans of shoe polish and dried milk.

"Yes, Koizumi would like to know a bargirl like this."

*****

They searched in vain for the Kims. Hobson took the opportunity to provide a cultural tour, gardens, temples, shops, even taking Sabatelli to a judo hall. Their students practiced a new sport with ancient self-defense origins developed by a Japanese educator. It was part of the national curriculum and Hobson had become acquainted with the sport as a student growing up in Japan. The Japanese educator bore a temperamental resemblance to TR, spindly in youth, who had grown to be a physical tiger and an irresistible organizational dynamo.

Sabatelli decided they needed to know more about the Royster Lines, so they backtracked to the waterfront.

*****

Sabatelli guided Hobson to a small chandlery on the waterfront adjacent to a long brick ropewalk.

Upstairs, in what he assumed were the living quarters, Hobson could hear a terrible argument being conducted in Japanese, but the exchanges did not approach the customary Western volume and intensity. An adolescent in flashy Western dress brushed the sliding door aside and stormed by them. Hobson could not tell if the youth was Western or Asian, but he was tall by either standard. A cigarette dangled from his lips and his shoes were two-one leather. Behind, appeared a middle-aged man equally tall, with grizzled muttonchops. He came toward them with a stern look of almost Biblical gravity, walking with a pronounced limp, and dressed severely in a dark business suit with a hard celluloid collar. The jacket was double breasted and came nearly to his knees. He was nimbly working a short splice onto a brass shackle. Hobson noticed his eye movements were very quick in a way that Hobson associated with nervous intelligence.

The man regarded Hobson with interest. "Wondered when the U. S. Navy might need a little rigging work. That's what you're here for I reckon."

"Er, no sir. I'm the man who replaced you as a shipping agent."

"Ha, so you're the new wonder from back home. Well, luck to you. Got darn tired of getting squeezed between cheap owners and skinflint captains. Better ship a cargo some time for your own account before they break you. Had enough of it anyway, looking for something different. Captained for a bit 'til I broke my leg and couldn't get it set right, not in the middle of the Pacific. It was about time I came ashore, rounded both Capes twice. Shipwrecked once. Then shipping agented a bit. Sail, steam, Yankees, Limeys, but got caught in the middle maybe once too often. Well, now I got this chandlery and manage this ropewalk and I'll hold to them 'til they bores me, I reckon. Good thing the wife speaks the language better than I do. Don't think I was meant to do one thing for long."

Hobson could make out the silhouettes of the spinners twisting rope through the window of the longest brick building he had ever seen.

"I've applied for a patent on a set of boat davits. Got the drawing back in the house if'n you want to see them. Name's Aegir Talmadge."

His eyes darted from Hobson to Sabatelli and back several times a sentence.

"That was my son. Heck, he'll be the death of me. Married one of the gals out here. Fine enough woman, but maybe that boy's some sort of punishment for my shiftless ways. Well, if this isn't Navy business, what are you here for and when did naval petty officers begin marching escort for a shipping agent?"

Sabatelli told him.

"Well, the Royster Lines is the tightest of the lot. Don't let that play of words...rooster-Royster make you think they had much of a sense of humor, or a sense of business either. *Jade Rooster*'s a sailing barque, but the owners of the line fell in love with steam afore it was really practical and they been payin' ever since. They been a hard luck line. Those steamers are always runnin' into somethin' or disappearin'. Some of them are wood hulled and not efficient. Lost a mail packet contract recently. I think it's 'cause the owners are tough, too tough on their skippers. Each skipper had better turn a profit if'n he knows what's a good for 'im. It seems every ship they lose, they increase the profit they want their skippers to haul in each cruise. More pressure on the sailing ship captains to cover the steamers. They're the ones that can take cargo across the Pacific. Steamers need so much coal; they can only carry passengers. Hull design, hull design, don't think people pay enough attention to hull design."

A Japanese woman not much bigger than a doll came to the door and gave Talmadge a dressing down in gentle Japanese. Hobson understood every word, but she did not realize it.

Apparently, the boy was difficult. His mixed heritage did not sit easily in a strictly ordered society, even in westward-leaning Yokohama. Probably his father's professional instability did not help, but his father was too intelligent to settle into just one challenge.

Hobson watched his eyes dart about their attire and sensed him weigh a series of conclusions. Hobson suspected his observations would be fairly accurate and based on broad experience.

"That all I know. Can't say I can give you any answers right now, probably because you fellows don't know enough yet," the ropewalk man concluded.

"Say, either of you ever sailed the Southern Seas? Some people say a penguin is a bird. "Cept it doesn't fly. I'm of a mind to challenge that categorization. I've been doing some thinking on it. Seems I should write one of those scientific societies."

Sabatelli eventually decided their investigation had reached an impasse. Hobson headed to Tokio before returning to Yokosuka and *Pluto*.

*****

Draper gave Hobson only half his attention. As they sat down Hobson noted he was a head shorter than he was and appeared to have slept in his uniform. He was poring over reports and gave polite indications of concern as Hobson recounted his visits and interviews. Then his aura of distraction fell away.

"What was the name of that high-rolling businessman again? You say he's got businesses in two major manufacturing towns in Connecticut and doesn't know anything about guns? That's pretty much all they do in that state, make guns. Like some hillbilly from the Ozarks 'not knowin' nothin' bout no 'stills.'"

"That's what I thought. Not a name that can be confused with any other, I expect. Now where did I see that name?" He riffled through several mounds of written reports. Most were handwritten, but some used the peculiar appearance left by a new machine called a typewriter. He reached behind him and opened an oak filing cabinet drawer. Hobson noticed a revolver nestled in one folder. Hobson always viewed officers as a singular and distinctly separate species. He wondered if the revolver was filed under "Small Arms" or "New Navy Colt" or perhaps, "Tack hammer, expedient, one."

"There, Everett Atticaris. You say he was here in Japan? Well, I will have to go visit the man if he is still around -- which I expect he is not. Probably gave him heart palpitations seeing you. I expect it did, " Mr. Draper grinned removing his glasses.

"He never showed so much as a tremor, though now that you mention it, he was out of that naval hospital pretty quick."

"Manufactures sewing machines and typewriters and doesn't know anything much about guns? He admitted to being from two of the three biggest arms cities in the U.S., Bridgeport, New Haven, the only one he didn't mention was Hartford and they're each a dogcart trip away from each other. You want to know who makes sewing machines and typewriters? The big gun companies. Can't live in those places without eating, drinking, and breathing the virtues of small and not-so-small arms. Mr. Atticaris is in the gun business in a big way, Hobson. A big way. Now the United States government doesn't mind arms sales one little bit. No, not one little bit."

Draper's head tilted as if he was viewing a picture from a different angle.

"Except to certain places, like the Philippines. He can sell anything he wants here in Japan, in China, even in Korea, but the only people he's going to sell to in the Philippines is the United States Army or the United States Navy. I think I'll get a message off to my counterpart in Manila. You didn't get any sense he's behind any filibustering? There's been a bit of that in the past years and it is hard to keep under control and can be embarrassing."

Draper looked over the papers a second time.

"You know what a Gatling gun is?"

"Yes sir."

"I suppose you do. Probably carry one or two in *Pluto*'s armory, those or Hotchkiss guns or Maxims. Well, he's got about two dozen to sell. How about a pneumatic dynamite gun?"

"Well wasn't *Vesuvius*..."

"Yes, *Vesuvius* was built expressly as a pneumatic dynamite gun cruiser. Used the Sims-Dudley gun. A little compressed air, a dynamite projectile, and baro-o-o-om. At best, that troublesome shore battery isn't there anymore or at worst, neurasthenia in epidemic proportions. The army bought a handful of them mounted on wheels...rolled them around like field guns. Then, after our little set-to with the Spaniards, the Army sold a few as surplus. They're a little short on effective range, but a splendid weapon otherwise. The Navy screwed up the pneumatic gun when it put it on *Vesuvius*, had to aim the whole ship at the target to fire it. The Army's weapon is on wheels. You just adjust the barrel. Fantastic demoralizer."

Draper opened a thin folder and ran his finger under several lines in one paragraph.

"Atticaris bought a few. He could fit out a small army, one that liked to fight bandit-style, about now. Filibustering or gunrunning, either way it is troublesome. Darn troublesome."

On Draper's desk was a letter opener. A bolo knife, the kind Hobson knew, that the Moros used in the Philippines. A doped-up Moro took a big round to bring down. Only then could you could take his knife as a souvenir. It occurred to Hobson that Draper might be as dangerous as he was disheveled.

"Hobson, I think you'd better tell me the whole story all over again, slowly. That man, Atticaris, must have just relished his interview with a representative of the federal government. Seems like we ought to keep on poor Mr. Sabatelli's good side. Never tell what that ol' 'Watch the Pea Carefully' Sabatelli might turn up.

"You know," he mused, "I can understand why we should be taking *Jade Rooster* seriously. What I can't figure out is why Sabatelli is devoting so much time to it."

CHAPTER EIGHT

After the war, the U. S. Navy had taken over the Spanish naval base and coaling station at Sangley Point, but found these too small and began developing facilities at Subic Bay. Many viewed Cavite – nearer Manila -- as difficult to defend, and from time to time, policy makers toyed with withdrawing from Cavite and developing a major base at Olongapo on Subic Bay, but nothing came of it. Olongapo was a backwater, and Cavite and Sangley Point permitted liberty in nearby Manila.

Pluto's job was to provide coal to U. S. warships. It spent most of its time in a triangle bounded by Japan, China, and the Philippines. Generally, the Asiatic Fleet summered in China and wintered in the Philippines, but operational requirements could prompt adjustments to that pattern. It had done so recently. From time to time, it went eastward into the Pacific – to the former Spanish possession of Guam, or to Samoa, and even occasionally to Hawaii, for instance -- to support a warship making a Pacific crossing. For the most part, *Pluto* spent its time -- like most colliers -- extending either a U. S. warship's radius of action or the time a U.S. a warship could cruise on station. The several colliers of the Asiatic Fleet divided their time among the three corners of the triangle transporting coal originating from the United States, but occasionally from local sources.

The Russo-Japanese War had underscored the need for coaling stations and colliers as an integral part of the fleet. The Russian Fleet, in its run from the Baltic to the Straits of Tsushima, had been plagued by its inability to find reliable sources of fuel. Political pressure had dried up its sources of fuel. Coal had to be stockpiled in safe places and be brought to the fleet in ships the fleet could rely on.

*****

The Asiatic Fleet was a vast bureaucratic organism. A recent occurrence in this one corner of *Pluto*'s operational triangle, the Philippines, stood to have an unsettling influence on *Pluto*'s routine for some months to come. It would have an unsettling influence on Hobson's routine in particular and would culminate in another corner of the triangle.

The occurrence that would affect both *Pluto* and Hobson saw its genesis months before, during a meeting between the local commanding officers and the admiral. An offhand discussion of fighting spirit aboard the flagship had become heated. "Fighting spirit" was a concept of near-religious significance. The flagship or the "Floating Palace" as it was known, was a worthy forum for such discussions. Its place in Western Pacific naval theology left it somewhat less visited than Mecca, but only slightly less important than Rome.

During the meeting, the captain of *Baltimore* had gratuitously observed that the crew of a collier could not be expected to have the proper "attitude or spirit of warriors" in view of their auxiliary status, and so should be excused from certain routine naval tasks. This had prompted a coughing fit by Mr. Wheelwright, captain of *Pluto*.

"They all start with the same training and all serve on steel ships and all serve in the same fleet, why should their attitudes be different? How do you measure warrior spirit?" Wheelwright said when all eyes turned to him.

"Hmmm, yes," the admiral was in his seventies and getting a bit bored with inventories and discussion of English and Japanese naval developments. The topic sparked his interest. "A test of spirit, yes. To measure it, how to measure it. A competition, yes, a competition. A challenge. Challenges are always a test of spirit."

"An athletic competition?" *Baltimore*'s skipper, a commander with the full three stripes rather than Wheelwright's two and a half, smiled slowly.

Wheelwright saw the trap he had fallen into, but far too late. *Baltimore* was the cock o' the fleet; it had taken gold trophies in each of the competitive divisions, boxing, fencing, football, swimming, sailing, and rowing. *Baltimore*'s crew was almost ten times the size of *Pluto*'s. Wheelwright tried to make his brain think faster, but he could not see a way to change the directions of the conversation. Control it, he thought, somehow figure an advantage that you have and work it against them before it is too late.

Wheelwright knew he was in a short-fuzed frame of mind and struggled to maintain his self-control. The list had been circulated of officers ordered to appear before the Naval Examining Board "for examination preliminary to promotion." He had not expected to be on the list yet, but it reminded him that one of the seven subjects of the examination was ordnance. There was woefully little he would learn about ordnance aboard *Pluto*. But *Pluto* was his command, and a basis for his reputation as a naval officer.

"Pulling boats," Wheelwright heard the words come out without his conscious desire to say them.

What advantage did his collier have? Virtually the entire crew spent hours a week loading coal, a slow, backbreaking, arduous undertaking. Not an undertaking requiring great skill, just strength, endurance, and consistency.

"We'll beat *Baltimore* at rowing, on warrior spirit alone. No boat officers, strictly crew, if this is to be a measure of the crews' warrior spirit." Wheelwright did not know why he had added this proviso, but it had somehow seemed the right thing to say.

"And the stakes?" The captain of another protected cruiser thought it prudent to participate. He, too, had sensed the admiral's boredom.

The Admiral decided this was his meeting and he was going to take charge. "A warrior's competition, a navy competition, must have a navy award. Rowers vie for a rooster. That's the tradition."

"We've already got a gold rooster," *Baltimore*'s captain chimed in. He also had a gold everything else, but he anticipated that this competition was going to lead to an interesting round of off-the-record wagering among the fleet wardrooms.

"Yes and we have a bronze rooster." Wheelwright remembered because it was the only athletic award his ship had ever won. Bronze was the metal for awards for ships with smaller crew sizes.

The Admiral looked around the cabin. The word rooster had triggered a recollection. He fingered some work a jeweler in Hong Kong had done for him as a present for his wife. Feeling a sudden serge of Solomonic wisdom, he said with finality, "Then a jade rooster it will be."

*****

Lieutenant Commander Coley Wheelwright was in the in-port stateroom of the captain of *Baltimore*. The skipper of *Baltimore*, a commander by grade, was an insufferable old sundowner. His habit of wearing a stopwatch around his neck was well known.

Now they were to iron out details. The Admiral's flag lieutenant was serving as a mediator. *Baltimore*'s captain cabin had paintings. The flag lieutenant had never seen paintings on the bulkheads of a ship before, and he was impressed.

"We have worked out a four-mile course off Shanghai." He pointed to two points on a chart. "Slack water or with a current running?"

"Seamanship, this must also be a test of seamanship, we are gauging naval warrior spirit." *Baltimore*'s skipper had been advised by his executive officer that collier coalpassers were forged of steel, had bituminous between their ears, were habitually sullen and dirty, and that it was of the greatest importance to do anything to keep the collier boat crew off center. The hell with seamanship, he wanted to throw large chunks of excrement in the game.

Wheelwright winced since it was going to be useless to argue with a fellow skipper who wore three stripes to his two and a half in front of a mediator who wore only two. *Baltimore* may have been a second-class cruiser, but she outgunned and outmanned *Pluto* significantly. He decided to chart a conservative course. The Navy was built upon hierarchy and he had already acted radically in challenging a cruiser skipper.

"Let's do it with a current running."

"A pulling boat race between Naval Constructor's Standard Navy cutters…" the flag lieutenant began.

It was *Baltimore*'s skipper's turn to flush. He opened and closed his mouth. *Baltimore* had a special racing cutter that was its pride and joy. He had assumed its light weight and fine lines would bring his ship victory. Standard Cutters were barges in comparison.

"When?"

For some reason they looked at Wheelwright. He supposed it had something to do with giving a man his last wish before an execution.

"During the Christmas leave period. That's the first time we'll have enough down time around Shanghai to train."

"We'd be glad to change the site to Cavite," *Baltimore*'s captain offered.

"No, you have the largest pool of manpower to draw from, we want some time to train up to this."

"Train up?" The sundowner smiled broadly.

The flag lieutenant nodded and set a date for a pulling-boat race between the twelve-oared cutters of a protected second-class cruiser, a ship of the line, and a first-class collier, an auxiliary, to be held in Shanghai harbor in two months.

"There'll also be the river current." The flag lieutenant added.

*****

The tall man fingered the edge of the executioner's sword. It was the real thing and would fetch a significant sum in San Francisco. He gave it a swing, then whiffed it several times back and forth, up and down. Too heavy to apply in any other purpose. Horizontal slashes were awkward. The victim had to be stationary for it to do its work properly. This was not a weapon of war, but an instrument of policy enforcement. Weapons of war were far more complex. They all involved trade-offs. If a weapon had a valuable feature, it also had a drawback. He had made a study of these things. It could be said that the study would someday result in a great return on his invested effort, he thought with an inward chuckle.

This appliance, this artifact, this trinket was a mere diversion. The warlord had given it to him because he liked him.

In the courtyard below him, he could hear chatter in the Shantung dialect. A washerwoman and a watchman were discussing the event to take place at noon. He was in Chefoo, Shantung Province, within walking distance of the harbor.

He found that that was the secret, to be clever and have people like you. He knew he was clever, and better yet he was educated, clever with a gilded edge. Getting people to like you was an art that he had studied. His appearance was good, he had been fortunate in his breeding, and he attended to those details of dress and grooming which made a favorable impression. He had been schooled in looking the part and exuding "presence." As for the matter of personal charm, he found it easier to be charming when he did not care. It was strange how that worked. If you did not care, you could be irreverent, and irreverence and charm often went hand in hand. He did not care about much, but there were a few things.

He looked out the window and noted the washerwoman was carrying a basket. That set him on a different line of thought.

He had seen the photos, Brewer and Hoyt and the others. They had failed him. Things had gone wrong and they had paid the price. This would not happen again.

He did not feel threatened. Questions were being asked, but he knew how to play the edges of the map, confuse the jurisdictions, pit fiefdoms against each other. Bureaucrats went through the motions and soon lost interest. Really what was their incentive? That stout office clerk, Sabatelli, would have other problems on his plate in due course – how could it be otherwise? -- and *Jade Rooster* would be forgotten. That lower-than-dirt gob he had tagging along, what would he add and how long could the Navy spare him? What did he bring to the investigation anyway? No, time and inertia were on his side.

The Kempeitai were going through the motions, too. They knew more but were not going to share it with Americans, let alone investigators pursuing an insurance claim. The Kempeitai wanted answers, but for other reasons. How big would the claim be, and what could they do about it? He did not know where *Jade Rooster* was, what chance did they have?

He knew the significance of four heads in baskets.

A runner came up and knocked on the door. The surrey was here. The warlord had two women with him, both shielded from the sun. He knew who they would be and that they were two of the most beautiful women in China that day, in his opinion. One was Asian and the other European. Beside the driver was a battleship of a man whose eyes were always moving. He was the American woman's bodyguard. Next to the warlord sat a woman, equally formidable in bulk -- a battleship in the company of a cruiser. If one took the Grand Tour by way of China, one secured a bodyguard and a chaperone. He wondered what a bodyguard could do against a warlord's army. Probably very little, but the American woman was well connected politically, the daughter of a senator, and the warlord likely had enough concerns without facing an international incident. Raisuli's taking of Pedicaris and Varley in Morocco were still on everyone's minds. Foreign armies did not need much of an excuse to go tramping through China these days. The warlord would prefer his domestic armies go tramping to acquire territory. The warlord was from a province in the interior. When he wanted to relax he came to Chefoo or Shanghai.

Here in Chefoo both he and the warlord played it straight arrow. The warlord was his friend and his business was direct. He could not stay for long, even as conveniently out of the way as Chefoo was for him. He had matters to attend to elsewhere, matters he cared about. He would not be charming where they were concerned. Yes, it was a revelation; charm and concern were rarely compatible. It was a matter of straightening out relationships and removing hindrances. What he wanted required efficiency, not size, nor flash, but a type of discipline.

The American woman wore a wide-brimmed straw hat with flowers and a cream-collared, high-necked blouse with leg o' mutton sleeves. She had that haughty look reminiscent of a Gibson girl and he though he had detected the glimmer of a derringer above her high-button shoe as she shifted restlessly in the surrey. Did anyone trust anyone out here?

He put on a Western jacket and hat and descended the stairs. As he left the door he saw a wicker basket stowed in the boot of the surrey.

They were going to watch an official beheading, and the warlord had thoughtfully packed a picnic lunch. It was surprising how many uses a basket could be put to in the Realm of the Golden Dragon.

*****

Pluto was on a mooring off Sangley Point and her cutter bobbed at the bottom of a rope ladder suspended from the strong back, a large beam that paralleled her port side.

"Don't worry about your elbows. Everyone gets self-conscious about their elbow placement when they begin rowing. Forget it, just row. We'll attend to the proper style and grace accorded manly naval maneuvers later." Hobson commented. Merchant barques and gunrunning were distant concepts.

Hobson had a book on rowing he had been lent. He read it just before each practice so he had something authoritative to say. He'd rowed dories and had some Navy training in double-banked rowing, but you had to say wise things if you were going to be the coach. It was his charge. The ensign had a dozen reports and forms to complete and had looked at the crew and despaired. Hobson encouraged him to complete his reports aboard *Pluto* and leave the rowing to him.

In the coxswain's seat was the Cabin Cook Second Class "Tiger" Cheng. Hobson believed he had been scientific in recruiting him. Cheng was the captain's cook and by osmosis carried the captain's presence. He'd figured Tiger had one of the best strength-to-weight ratios on *Pluto*. Cheng was indispensable and his loud deep voice and high level of animation assured that he would never be overlooked in a crowd. Everyone on the ship knew he was the essential go-between with the overseas Chinese in the Philippines and Japan, and with the Shanghai Chinese. Additionally, he maintained a store of Eight Diagram seasickness pills and postcards and fans and umbrellas for the benefit of the crew.

Tiger had been a coalpasser on Nanshan, one of Dewey's two colliers, at Manila Bay. He had been one of the considerable numbers of Chinese in Dewey's Fleet that day. In the intervening years, he had signed on with the regular Navy and become a cook, though cook was an inadequate title. As further evidence of his indispensability, he doubled as the ship's bugler.

Tiger was an adventurer in the Chinese tradition of the Three-Jewel Admiral who had explored the Asian Seas. A Marco Polo in reverse, he was a translator not so much of words as of missions. He, like so with many Chinese sailors, could never make a complete break with the ancestors by sailing too far. Yet the Manchu world was collapsing around him, these were uncertain times, and he must go where his ship and his luck took him.

There had been grumbling whether cooks and stewards were really part of the Navy, but no one had the nerve to go toe to toe with Cheng who was all of five foot tall and about 115 pounds. He was one of those small men who did not know how to back down and who gave ground to no one.

Cheng had been born on a junk and had sculled sampans until he'd found his rice bowl on *Pluto*. He understood wind and current.

At stroke was a native of Sausalito known as the "Oyster Pirate." He had the most rowing experience, most of it gained dredging by moonlight in other people's oyster beds. As a child, he had even seen the great Canadian oarsman, Ned Hanlon. The Oyster Pirate avoided all non-technical accountability and positions of responsibility. Things performed in a predictable manner; people did not. He could be highly competitive, but only if he could sense fear among the competitors that was strong and palpable. Only fear could shake his lanky, laconic body into action. His most memorable physical attributes were his pronounced Adam's apple and gunboat-size feet.

The Oyster Pirate was an oiler and one of the black gang. He had bought a sewing machine somewhere and made money on the side sewing "tailor-mades." The concept of sport was alien to the Oyster Pirate's view of the world. There were angles and there was financial gain. A sewing machine gathered small amounts of money and useful scuttlebutt. No one did things just to do them, not in the Oyster Pirate's world.

His hands would gesture with the grace of an orator and his mouth would open several times before the words ever came out. It was as if he had to pump up steam before he could generate sound. "W-w-we've got to rig stretchers and sew leather seats on our pants."

"Leat'er? What we need leat'er for? You some kind of busted ludder…rudder slipknot sailor?" Cheng screamed.

"We can grease the leather and slide back and forth on the seats. That w-w-way, braced to the stretchers, we get more use out of our legs."

The Ensign casting one last glance as he returned to the bridge, looked doubtful. "I'm gonna have to check the Luce rules. I've heard it's naval constructor boat standards and no adaptive work."

Cheng looked enthusiastic. He lived by the power of force of will.

They rowed from *Pluto* to a buoy off the point and back four times. Cheng was screaming most of the time. "Don't dig in. Keep top edge of the blade close to surface."

Cheng was not going to approach anything that wasn't cutthroat serious.

He was, after all, the captain's cook though the title "logistical factotum" would have been appropriate.

The oar tips flickered like synchronized silver blades giving the appearance that the boat's progress was more glide than effort. "L-l-like a big ol' water spider stretchin' her legs!" the Oyster Pirate blurted, perking up. It was a good start.

"Well, not long and we'll be scuddrifting, just scuddrifting along those waves." One of the old salts invented words, or invented new meanings for words. Hobson admired that. He believed this strange form of deckplate erudition showed imagination and that imagination was one of the keys to true leadership. "Look, if were gonna do this, we got to do it first rate. We have to build on a routine and we gotta stick by it. Tiger we gotta eat more eggs and beef and milk."

Tiger looked thoughtful. The officers were going to eat a bit leaner for the next few months, but he could work it so they'd never know it.

"No cow milk, maybe goat milk."

Their hands were raw and they were stiff from the new pattern and rhythm of exertion.

*****

Manila's principal shopping district, the Calle de Escolta at the north end of the Bridge of Spain, was a good place to start liberty. Manila smelled of mildew, barbecued meat and opportunity. Tiger, the Oyster Pirate, Hobson, and several others from the cutter's racing crew enjoyed extra liberty as an incentive. The three had separated from the rest of the crew, when Hobson caught a glimpse of a hat out of the corner of his eye as they passed the opera house. It was a hard straw boater, a straw boater with a distinctive blue and white band, and a lanyard. The straw boater could be seen in the back panel opening of a maze of hackneys. Hobson excused himself and began to follow the straw boater as a heavily laden Carabao drawn cart blocked his view. Further frustrating him, the Oyster Pirate and Tiger, sensing his excitement, would not let him break free.

"I think that's a fellow I talked to once, turns out he's some sort of filibusterer or ordnance honey-fuggler, a gent named Atticaris, and the ONI fellows – the intelligence fellows -- are interested in him. He's involved in some form of treacheration. Three white suits and he'll spot us as easily as white sails against a wooded headland.

"We figure out where he's staying, and even better what he's up to, and they'll be somethin' in it for us or maybe *Pluto*."

The Oyster Pirate began to wave his hands to speak, but Tiger interrupted. "Many uniforms around, US Navy, and Royal Navy, Kreigsmarine and Japanese. Many uniforms."

The Chinaman was keen for the chase. Tiger was keen for everything, Hobson was not surprised.

Hobson shook his head. "See if you can scrape up the ONI representative. Start at the Governor's office."

The Oyster Pirate, who appeared eager to follow, was not enthusiastic about squandering liberty time on anyone official, but Tiger managed to drag him off stammering. Tiger knew that a lone Chinaman, even one in naval uniform, had a Chinaman's chance of getting help at the Governor's office.

CHAPTER NINE

Hobson wended his way through the street stands and the alleyways trying to keep up with the hackney. It stopped and it passengers descended. Atticaris was not alone. He was talking to another shorter man with a deep tan. The man was a little over five feet tall, carried his arms away from him like a stevedore, and wore a battered bowler. They went to a shop and Atticaris picked up a package. Hobson made note of the sign, "Stewart's Fabric and Dry Goods." They changed course several times. The shorter man walked with a singularly upright posture and occasionally looked over his shoulder. Atticaris and the shorter, more powerfully built man walked a distance and stared into a shop window.

Suddenly they doubled back and came directly at Hobson.

"White suit stands out in a shop window's reflection. Well, my fine young crackerjack, you are a ways from Japan."

"Well, join the Navy, see the world. *Pluto*'s in at Sangley Point, y'know. Simply enjoying the sights courtesy of the U. S. taxpayer."

This seemed to tickle the man in the bowler who broke out in a grin. He had a first-rate handlebar moustache which accented a very badly broken nose. Hobson sensed that luxuriant handlebar was a point of pride. One hand was constantly stroking it. The nose had to have been broken repeatedly, to be that flat. Hobson's gaze ran down to his hands. They were broad, the knuckles enlarged. A bantamweight… smoker fighter or bareknuckle boxer.

"Let me buy you a drink. I wore a white suit once. Atlantic Fleet, not out here among the tigers, dragons, and bamboo breezes."

The man in the bowler took Hobson by the upperarm firmly. He guided Hobson and Atticaris through several alleys. They ducked into a barbecue parlor with beaded curtains and a dirt floor. Hobson thought he saw a rat scurry under a table. The man in the bowler hat seemed to know the place and said something to the proprietor in a language that was not English.

"You're a talented fellow, Hobson. Navy man, navigational skills, weapons training, and language ability." Atticaris said with interest. "It seems I might have a project or two you could help me with."

"You know that white suit will use you up. It used up my father and it would have used me up, if I'd let it."

Atticaris' look mixed charm and intensity. And confidence, he was ever so confident.

"A lot of talk about honor and status. Yes, status. Most people don't want to have anything to do with the Navy, officer or enlisted. Won't even let you in their houses. You know that."

"Were you an officer?" Buy time and play to his ego. Hobson studied Atticaris' face. Clean shaven, so soft and smooth, not a wrinkle and somehow vaguely top heavy. Atticaris was always smiling. Life came easy to Atticaris, he had everything under control, and he rated only the best. The best came easy.

The Filipino owner opened two warm beers. As the man with the bowler reached for his beer, a tattoo of an eagle, globe and anchor showed under his cuff. That helped Hobson place him, an ex-service expatriate – Philippine service probably with Waller at Samar.

"Of course, commissioned just before the old man began playing the market. He told me not to do it. It's a burnout profession. Lots of obligations and standards, but no payoff. I'm a businessman and figure out how to get that tired professional knowledge to pay, something my father never learned how to do. Farragut took all the credit and left my father with nothing. That book never made him much, he died bankrupt. I'm never going to die bankrupt."

"You don't talk like an officer, they're always talking about duty and honor and obligation…and how it's a …." Hobson began.

"It's nonsense." He dismissed the thought with his hand.

"…a vocation."

An unidentifiable meat came on skewers.

"You know they talk about that in churches sometimes, about vocations…" Hobson began again.

"Yes, that should be the only place, in churches. Somewhere that's got a firm grasp on total unreality"

Hobson studied the dragons on his cuffs. "Well, my parents were in the church go-to-meeting business. Vocation, it means a calling, I think. Something more than a paycheck. Something special about whatever it is you're called to. People look on vocations as a destiny. People who think about vocations, they feel they are going to be needed for some great purpose, someday."

"Great purpose? No one believes that."

"I think maybe my skipper thinks like that. Maybe some other officers. It's not just officers get to thinking like that."

Atticaris eyes narrowed. "You don't believe in that hokum. There's no lofty purpose in plotting lines on charts and passing coal."

"Don't rightly know what I think most of the time. Of course, on occasion, my leading petty officer tells me what I should think, and if he doesn't about half of the crew and all the officers do. The benefits of disciplination."

"So how about being a business man out here in the Pacific with me. Make more money than all the men who swing a hammock aboard *Pluto* make in a year. You can buy a collier and have change left over and mix a few diamonds in with the lumps of coal."

Hobson rubbed his chin noncommittally and began to search for his pipe.

"People around you, off Korea, haven't had much chance to spend their money lately."

Atticaris stiffened and looked at his pocket watch. The man in the bowler gave Hobson a wry look of indifference. Atticaris rose to leave and the man with the bowler followed his lead. "Sailors are fools. Always have been, always will be. You'll die drunk in the shadow of a piling with a hooker going through your wallet."

The man with the bowler grinned, "Yup, sailors is fools." He chuckled as if it was an old joke.

"Well, sir, can't say I agree with your opinion, but thanks for the beer and monkey meat. Take an even strain."

*****

Hobson, Tiger, the Oyster Pirate, and a very bored clerk from the Governor's office searched the area later, but Atticaris was gone. They found his hotel and learned he had checked out.

"Fl-fl-flew the coup." The Oyster Pirate observed, his Adam's apple bobbing. "Shady sonuvabitch, cutting into my liberty time. Low life. Some fellows are always playing angles, gotta watch 'em. Gotta watch 'em real close."

The Oyster Pirate looked particularly thoughtful and sincere as if he had revealed a great truth. "Did he say he was an officer?"

"Yeah, well, can't watch 'im. That's problem. Big darn problem."

Hobson went back to Stewart's Fabric and Dry Goods and learned that Atticaris had placed special orders for goods that were delivered to the dry goods store. Atticaris had essentially paid them for use as a mailing address. The staff was all Filipino; no one named Stewart had been associated with the shop for years. Several crates had arrived but no member of the staff knew what was in them more than the fact that one package was ripped and had contained what looked like woolen long underwear. One damaged crate's contents had resembled an overgrown coffee grinder.

The Governor's office clerk rolled his eyes, convinced pranksters had dragged him off on a fool's errand. "Not much call for wool long underwear in the Philippines. You sure this is the fellow running guns to the Moros? Anyone who can sell long underwear in the Philippines has a promising future in retailing."

PART II

Coaling Ship

Coal! Coal! There is no escape from it; the choking dust lies everywhere, there is no getting away from from the thunderous rattle of the cobs as they pour into the yawning holds, nor relief from the labour of warping ship back and forward to suit the trimming of the cargo. Coal! Coal!

-David William Bone

CHAPTER TEN

The Navy Department had grown fitfully during the last two decades, but now gloried in an all-out renaissance. Though its ships-of-the-line were all United States made, graced by the technology of America's burgeoning economy, the same could not be said of many of its auxiliary vessels. *Pluto* was a Spanish merchantman that had been converted to provide coal to the fleet. She was part of the spoils of the Spanish-American War. For the past few weeks, she had prowled the Philippine Islands, America's possession, and it was rumored she'd be headed for Shanghai shortly. As part of the Naval Auxiliary Service under the Bureau of Navigation, some colliers had a merchant seaman component to their crew, but not *Pluto*. She was all Navy and an experiment in efficiency.

Every morning the department heads reported to the bridge for 0800 reports. Since the bridge was Hobson's normal station, he often had the treat of observing senior management in action and picking up valuable scuttlebutt.

Hobson paid only passing attention to most of those present, but he watched four of them keenly. They were the skipper, Mr. Wheelwright, Quartermaster First Class Phipps – Hobson's supervisor, Yeoman First Class Jackson, the black petty officer who handled correspondence record keeping and administration, and finally there was the Prince of Darkness. The Prince of Darkness was a massive, battered, Warrant Officer from somewhere in the Ozarks. It was rumored that Warrant Officer Crottle – for that was his real name -- had killed a man in his adolescence and had been "encouraged" to enlist. It was also believed he'd killed a Navy chief at Cavite when he himself had been a chief. There had been an investigation, but nothing had come of it. Everyone seemed to accept that he had, and that the chief at Cavite had had it coming to him. Hobson had come to *Pluto* after the event and no one seemed interested in talking about it. Hobson had been warned, however, that Warrant Officer Crottle was not a man to be crossed, and to give him a wide berth. As a warrant, Mr. Crottle experienced a limbo-like social status; no longer enlisted, yet not quite a commissioned officer.

Crottle always appeared on the bridge in soot-covered denim coveralls. Phipps assigned a striker to walk discreetly behind Crottle and clean up after him when he appeared on the bridge. Crottle did not seem to notice. He never smiled and on the rare occasions that he talked about anything except the responsibilities of the Black Gang, his comments were pure vinegar.

Though Crottle's social status might have been ambiguous, his place in the naval pantheon could not have been clearer. Black Gangs inhabit a special kind of naval Hell. In the tropics, the temperatures below normally exceeded 100 degrees Fahrenheit and members of the Gang had to stoke the fires which kept steam up in the boilers. It was hot, strenuous, noisy, dirty work. In battle, the stokers and rest of the Black Gang were locked below. There was no alternative; movement and maneuver were the keys to survival in an engagement at sea. The Black Gang's duty station was in the hot, sooty bowels of the ship... and that status could drive men mad. On liberty the wildest, meanest, most dangerous section of the crew was the members of the Black Gang. Crottle was King of the Black Gang.

The skipper and the three department heads exercised four distinct styles of leadership and each was successful. Mr. Wheelwright was a gentleman. He was known to be thoughtful, intelligent, and fair, but he was not anyone's friend, he was everyone's boss. The smart money said he would not be on an auxiliary long. It was said he came from an Eastern family with money, but if he did he did not make an issue of it.

Yeoman First Class Jackson was likeable. Everyone liked him. His eyes lit up when anyone entered his workspace and he had this laugh. He seemed to seek every crew member out and he tried to joke with each one. People did things for him, just because they liked him. He had a smile that made you think of a piano keyboard. He was a good musician, better than most of the members of the marine band at Cavite. And he could dance…not ballroom dancing, the other kind.

Quartermaster First Class Phipps was the oldest, older than Mr. Crottle. He'd been everywhere and done everything twice. He knew more about navigation than Columbus and all the officers combined, and one or two of them had degrees in pretty fancy scientific areas of engineering. Wizened, gray, and heavily tattooed, he had a naval homily – always slightly negative in tone -- for every occasion. He'd been a petty officer in what he called "the Cubic Wars," the series of affairs including the Spanish-American War involving Cuba, before coming to the Asiatic Fleet.

Crottle led by intimidation. He looked right through you and the corners of his mouth were permanently curled downward. It seemed like a good idea to do what he told you. He'd used his fists coming up, and still used them to make a point. He had never fought in a Navy smoker, but there was frequent speculation on his ability to take the fleet title. Now that he was a warrant, it could only be speculation. To whip him, the speculation ran further; you'd have to kill him.

Warrant Officer Crottle didn't think much of the Navy sports program and rowing in particular. And Hobson was the unofficial coach and manager of the rowing team.

Technically there was an ensign who'd rowed crew for two semesters at Annapolis assigned to run the team, but he was overburdened by official duties, and Hobson was the one who made it work. He cajoled volunteers and figured a practice schedule. He smooth-talked his recruits into regular training which went beyond rowing and included running, speed walking, and work with Indian clubs. Hobson, who had grown up among sampans and schooners, had the most small-boat training of any of the crew, many of whom were from landlocked Western and Midwestern states, except the Oyster Pirate and Tiger.

"Coaling *Baltimore* at 0830. Make sure *Baltimore*'s infernal gun sponsons don't gouge our sides." Wheelwright announced at the end of reports and the captain nodded.

This was no revelation. Coaling was simply a matter of pain, pain to be endured, and accustomed pain.

He did not mention the pulling-boat competition; he did not need to. *Baltimore* would bait *Pluto* and *Pluto* would take it, for the time being.

"As is our lot in life, we shall be dispersing black diamonds to the needy."

*****

"Bring back sail, bring back sail," was the chant that started somewhere on the *Baltimore*'s foredeck and then died. The skipper of *Baltimore* holding his stopwatch scowled and looked at his executive officer. Somewhere amidships *Baltimore*'s massive master-at-arms brushed aside lined-up bodies with a snarl as he made for the miscreants. There would be no counter-productive frivolity, let alone unnecessary time-wasting talk, on *Baltimore*. The time it took to take on coal was one indication of operational readiness. The skipper of *Baltimore*, like every other protected cruiser skipper, timed coaling.

"These Baltimores is full o' beans, ain't they?" Jackson said to Phipps. Phipps gave the black yeoman a sidelong glance. "Them cruiser sailors are no stranger to arrogance, that's for sure. A few weeks ago they caught some 'Frisco gunrunner trying to smuggle Gatling guns to the Moros on Mindanao. Admiral loves 'em now, more than ever. Heck, they'll be totally insufferable for months. Cruiser sailors, hah, no liberty port's gonna be big enough for their swelled heads."

Pluto's mascot, Admiral Fu, a goat with a coat like obsidian, bleated eagerly from his station on the main deck.

Baltimore and *Pluto* were rafted up on *Baltimore*'s anchor in a still cove off Formosa. Enormous hemp fenders had been rigged, as well as a series of "clotheslines" and brows for small carts. *Pluto* was the larger ship. She was black and forbidding with buff colored decks that would soon be black, too. Alongside her -- nearly as big -- bristling with six-inch guns lay *Baltimore*, with buff decks, too, but painted a virginal white. The coal would be in sacks primarily, but any container would do. The coal was wheeled in coaling trucks to the round bunker scuttles and dumped down chutes into the bunkers. There trimmers shifted the coals around evenly and jammed it evenly. This was a timed maneuver, considered a measure of a warship's ability to operated under wartime conditions and was an indirect measure of a warship's endurance.

The amount of coal shifted during the preceding hour was announced on the hour. A good ship could shift 100 tons of coal in an hour. It was relentless, grimy, backbreaking work.

As the first coal went into *Baltimore*'s bunkers the cry came up like a wail, "Nip diamonds." The lament "Nip diamonds" was echoed throughout *Baltimore* and *Baltimore*'s crew gave *Pluto*'s crew a collective look that was not, as Phipps described it, "Christian." Philadelphia was the City of Brotherly Love; Baltimore as far as anyone could tell was the City that Hated Nip Diamonds. Japanese coal burned sooty and fouled the ship. Japanese coal was the dirtiest coal a ship could burn.

As a rated quartermaster Hobson did not have to pass coal. In fact, Phipps actively discouraged him from doing so; it might set bad precedent. If the ship had been underway, there was no doubt Hobson would not have been allowed to pass coal. His quartermaster skills were too important to the running of *Pluto*. But they were at anchor and Hobson had submitted a chit to do so. The system couldn't really stop you from doing extra work without a good reason. That too might set a dangerous precedent.

Warrant Officer Crottle looked on in his sooty coveralls. Coalpassers, a distinct rate, came under the engineering.

"Black Gang don't need no 'exercise,' " said Crottle with disdain and flipped the remainder of his coffee over the side. The surly engineer wiped his brush-like walrus mustache, which arched gloriously and seemed to accent his massive shoulders.

He knew why Hobson and the rest of the rowing team had volunteered to pass coal. Only a few of the engineering rates had joined the rowing team and Hobson suspected Crottle had discouraged others from rounding out the team. The Oyster Pirate, an oiler, was one of the few that had risked Crottle's displeasure.

"Exercise is for skaters, for people who don't have no real work. Exercise's fool's work for people with nothing better to do. You don't get paid for 'exercise,' do ya? So what's the point? Somebody else's entertainment?"

"Just taking an even strain, Mr. Crottle," Hobson returned. There was nothing to be gained getting into an argument with Crottle. Was Crottle looking to start something, or was he making a point?

Hobson crawled down into *Pluto*'s bunkers with a shovel and began loading 100-pound bags.

He could hear Admiral Fu bleating derisively above him.

Another sailor in the bunker mused about more efficient ways to pass coal. It was said experiments had been conducted where coal could be passed at sea using shear legs, tensioned cables, and trolleys. Some said oil would change things. No one on either ship could truly visualize a Navy that ran on something poured out of a can.

*****

Lunch was on station. Salted beef on crackers that turned black with handling, and water, was passed among the crew. The sailor next to Hobson looked out of the scuttle at *Baltimore*.

"Hey, look they've got soft tack, bread. Fresh bread or biscuits maybe."

A protected cruiser stood a high likelihood of having a baker and serviceable ovens. *Pluto* had none of these.

"Criminy, wish-t I was on a cruiser."

Crottle appeared behind him out of nowhere. His battered form loomed over the edge of the scuttle and with the sun just behind it. His massive shadow covered the scuttle. He spit over the side, a good distance.

"Brass and brightwork and fresh paint and fresh bread don't make no ship. Each of these magic carpets made of steel can take you some place better'an you been.

"Who's to say what ships better'an another. We're here to make sure the Navy lays ordnance on a target some place, anyplace, when it wants to. It's like we're all links in one long anchor chain. If *Baltimore* can lob shells into Shanghai or into a limey battleship, who's to say whether they could do it 'cause we gave 'em the coal to get there, or it's because some slick gunner's mate can do math or the stewards served a good enough meal to the officers to give'em gumption. It all goes into the forgin' of the chain. Well you jus' remember '...on the strength of one link in the cable, dependeth the might of the chain...'

"I'd check any new bosses and shipmates afore you get it into your head to jump ship. Don't jump outta the boiler into the firebox, you scrawny excuse for a sailor. You so sure that you got it so bad here?"

Crottle turned away just as suddenly as he had appeared. The sailor ducked down into the scuttle muttering under his breath, "Tarnation, the Prince of Darkness has spoken and he spoke to me."

The Prince of Darkness. No one ever said it to his face.

CHAPTER ELEVEN

"Secure from coaling." The boatswain's whistles trilled.

Coal dust covered everything. It was as if the world had been scorched and covered with black pepper.

"The Great Black Fleet," the sailor next to Hobson mumbled as he poked his head through the bunker scuttle. They looked at each other. They were totally black except for their eyeballs, and little white cracks radiating from their eyes. "The stacks have gone to war with the decks."

Hobson looked out of the bunker scuttle and recognized Gunnarson on *Baltimore* lounging on a gunmount just above him. Gunnarson did not recognize him.

Crottle mustered the coalpassers on the fantail and they stripped. They stacked their clothing in bins. Later the clothing would be tied to lines trailed over the side leaving a squid-like line of ink. *Pluto* fouled both the skies and the seas.

Crottle chuckled mirthlessly. Before him were dozens of men jet black from the neck up, with pale pasty bodies, gritting their teeth and naked as jaybirds. He gave the order to turn on the hoses. The hoses were none too gentle. Black faces and pale white bodies.

*****

"*Pluto*'s Black Diamonds, best damned minstrel show in the Pacific," a quartermaster yelled down from *Baltimore*'s signal bridge as *Pluto* pulled away and the coaling detail began its wash down. The signalman cooing noises and held his binoculars like a dowager at the opera.

"Stow it, *Baltimore*," Crottle bellowed. One of the hoses seemed to turn toward *Baltimore* and the quartermaster sought cover.

Baltimore, conducting a similar washdown, crossed *Pluto*'s hose stream with its own in warning. Then both hoses turned back to their naked crews.

"Hey turn the hose on Wild Irene," yelled one coalpasser pointing to a tattoo of a winking Gibson girl on one buttock. "She don't like no black diamonds, just the white, sparkly kind."

"With a tattoo, you ain't never really naked, ya know," he pronounced to those around him sagely.

*****

Hobson saw Lieutenant Commander Wheelwright bridle.

Wheelwright was proud of *Pluto*'s minstrel show, one of the best in the fleet. To the coal dust covered crew, the reference had a double meaning. Minstrel shows were standard shipboard entertainment throughout the fleet and had been so for decades. They were a long established ritual of jokes, songs, music, and dancing. The humor was broad; subtlety had never been regarded as a naval virtue. The First Class Yeoman, Pompeii Jackson, was an accomplished buck dancer, and one of the crew's most respected and well-liked members. His father had been a minstrel on a riverboat. Yet, the comment had been meant as a slur. Perhaps minstrel shows themselves carried the undercurrent of a slur, Hobson thought. It was just easier to draw sailors out and get them to them to take their lot less seriously, if there was an accepted ritual. Like the Crossing the Line ritual, everyone knew the jokes and the parts, but it was still taken as fun where the whitehats were the stars. Everyone had seen or heard of a minstrel show and knew when to laugh or applaud. So if a sailor took part and seemed a little fouled up, well the sailor was just playing a part and who knew if it was he or what the part called for. Everyone participated at some point. Many looked forward to them.

"I think we are going to do away with black face from here on out," Wheelwright said to no one in particular. "Our shows don't need it."

Later someone had said something to Jackson about it and he had rubbed his chin thoughtfully, "Naw, don't need it. 'Cept if this catches on, I don't know whose rice bowl is going to get broken back home. Some of us," he grinned knowingly, " didn't have to put much on. Yes, we used to save a lot of money on that black face make-up. Me, I won't miss it. Just nobody mess with my dancing. Ha, you folk won't ever learn to dance right."

Then Jackson laughed that laugh that everyone liked.

No one seemed to mind except the machinist's mate who had come up with a goop for cleaning the stuff off and charged a whole two bits. "Point out that signalman to me when we get back to Cavite."

"I'd would kind of like for us to beat *Baltimore* in that pulling boat race," Jackson said to himself as he descended the ladder.

*****

A day out of Olongapo, Hobson was on the signal bridge. Quartermasters, in addition to navigational duties, handled flags and signals. Another U. S. N. ship was in the area and he was searching the horizon for it.

Hobson was particularly alert in the first dogwatch as they emerged from a rainsquall. Tiger had smuggled a mango out of the officers' mess for Hobson and he was carving slices out of it on the sly. The trouble was that Admiral Fu one deck below had detected the existence of the stray mango and had begun to bleat.

As the shadows lengthened, they began overtaking a good-sized prau and Hobson gave it the once over. A man and his wife tended its lines.

In the foresheets of the distant prau was a man about average height for a Filipino wearing little more than a loincloth and a scarf around his head. Tucked in the loincloth was a bolo knife. At the tiller was a very young woman wrapped in little more than a towel. He seemed unusually well developed in the shoulders for a Filipino. A long luxuriant moustache arched below his nose like a miniature woman's boa. It would have made a wonderful handlebar waxed. The man's hand drifted unconsciously to stroke it.

Hobson remembered their course would take them in the general direction of Mindanao and called down the speaking tube, "Phipps, suggest to the skipper we come closer to that prau."

"Hobson, we can't be inspecting barebreasted jail-bait just because you learned how to use a set of binoculars today. You're gonna haf to learn a-nat-tummy on your own time."

"No, Phipps, I'm serious. Suggest he change course to get closer to that prau. Something a mite unchristian there. Just a mite, tell'em Hobson said so. Just a mite."

A ten degree course alteration brought the prau into fuller view. Thirty minutes later Hobson could make out fishnets in detail and a man had a badly broken nose and a tattoo on one wrist.

"Phipps? Tell the skipper I think it's a gunrunner. Guns to the Moros on Mindanao. We better get to her before sunset."

Tiger sounded the bugle and *Pluto* came to general quarters.

*****

Pluto raised the code flags for "heave to, boarding" which were ignored. A gun crew prepared to fire across the prau's bow.

At three hundred yards all hell broke loose. The prau suddenly bristled with Winchesters and two *Pluto* crewmen readying the steam launch for the boarding party fell dead. At the same time the searchlights were shot out.

"Gutsy bastards." Phipps said with heat. "Gutsy, dead as a tin of corned beef, bastards."

"Open up with the Maxims." Wheelwright commanded. The prau was laced from stem to stern with ball.

All the prau's lines parted and its sail came crashing to the deck. In the twilight, they could see a half dozen Moros rushing on deck as the prau was holed below the water line. *Pluto* gave no cease fire command. They dropped into a bloody tangle. Hobson could not see the girl, but assumed she was dead, too. The man with the flowing moustache had found concealment and continued to lay down fire. The Maxims probed for a while and eventually found him.

*****

Hobson was part of the boarding party. The prau was settling. The man with the moustache was indeed the man with the bowler.

"Eagle, globe, and anchor." Phipps said looking at his tattoo. "Hmmm, didn't put enough aside for retiry-ment. Should have bought a bar instead. One of Butcher Waller's boys, I'll bet. Decided to play both sides. I'd say he was the boss and it looks like the fellow in charge of the project has to know the locals in this operation."

They found brass cases of Winchesters elaborately encased in oiled leather bags stored in watertight brass boxes.

"Very, very polished." Wheelwright observed. "That's not a standard shipping package for ordnance. Someone must know about

92

ships and the sea and how to protect expensive hardware afloat, no matter how crude the delivery."

"Not just afloat," Jackson, the yeoman, interrupted. "These packages can be submerged. You could just drop them off the coast, and buoy them for pickup."

*****

Once stripped of her cargo, the prau was set afire and adrift. They would photograph the bodies of the gunrunners in daylight. The prau burned brilliantly with occasional bursts that proved they had not found all the ammunition.

When the prau had burned to the waterline the gun crew broke apart the remainder of the derelict with 30mm high explosive rounds.

*****

The boatswain's mate piped "all hands to bury the dead," the funeral service was read over the two crewmembers, they were consigned to the deep, and their personal effects were auctioned off to the crew.

The gunrunners too were dropped over the side, but with less ceremony.

Tiger was surprised to discover that Admiral Fu had fallen to a stray bullet. There was fresh meat in the crew's mess that night.

*****

The Admiral was very pleased with *Pluto*. The pulling boat race now -- for Wheelwright – was all risk and beyond any benefit, but the die had been cast. It could not win him favor above what had been earned intercepting a gunrunner to the Moros.

The crew positively swaggered around Manila. The Oyster Pirate for a beer would show shipmates Stewart's Fabric and Dry Goods if they could endure the thirty-second warm up period it took for him to get started on the story. At a higher level there was even talk of other colliers with all Navy crews.

That week, Calle de Escolta belonged to *Pluto*.

*****

Hobson found himself in an office in Manila describing his meeting with Atticaris to his commanding officer, Mr. Draper who had been called in from Japan, a local ONI officer and the flag lieutenant. He described the pursuit of Atticaris and the subsequent seizure of the gunrunning prau on its way to Mindanao.

In return, the ONI officer informed them that the man in the battered bowler had been O'Hare, an ex-Marine with many years' Philippine experience.

"Funny thing," the ONI officer said. "We have been paying O'Hare for intelligence for months. He provided good information on the Moros. We've rounded up several Moro insurgents and we foiled several of their raids based on his tips."

"Well, Atticaris and his buddies seem to fancy their greenbacks flowing from two directions." Hobson knew he was taking a chance offering his opinions, but he was somewhat flattered by the attention, and at the same time uncomfortable enough to reach unconsciously for his pipe. "They know that they best keep up the conflict. If any one side wins too fast, Mr. Atticaris and his gang lose a market, I expect."

"Well, Hobson, I know one thing. I don't want any of Atticaris' expensive ordnance going to the Philippines and I think *Jade Rooster* might have been carrying a shipment of something dangerous to our interests," said Draper.

"Well, my chief concern is that none of Atticaris' hardware gets to the Philippines. I wonder if this whole *Jade Rooster* incident is a matter of Philippine guns being diverted by Korean rebels." Draper's uniform was even more rumpled than usual. Hobson could see that the flag lieutenant had difficulty looking Draper in the eye and wanted to give him a wide berth in case whatever the naval militia officer had was catching.

"Two other matters. Are you familiar with the Sisters Rowbotham?"

Hobson drew a blank.

"Two Mucha-esque ladies who hang around the Grand Hotel."

Now Hobson remembered the long dresses and swirling strawberry blonde hair, two sisters who flowed rather than walked across a man's line of vision.

"One of them carries a knife and knows how to use it. She dispatched some blackguard of a drunken German steamship officer the other night as he tried to storm into her hotel room. Seems she and Atticaris were acquainted. It wouldn't surprise me if she made the acquaintance of Hoyt at some point...no intentional pun there."

No one laughed. Draper wondered if he should warn the British attaché to whisk them out of the country before Koizumi got his claws into them. He would have to give it some thought since the British and the Japanese were allies.

"There's a final matter. I also wonder why if Sabatelli didn't know what Atticaris was up to, why he's gone to so much trouble to determine what's happened to the barque." Draper speculated. "If we are right, it seems Atticaris portion of the cargo was worth the most."

*****

Warships were the greatest mobile concentration of applied technological skill and lethal force in the world and those who sailed them knew it.

Cruisers were the largest American warships in the Pacific and America's single greatest concentration of destructive might in that ocean. *Baltimore* had fought alongside Dewey at Manila Bay and its crew could not help basking in the glory of her great name and awesome power in the conduct of their daily lives. Cruisermen were the top warrior caste in the Asiatic Fleet. Only men's men could harness and direct the very might of the god of War. Only men's men could control the power that flowed through her mighty machinery and flamed through her thunderous guns. They were men's men, the select, near divine heroes who functioned on a plane rightfully above that of mere mortals. Who dare judge them or hold them responsible for their actions, especially ashore away from the terrible burden of their awesome power? Looking into the mirror, some cruisermen half expected to see sunlight radiating from their eyes, clouds swirling about them, and lightning bolts shooting from their extended fingers.

It was to be expected that the crew of *Pluto* found the crew of *Baltimore* insufferably condescending in their dealing with their smudgy brothers from the naval underworld.

CHAPTER TWELVE

Pluto was ordered to Subic Bay. There several ships coordinated a minstrel show at the Navy Theater in Olongapo. Often only one ship put on a show, but in this case the performers came from different ships. The idea was inspired, for as luck would have it, the ships in port boasted an unusually good selection of amateur entertainers.

Jackson, for one, of *Pluto* was well known and his name was used as the top draw. He would perform near the end. Several groups sang spirituals or did barber shop quartets. A smattering of comic routines in the "Mr. Bones" vein followed them. At the conclusion of one of these, Tiger chased the Oyster Pirate into the aisles with a butcher's cleaver in a time-honored burlesque that they improved with a run of headless sailor jokes. A slapstick send up of the naval hospital at Yokohama was well received. Three performers did impressions including a brave coalpasser from *Pluto* who did fairly respectful impressions of Mr. Wheelwright and Mr. Crottle. Crottle never smiled. Not to be outdone, a boatswain from one of the harbor tugs did an impression of Theodore Roosevelt and the Admiral. A yeoman visiting from a submarine in Cavite recited poetry by Sir Walter Scott, and a corpsman did "The Village Smithy." *Baltimore* had a jug band with a few ukuleles that played several contemporary selections which were generally held to be of high order. A painter from *Baltimore*, who was also part of the jug band, broke away and pulled out an English 48-button concertina. He danced an awkward hornpipe and did a medley including the ever popular "A Life on the Ocean Wave."

It was raining outside the theater. This time of year, it rained daily. The roof of the theater was tin and the rain had a soothing, sizzling effect.

A sailor attached to the naval station did a selection of fiddle pieces, which he sang with a pronounced country twang. He encouraged the audience to join in the chorus of "Comin' Round the Mountain" as he improvised mildly off-color lyrics, which brought scowls from the officers with wives. Hobson was surprised to see Crottle smile.

The ship's crews seated themselves by ship. *Baltimore* was the largest ship in port and its crew occupied the greatest number of seats. Like most cruisers and battleships, *Baltimore* had a marine detachment. Also occupying a large number of seats was the Station's marine detachment. *Baltimore*'s marine detachment was of two minds, and uneasy in the presence of this other marine detachment. Although they were crew of *Baltimore*, as marines they were the organization that enforced order on sailors. By tradition, marines in addition to sniping from on high, provided colorguards, and reinforced landing parties. They also constituted the thin blue and red line which defined the demarcation between labor and management aboard ship.

*****

Up until the concertina selection, *Baltimore*'s superiority had gone unchallenged. The most popular performances had come from *Baltimore*. Most of the performers from the other ships were in blackface, but *Pluto*'s performers were not. Petty Officer Jackson now caught the spotlight. Jackson was as near a professional as they would see that night. He was a buck dancer and buck dancers did very athletic performances involving jumps, slips, and the intricate tapping of shoe heels and toes with special shoes. His father had been a professional dancer and his father before him. Dancing had taken them out of the cotton fields and guaranteed their survival during the Reconstruction. No one could simply decide to become a buck dancer. A buck dancer had to be coached and had to practice buck dancing for several years. First Class Yeoman Jackson had met the requirements.

And with little more than a drum and a trombone as accompaniment, it showed. The Oyster Pirate played fairly basic trombone with a battered, borrowed instrument. Hobson, who was part of the assigned shore patrol, could not figure out how Jackson could practice or where, but he held no doubt that it was a practiced performance. The crowd sprang to their feet and demanded an encore. Most of the *Baltimore* crewmen however sat sullenly in their seats.

Shore patrol duty was rotated among the ship's rated personnel and considered "leadership" training. Members of the shore patrol had to know regulations and had to act to enforce regulations. For the most part, it was not bad duty, members of the shore patrol went where the excitement was and to many places for free. Problems for the most part were unambiguous and consisted of keeping the vertical drunks in line and getting the horizontal drunks back to their ships.

Jackson wiped his brow and did another performance. He gestured for the audience to keep the beat by clapping -- alternating strong and weak claps. Then he began to syncopate against that underlying beat. Many of the sailors, those who had grown up outside the big cities, had never heard syncopation and realized it was something unusual, but could not put their finger on what gave the performance its catchy, almost hypnotic quality. The Oyster Pirate launched into his single ragtime tune and a couple sailors began dancing in front of their chairs.

Though the majority of the audience approved, a significant majority of the audience from *Baltimore* did not. It was unfitting for an auxiliary to steal a minstrel show. The battleships put on the best shows, then the cruisers, then whatever was left. Here, a 'what's left" was upstaging a cruiser.

For a moment, Hobson thought he saw the burly Gunner's Mate, Gunnarson, moving restlessly in the midst of the Baltimore seats. He made note to keep an eye out for the cruiserweight boxer.

At that point the monsoon broke and the rain began coming down in wind-driven sheets. It prompted one of those quiet moments during any performance, during which one of the Baltimores was heard to say in a loud voice, "… black as a skillet…" No one could say what the context of the statement was, but it was widely taken as an insult. *Pluto's* crew of about three dozen arose en masse. Hobson and the other members of *Pluto's* shore patrol jumped into the aisles and put themselves in buffer positions. *Baltimore's* shore patrol did the same.

The officers and chiefs who had brought their wives began edging them toward the exits.

Jackson stiffened for just a moment. Then his routine seemed to extend and build in intensity and bravado. His performance assumed a power, a style, and anger. It had become "make-see pidgin." He ended with an aerial and a split and then raised his hand in a well-known gesture of defiance. The gesture was made in the direction of the Baltimores.

Had the chairs been permanent and bolted to the floor, it would have been different.

A chair was thrown, the rain intensified, and then the wave broke with force. Several chairs flew.

Suddenly it was shoulder to shoulder and there was outraged yelling that was hard to follow. Hobson could see Gunnarson with several of his shipmates. They were inching toward *Pluto's* seats. Hobson turned to face his shipmates, but had his truncheon up and stood so he could turn quickly.

Olongapo's marine detachment started plowing a path through the hall, back to front. Several assumed positions around the Admiral's party. No one could figure out how, but they too had truncheons. *Baltimore*'s marine detachment wavered. There must have been grudges aboard *Baltimore* because several *Baltimore* bluejackets saw their opportunity and started windmilling into the leathernecks in their own ship's detachment. The crews of two destroyers turned and faced the cruiser sailors. If you were going to fight, you might as well take on an adversary that would add to your legend. Gunnarson and his following suddenly realized they were now dangerously distant from their engaged shipmates.

Gunnarson was angry and frustrated. He wanted to say something that would remind the collier sailors of their insignificance in the martial universe.

He thought and thought and as he did so, he found himself being swept backwards by the crowd.

"Screw *Pluto*, screw you slipknots. You're a bunch of third rate minstrels who can't even put on blackface right. We took this show. You no account sleeves aren't gonna win no pulling boat race either. In a pig's eye."

"Who says, no neck?" A voice from *Pluto*'s seats cried out. Followed by, "Yeah, who says, put money on it."

Gunnarson was trapped. It was bad enough that he was being swept along in a way that might be viewed as a retreat, but now he was going to have to take a financial risk. The only thing he could think of doing was yelling a figure that no one would match. He could have kept quiet but that was not Gunnarson's way. He could not see anyone he recognized so he might still get away with a bluff and a quick pull out.

"Yeah, in a pig's eye. Three hundred says you slipknots are gonna lose and lose bad."

A general intake of breath ensued. Though most of the hall was in an uproar, it was quiet in that small section. First the basic challenge itself was enough to give pause. Three hundred dollars was just about a year's pay. Second, no one seemed to know the no-necked gunner's mate's name or reputation. How seriously should they take the bet?

Hobson turned to face him. Gunnarson had had his attention on the crew. The shore patrol had been invisible to him.

"I'll take your money. Three hundred, cash, Gunnarson. Yeah, you, Gunnarson, I known your name. Three hundred in greenbacks. My name is Hobson, if you forgot. Quartermaster Third. Am I right? That's Gunnarson of *Baltimore*."

Gunnarson nodded slowly with a look that was later described as "downright unchristian."

*****

You got that much Hobson?" One of *Pluto*'s coalpassers asked.

"With what you other fellas throw in. Maybe. Anyway we're going to win."

"Others pitch in? Hobson, you're screwed."

CHAPTER THIRTEEN

At a different latitude, a few degrees of longitude away, the weather had assumed a dark and ominous aspect. There were those who attributed the same strengths and frailties of human character to the most subtle appearances of the sky. "Dark and forbidding" or "light and airy" for instance and certain color combinations and effects of light and dark surely conveyed a sense of mood. On this occasion, it was the very darkest part of the night in terms of cloud formations, celestial illumination, and of what was in store for several men on a distant Korean mountain.

On that mountain, several prisoners were shackled with their wrists bound behind them to waist-high posts. There were sacks over their heads. Several had endured torture to the extent they could barely stand and could never return to normal life.

It was very quiet. The few Japanese noncommissioned officers stood stock-still and seemed to almost hold their breaths. They were in a field on a mountain crest overlooking a valley. The spot had a pleasant yin and yang aspect.

A sword was drawn from a scabbard and, from the sound, the prisoners sensed instantly what was in store.

"Mansei!" they began to yell in unison over and over again with the hope someone would hear them.

The Japanese officer in jodhpurs and puttees made a couple practice swings with his sword. He would have liked people to think the sword had been in his family for centuries, but like most Japanese officers he was from non-Samurai stock hoping to rise in status.

He folded his uniform blouse and placed it on a stone monument. Someone long ago had noted the pleasant yin and yang to the clearing and used it as the family plot. Korea had few formal cemeteries in the western sense, and there were only those family plots situated in places with the proper mystical balance.

"Mansei!"

He was very accomplished in the use of the sword. He had not been born to it, but had studied its use rigorously. He had studied Kendo at the university -- he was one of those rare, university trained Army officers -- and accepted the fact that the day of the sword as a primary weapon had past. His university degree explained why he had been assigned to intelligence, and eventually the Kempeitai, the Imperial Japanese Intelligence Service. . The Meiji emperor had eliminated the status of samurai and it was now illegal in Japan for anyone, except a military officer, to wear a sword. This sword gave him a tradition and validity

"Mansei!"

He was good at languages and spoke English and, more importantly these days, Korean. Korean had been easier to learn than English; its grammar was similar to Japanese.

One sweep of the sword and he beheaded one of the prisoners. It was so swift and clean that the prisoner was stopped in mid-syllable. The sword was extremely sharp and the head had been severed cleanly and dropped not far from the slumped body at the post.

"Mansei!"

The waist-high posts had been arranged in a circle, sort of a low-lying Stonehenge. He criss-crossed the interior of the circle, back and forth, as if he was doing the kata, the sequence of practice movements, of a swordsman engaging several assailants.

Beheading was the historic privilege of an opposing samurai captured in battle. Indeed, it was an honor for those taken in battle. On the other hand, it was once the privilege of a samurai to behead anyone for "unseemly behavior." Was this war or peace? Were the Koreans opposing warriors or just unruly serfs? Hopefully he viewed the recent events as war and though the Kempeitai officer was not so sure this rabble deserved the honor, he sought an opportunity to test his sword and his warrior's heart.

"Mansei," the group chant was getting weaker as one by one the voices were stopped.

"Man…"

The last voice was stilled.

Major Koizumi of the Kempeitai wiped his sword with a clean cloth and gestured for the noncommissioned officers to deposit the bodies in a mass grave. He was pleased to begin his second tour here in Korea, for Korea offered many opportunities.

Mansei, he recalled, was the Korean word for freedom.

*****

The crew of *Jade Rooster* started to show up in Chefoo and other Chinese treaty ports in ones and twos. They all attested to the fact that *Jade Rooster* had been seized in the islands off Mokp'o. Sabatelli found his desk snowed under with the telegrams of beached seamen. The Royster Line's agent in Shanghai related a sad tale of stranded seamen drifting onto his doorstep and seeking backpay and return passage. The Korean fishermen who put them ashore on the Chinese mainland to the north always disappeared.

A clerk with a visor brought in a sheaf of bills of lading in a heavy binder and plunked in it down on his oak rolltop desk, the emblem of his exhaulted station. It was littered with tide and current books, coastal pilots, blotters, stamps, and back issues of the Police Gazette. On the walls were yellowed etchings of ancient square-riggers running before the wind with their pennants flowing in the wrong direction.

105

The story was always the same. *Jade Rooster* had been afloat when they had last seen her. There had been a gunfight.

This was a new development, no one had mentioned a gunfight. Had that occurred before or after the passengers had been set adrift? After gunfight some were made to sail the barque at gunpoint. They had last seen her in the night; her captive crew had threaded her through a rocky chain of islands. The *Jade Rooster* sailors were sure the fisherman and pirates had been Korean. There was the prevalence of garlic and fermented cabbage in the food they were given, the characteristic "eh-yo" at the end of sentence after sentence, and they had arrived at Shanghai from the East. One or two who had sailed Asian waters before were sure they had been taken off Mokp'o. No one was sure about the passengers. Some had been put over in boats. Some were held perhaps for ransom. Some, including the captain, had been either shot or executed.

Discussion of the passengers reminded Sabatelli of his initial contact with the surviving passengers. The Kims had disappeared. Sabatelli had lost track of Atticaris. He and Atticaris had tripped the light fantastic with the Sisters Rowbotham, the sinuous strawberry blondes with the continental manners. The man knew how to have a good time, Sabatelli mused with a smile. Edwina Rowbotham was something to remember, British, but really rather worldly in a Gallic way. He had grown to believe Atticaris was a beau, probably a bed-presser and cheated at cards, but pursued none of these vices to ungentlemanly excess. Atticaris had eventually headed on to Hong Kong as far as Sabatelli knew.

A Japanese runner chattering to the Japanese staff bustled into his office with a written notice of an arrival. He came from the mechanical semaphore station, part of a network of mechanical semaphore relays which monitored arrivals.

With the rush of faces and questions, Koizumi came to mind. He too, had left Tokio on some assignment. One of Sabatelli's commercial contacts had provided him with that information. The contact seemed relieved that Koizumi was gone. Koizumi seemed to know quite a few Westerners in the shipping business. He sensed that Atticaris and Koizumi were men who should be watched yet he could not say just why.

Well, time to get hold of Hobson again. Set him to work on finding *Jade Rooster*. He spoke the language, actually he spoke the languages. Korea seemed the next stop and that required knowledge of the rulers, Japanese, and the language of the ruled, the Koreans. Well, how was he going to get a hold of that bluejacket? And what was the name of that rumpled, bespeckled naval officer at the Embassy? That young, walking laundry bag of an officer would set the wheels in motion if he knew what was good for him. Yes, start there first.

As Sabatelli began to figure the best way to distribute cargoes to three ships still in demurrage, a pilot came in and roared his displeasure with the captain of a lumbership from Seattle. Tea, jute, silk -- he was always juggling, fitting, measuring, loading. It took Sabatelli a half-hour and a fifth of bourbon to mollify the disgruntled pilot.

One thing he had meant to pass on to Hobson. There was no Sato on the barque's passenger manifest. The nearest unaccounted for name was Moon. Sabatelli doubted it was a Japanese name. In his short time in Yokohama, he had begun to notice that, for the most part, Japanese names had several syllables, while Chinese and Korean names tended to have less.

Too many ships in demurrage, waiting to be loaded, a good sign if he had the time to take the long view. Perhaps Yokohama might catch up to Kobe.

On one very minor item, Sabatelli had not been completely forthright with the Navy. The matter was simply none of their business. He doubted if it would amount to much. Piracy had been committed on the high seas, or on some seas somewhere, and if no one else was interested, it was the Navy's duty to do something about it.

*****

Hobson had the evening watch as they neared Shanghai. After taps he took a round and noticed someone acting peculiarly on the fantail. He picked his way among the dozing sailors and caulking mats. As he approached, he realized it was Jackson doing something physical. As Hobson approached, he realized Jackson was working on his buck dancing and he was using the thump-thump-thump of the propeller to synchronize his movements. He was singing a ragtime melody softly to himself.

Jackson was a marvel. His movements made him appear to slide backward and forward, and then side to side. Sometimes he seemed to waver like beach grass buffeted by a spring tide. Gravity seemed to take a vacation where Jackson was concerned. The black man went an hour and then collapsed in a heap on one of the coalscuttles.

"Skipper lets me do this after taps. Have to work at it. I lose my dancing, I lose my connection, my..." he pointed panting to the life ring on the rail, " my life buoy."

"Just shy of excellent at that rigmarole. Lotta work staving around like that, I expect."

"Have to keep at it. I asked for a big ship -- something big and stable --with a reciprocating steam engine --for a beat. Tonight was a good night. Often the swell makes it impossible."

He took several deep breaths.

" I like what I do in the Navy, but the people out here are right. You have to respect the ancestors and save what they pass down. Not all of it, mind, just the good part. Without dancing, don't know how my family would have survived. Yup, these people out here, they're no fools. Problem is figuring what's the good part to save and pass on."

He wiped his forehead. "But I am in the Navy. Somewhere way back, my African ancestors got into it with another tribe and lost, and were sold off to Arab traders. Then to someone down South. The ancestors weren't strong enough."

He took off his shoes, stuffed them with paper, and put them into a bag.

"Don't want to be on the losing side, especially if the winning side is worth something. My grandfather saw the Confederacy and what some people call the Reconstruction. No, don't pay to lose. Kind of gives me the right feeling knowing how to use those. The great equalizers, jumbo size."

He pointed to where the Maxim guns were normally shipped.

"Steel is hard on the knees and ankles. I go lighter when I work out shipboard. Sometimes I wonder if I shoulda asked for a cruiser with their teak decks. 'Course, there's steel under the teak, so not that much more give. Well, after what I know about *Baltimore*, I 'm glad I got *Pluto*."

*****

Hobson returned to the Signal Bridge as *Pluto* steamed into Shanghai. He tallied sets of vertical red and white light signals that blinked in the collier's direction. Various combinations of lights composed the new night signaling system and the flagship seemed to be waiting for radioless *Pluto*'s arrival. Hobson read the lights, deciphered the code, and realized he was the subject of the message. "Qm 3c Hobson report flagship detached duty NE x E." He was being ordered to Korea.

Code or no code, the Oyster Pirate knew within an hour. "W-w-w-we're going for liberty in the Bund. Scuttlebutt is you're headed for the land of Asian hillbillies. Madame Kwan's, pocket billiards, cold beer, and cross country horseback riding for us in the Middle Kingdom and thatched huts, fleas, oxen, and garlic for you in the Hermit Kingdom. Tell you, we ain't gonna train very hard, rowing without you."

"Yeah, well they sing pretty good. I'll put a team of Koreans against a team of Chinese singing "Darlin' Clementine" and the Koreans will win every time, words and all."

The Oyster Pirate sniffed.

Madame Kwan was the proprietress of an anonymous establishment that catered to the bluejacket trade, beer, whiskey, girls, tours, music hall tickets, postcards, and a horse livery. Occasionally a neighboring house wafted the chestnut odor of opium and bad joss over the establishment, but directly upwind was the incense-washed Temple of T'ien-hou, the goddess of heaven and protector of sailors, fishermen, travelers, actors, and prostitutes. There was a pocket billiards table on the ground floor of Madame Kwan's, an acey-deucey game on the second floor, and she'd even had jury-rigged a horseshoe pit on the roof. Her cigarette holder was her trademark and she imported OB Beer from Hong Kong. Dressed in a frogged silk jacket and silk trousers, she greeted every new American sailor with a handshake, a slap on the back, and her business card, "Kwan, Soon Lee, Factotum." The card had a wire address below and it all repeated in Chinese pictograms on the reverse. Tiger was the only Chinese male allowed as a patron since he was Navy, though no one ever saw him there except for an occasional drink. It was known as an American sailor's saloon though British, French, and German sailors, in small numbers, could visit if they showed proper deference.

He looked longingly at the harbor lights of the city that was like a boomtown. It was a sailor's delight, wide open and anything for a price. Once during every Shanghai visit, Jackson organized a bicycle expedition to an old camelback bridge under a willow tree in the interior. *Pluto*'s crew looked on the bridge as its own. Perhaps a better site for croquet, it was the site of innumerable, never finished football and baseball contests. Once, the Oyster Pirate bought a whole stand of kites, and they had beery kite fights. Sometimes they even invited the officers.

His eyes drifted down and he saw Warrant Officer Crottle scowling in his direction.

Well, Korea could be good liberty, too -- for him anyway. It was home. He had loved its rocky mountainous beauty and had longed for an excuse to go back.

Phipps did not allow him to leave without firing a salvo of naval-sounding proverbs. Sailors ought to be on ships. Sailors ought to be on their own ships. Sailors ought to be on their own ships doing naval business. Nothing good ever came of dealing with civilians. All civilians were corrupt, and tried to get the best of sailors. Foreign civilians were the worst of the lot, thieves and honey-fogglers. Nothing good came from having anything to do with civilian ships. Ultimately, nothing good came of sailors being off their own ships and dealing with civilian ships in a foreign country. This was a hoodoo set up. Any right-thinking sailor would plot a reciprocal course, but quick.

Though not entirely in disagreement, Hobson gathered that Phipps was not happy with the prospect of being short one Quartermaster.

*****

Hobson caught a bumboat over to the flagship before breakfast. The Shanghai paymaster was there and gave him his orders and a ticket on a passenger steamer to Chemulp'o. He was told to keep a journal of any navigational observations that he thought might be useful for Sailing Directions for Korea and identify hazards of any sort to U. S. merchant shipping. He was issued a significant sum in "Mex," Mexican silver dollars, for expenses.

Riding a civilian steamer to Chemulp'o as a passenger and watching some other poor seaman sweat would be a total pleasure. A politically well-connected landshark, a fellow named Sabatelli from Lighthouse Insurance, would meet him there, he was told. Ah, the galley grapevine, Hobson chuckled. He'd taken liberty in Chemulp'o before several years back, but that was different and politics of the region were changing rapidly. He was just one member of an American crew in a relatively cosmopolitan port and by the time anyone had realized he was the strange American who spoke Korean, they had left. Who knew where he'd be going after Chemulp'o and where his past might meet up with him. It had been six years. They'd put in to Pusan once or twice, but this would be different.

This would be different. In uniform and asking awkward questions in Korean, he'd be watched and he wondered if he could weather the scrutiny. He tucked most of the Mex into his moneybelt, which never left his body. Living out of a hammock and a bucket, a sailor was left with few ways of storing valuables. It was not a widespread problem.

*****

The Japanese carefully regulated Western entry into Korea. Sabatelli was told to conduct his investigation out of Chemulp'o, the western port not far from Seoul. He would be under the watchful eye of one of the larger Japanese garrisons. Chemulp'o was a poor version of Yokohama. It was sooty and muddy and littered with dunnage. Japanese ships dominated the harbor and were loading an unending cargo of Korean raw materials. Sabatelli noted that the Japanese ships deadheaded, arrived nearly empty. Non-Japanese foreign ships, carrying cargoes to or from Korea were rare indeed. Korea was now a colony in all but name and she existed to serve Japan. The few other foreign ships were just passing through, looking for shelter or maintenance. Koreans performed any task that looked like physical labor. As a group, they looked ragged and ill fed.

The houses were small and more hut-like. Most of the roofs were thatched and had gourds and vines growing on them. Most had walls and small courtyards. Few women above the station of laborer walked about within the city.

Usually self-important, Sabatelli felt lost. He had found some overseas Chinese to cook and take his laundry. He had found a seaman's inn with a tiled roof, but he still hadn't established a rhythm when Hobson arrived. As out of place as he had felt in Japan, here, he was totally out of his element. There were few English speakers and few to cater to Western tastes.

Most of the Koreans wore white and little horsehair tophats. The husky blocklike Korean men carried loads in wooden backpacks and tied their hair up in buns despite a Japanese proscription against traditionally long hair. The few women carried babies like Indian papooses either tied in front or tied on in back. Where it wasn't muddy, it was dusty and as in Japan, the primary fertilizer was nightsoil.

They checked in with the Japanese military police who, after a day or two's official hesitation, gave Sabatelli and Hobson permission to ask questions as long as they shared their results. Hobson and Sabatelli combed the docks for any word of *Jade Rooster*. There was a reticence on the part of the Korean fisherman, but also, Hobson sensed, true ignorance. Sabatelli led the effort with the merchant fleet, but there was no help there, either. Several Japanese skippers seemed interested and the other foreign skippers, too -- their ships might be next. Yet no one could offer a clue.

Hobson and Sabatelli took day trips down the Western coast, but were no more successful than they had been in Chemulp'o.

CHAPTER FOURTEEN

Hobson had learned in his brief years with as ponderous a bureaucracy as the Navy, that there were official sources of information who passed the "Word." In this case, the official Japanese word was that there was no word about *Jade Rooster.*

Experience had also taught him that there were unofficial sources of information who circulated "scuttlebutt." This second category, too, was subdivided into two parts. Scuttlebutt in its unofficial fashion basically flowed from two directions: downcurrent from the authorities, who in this case were the Japanese, or upcurrent from the rank and file, in this case the Koreans.

He had learned that the Word was not always true and scuttlebutt was not always false. Hobson went hunting for scuttlebutt.

He began by visiting the police gym in Chemulp'o to develop a contact or two. He carried a judo gi and asked permission to practice. Several sailors from *Pluto* had begun to study the sport. It was beginning to gather a following in the US. It was said Teddy Roosevelt had studied it. Hobson enjoyed it far more than cutlass drill twice a week with Warrant Officer Crottle. His shipmates regarded cutlass drill as a useless holdover and little more than calisthenics with an old piece of steel. Hobson on the other hand had used judo three times. No, four, he recalled. Three times to break up bar fights, and the final time to drop that gunner's mate off *Baltimore.*

Since the 1880's when judo had won a famous competition to determine the primary self-defense discipline of the Tokio police – a story known to every Japanese schoolboy, judo had become a regular part of every police station's routine. The mats at most stations were open to non-policeman to ensure enough participants for a workout. Though these were military policemen, rather than true policemen, the same tradition held true. Here perhaps was a place to develop unofficial contacts.

From the moment he set foot on the mat he was hazed. Hobson's time afloat had inured him to that custom, too. The new fellow had to show his stuff to join the group. Hobson found some very tough opponents among the judoka. Some of the most aggressive were Koreans working for the Japanese. Hobson wore the white belt of a novice judo wrestler. Initially the blackbelts ignored him, but left him with a smattering of uncoordinated office workers and clerks. He did not expect that to last. He would be expected to fight his way up the ladder, with a few initial victories before loss after loss. There was a tension in the air, subtler between the Japanese and Koreans, with a more open disdain for Europeans. These were the guardians of the New Imperial Japan, and the aspiring guardians from a subjugated land. Hobson knew to pace himself for a long evening. Eventually a few of the blackbelts did come over and each with courtly politeness asked if he wished to "play" judo. He found himself being used to sweep the mats. Rarely was he thrown where his feet did not rise to the twelve o'clock position on an imaginary chronometer. He felt like a ragdoll being thrashed about by a series of bulldogs. They seemed to take rather grim enjoyment in the process. No more than a few words were said. They were skilled, compact, and strong with low centers of gravity, a great advantage in judo.

Near the end of the line, a thick-necked fireplug of a blackbelt with a cauliflower ear walked up to him and smiled. "Faites-vous joué de judo?"

Built like a depot stove, Hobson thought as he shook his head. "Yankee."

"Ah, cowboy. Teddy Roosevelt. Buffalos."

Hobson wasn't sure being described as Teddy Roosevelt by a Japanese soldier was a good thing. Roosevelt had negotiated away Japanese conquests in the Russo-Japanese War and won the Nobel Peace Prize...but hardly Japanese admiration. Yet TR was reputed to have studied judo and the Japanese would have liked him on a personal level.

Cauliflower Ear bowed quickly and effortlessly threw Hobson over his shoulder. At the peak of the arch, Hobson's feet had chimed eight bells in the evening watch again.

Hobson got up and started waltzing Cauliflower Ear around to break his balance. He tried several leg sweeps which Cauliflower Ear countered disdainfully and put Hobson on his back again.

"You know American song, 'Daisy, Daisy'?" Cauliflower Ear said lifting Hobson off his hip and over his leg onto the mat. Hobson hit cleanly on his back with a resounding, "thwack." It stung, but strangely did not really hurt.

"Yes," Hobson.

He let Hobson try a few more attacks, and then, when Hobson stumbled Cauliflower Ear rolled him into matwork, first securing a few armbars and then coming just short of choking Hobson several times. He smiled and Hobson noticed several missing teeth.

"You sing 'Danny Boy?'" Cauliflower asked roughly.

Cauliflower began another shoulder throw and Hobson stepped behind him scooping him up by clasping both knees. The mat, really a group of mats suspended from ropes, rippled faintly outward. Cauliflower looked surprised. It suddenly became very quiet in the hall. Hobson had had his moment and waited for retribution.

"Well, the first verse only," Hobson said hedging.

"You play beisu-boru?"

Hobson, in fact, hated baseball. It was a slow sport with far too many rules, but Cauliflower Ear had just begun a choke.

"Love it."

"You drink biru, eh, beer, liquor, ne?"

"Been known to."

Cauliflower Ear did not understand the phrase, but figured it meant, "yes." In fact, Cauliflower Ear would not have been able to grasp the suicidal implications of Hobson saying "no" to a senior belt on the subject.

"After workout you, me, we go to hot bath, then drink, hokay? Maybe we visit kisaeng girls after"

Hobson was looking for conversation and fussy sailors never picked up the scuttlebutt.

As he painfully changed into his uniform and turned up the collar on his pea coat, Hobson recalled that overseas diplomacy in the face of brute force had always been the time-honored, though never entirely risk-free, role of the United States Navy.

*****

That night they did everything Cauliflower, whose real name was Matsuda, had promised. They repaired to a public hot bath. Matsuda liked judo, but loved to sing and liked baseball.

Late in the evening, Matsuda confided that he liked Korea, too, but that the Koreans hated him and his countrymen. He further confided that some of his countrymen deserved the hatred of the Koreans.

Matsuda was a proud member of the Imperial Japanese Army. He would have been glad to risk anything to defend it or to advance its interests in battle. Garrison duty as a military policeman, however, he found less appealing.

They eventually found themselves in a small side street restaurant eating pulgogi and drinking makkolli. Matsuda was so wide he had to go through the door sideways.

"Farmers, we are always throwing farmers off their land." He said with disdain. The Japanese, in taking over the Korean government, had issued edicts on taxes. Many farmers were told to register their land or lose it. This was such a novel requirement that many farmers never did register their land. A few years went by and they suddenly found themselves being dispossessed. The Japanese handled it in such a way that many were not aware of the edicts at all.

"Not warrior's way. My father is a rice farmer. Soldiers should not throw old men on sleeping mats out of their homes." He swirled makkolli in the bottom of his cup. He pointed to the mountains. "All trees are going to Japan. Mountains will be naked soon."

"Bandits in the mountains." He mulled that over. "Bandits, some good men. They yell "mansei!" They are warriors. If I was Korean…"

He looked around the table slowly.

"…I be bandit.

"I don't know which better, throwing old farmers off land, or hunting bandits. Ughh." He made a face.

"Major Koizumi, he can be very mean man. Much want higher, higher…"

"He is ambitious?" Hobson offered.

"Yes, he has ambition." Matsuda said. "He likes to scare bandits and trick them. Major Koizumi very tricky, very tricky man."

"You know I am here looking for a ship." Hobson decided that exploit the opportunity."

"Navy ship? Big guns?" Matsuda made motions that would have been more appropriate to big breasts.

"No, merchant ship, a barque. One of those canvas mercantileries. A sailing ship."

Matsuda struggled to get his tongue around the word, "barque."

"Koizumi, he goes on ships sometimes…down south in Cholla."

Cholla province. It would be the hotbed of resistance. Hobson's father's floating parish had been off the coast of the Cholla province…the baskets in the picture…

Matsuda suddenly realized he was talking too much.

The baskets in the picture had a weave that Hobson had recognized. It was typical of baskets woven in Cholla province. It was a double interwoven reed of blue. He thought of the heads, Captain Brewer, Carson the second mate, Hoyt the personal secretary, and the enigmatic Mr. Sato.

"You know kisaeng? Korean entertainment girls? Like geisha, but not so good?"

"Yes, I am familiar with kisaeng." Hobson decided he liked Matsuda.

*****

Sabatelli was eager to return to Yokohama, but Hobson told him he needed more time. There was a connection between *Jade Rooster*, Cholla Province, and the Major. They would continue to work the waterfront and Hobson hoped to elicit something of value from Matsuda. For no reason he could think of, Hobson felt he had a personal interest in this puzzle.

CHAPTER FIFTEEN

Setting foot in Korea once again unleashed memories that pounded over his sailor's heart like seawater against a coastal jetty. He had spent his formative years in the Land of Morning Calm.

His parents had been missionaries to a network of island parishes in Chosun, as they called it, circuit riding among the herons and egrets aboard an ancient schooner beneath heavily patched tanbark sails. His mother had studied to be a apothecary's assistant and his father had turned to the ministry when he could find no other outlet for his generous nature, seaman's skills, and gift for languages. A floating chapel was not so unusual. Christian scripture was replete with seagoing imagery from Noah to Jonah to Jesus, and so without a trace of self-consciousness the missionary schooner set to fishing for men. They liberally distributed the gift of literacy in western languages and familiarity with western health practices, in the hope that an acceptance of the highpoints of western religion and philosophy would follow.

His father had been a lay missionary for the Congregationalists. More "dedication than education," his father used to observe with a chuckle in Japan and Korea. "Not much white rice, and poor as church mice," would be Hobson's under-breath rejoinder.

His mother was the potent draw. Spiritual comfort was always a bit hard to measure and observe. The Koreans saw the tangible benefits of Western medicine. Chinese medicine had its uses, but it often missed what Western pills and powders addressed.

They had come to Korea from Japan just before the Russo-Japanese War. A few years later Hobson had been sent back to San Francisco for schooling. A year later in San Francisco he had learned that his parents were missing.

Letters from fellow missionaries hinted at foul play. The Japanese were having trouble with some Korean provinces and Western missionaries were sent packing...or disappeared. Cholla Province was obstinate by reputation, and Hobson knew his parents would have obstinately guided their flock in the best way they knew how.

Hobson had known that he would have to return to Korea someday and seek some form of resolution. Broke and friendless, he enlisted in the Navy. Assuming that he would serve in the Pacific, he signed on using another name. He was not entirely sure why he had done that, perhaps as much for a clean break with the past as for protection against his parents' enemies. The Japanese were everywhere and he wasn't sure what that might mean to him.

*****

There was the second part to Hobson's plan to gather unofficial information from the bottom up. He planned to draw it from the locals out of view of the Japanese gendarmarie. Chemulp'o was under the heel of the Japanese and an anchored barque did not just disappear in Korean waters without someone knowing something about it. Moreover Hobson sensed there was more at stake here than Navy socks and foodstuffs. Atticaris and his ordnance enterprises aside, four heads in a whaleboat was more about anger than about sundries or weaponry.

Hobson had lived in Korea long enough to know indirect ways of gathering information, especially in a country that valued the indirect. He and Sabatelli discussed their options and formulated a plan. Hobson found Sabatelli's willingness to take a risk refreshing. It ran contrary to his sense of the man, his job, and the industry he represented.

The following night Hobson headed south toward Cholla Province in the attire of a Korean day laborer. He wore a fur hat, carried a wooden "A" frame pack, a chige, and spoke Korean, only when he had to. His accent and appearance at close quarters would betray him as a foreigner, but he never lingered and he had left Sabatelli behind in Chemulp'o. A Chige was the Korean answer to a wheelbarrow and he loaded it up with produce, a mat, a blanket, and a razor. He zigzagged along the coastal roads behind pony carts and driven oxen. Early red peppers dried by the road. Tendrils of morning mist lay low in the mountain valleys and yellow squash blossoms draped over hedges and walls. During the warmest part of the day, he would see old men seated on straw mats near the road, smoking long-stemmed pipes around a pot of incense.

Following an unending procession of women carrying bundles on their heads, he noted that baskets of rice, millet, and common vegetables were not as plentiful as he had remembered. Goats, pigs, and chickens were closely watched and kept far from the road. He wondered at the unusually large number of men and women dressed in hemp and wearing straw sandals, the traditional dress of those in mourning.

Late in the first day he spotted a checkpoint in the distance. Checkpoints meant requests for documents that Hobson did not have. He looked back to see a drover with a herd of oxen leave the road down a ravine and followed. He had heard the Japanese were encouraging "voluntary contributions," especially of livestock. Voluntary contributions were made at gunpoint when the Japanese took what they wanted at a price they set unilaterally "to serve the Imperial cause." It was not petty pilferage, but a part of a systematic program.

Hobson approached the drover's fire after sunset. The drover eyed him sharply and asked in Korean, "Russian?"

Hobson noticed that he seemed to grow, almost uncoil, to his full stature. Dark and leathery, the drover to Hobson's surprise was taller than Hobson, and Hobson noticed for the first time that he had a lop eye.

"Yankee," Hobson responded in the same language.

The drover seemed to relax slightly.

"Missionary?"

"Once."

"Well, I was part of the Korean Army -- once."

"You must be very prosperous to have these many oxen."

"Not mine. I run them past the Japanese, away from the Japanese. Can't get the best price in Cholla, but at least we are putting them in Korean stomachs.

"They are slow, contrary beasts though. I could use some help. Looks like you could use some company. You are traveling light for a foreigner...."

He did not complete the thought, but offered Hobson some radish soup.

"I think you might want to avoid the Japanese, too."

Hobson only nodded

The next day, after shaking the frost from their bones, they plodded on and some miles later, they rejoined the main road.

The road was muddy and the oxen contrary. Several times, without explanation, the drover herded the yoked oxen off onto a byway. Hobson followed his lead and once or twice they convinced an ox to move along when he was disposed to graze. Sometimes a team would get stuck in the mud and they would hitch others to pull the stricken oxen out.

The second night, the drover looked toward the mountains at sunset and sighed. "Our island brothers have brought darkness. I was a soldier once. Not much of a soldier, taught to look like a soldier, and to respond to direction like a soldier, but little more. Our new lords, the

Japanese, have fought two wars in one generation and we have fought none. Their leaders can put together a course of action; ours have been deadlocked into inactivity. I have seen how the Japanese work here and on the Manchurian border. We have been a shrimp crushed among whales, the Chinese, the Russians, and the Japanese. We survive, but badly bruised and in a stunned state.

"Our empress they killed, and the Prince has been taken to Japan to be made Japanese. Our royalty line was hamstrung...like an animal.

"Before that the Chinese from whom we sought protection occupied the palace and provided the royal bodyguard. They too have suffered from the sickness of inaction and they were weak. The Japanese out maneuvered them with palace tricks and now the Japanese are here to stay "to help us protect ourselves" from whom I am not sure...the Russians or perhaps the Chinese. Who is to protect us from the Japanese?"

They built a small fire concealed behind a hill, boiled greens, and brewed barley tea.

"We are in a sad situation. Korea needs leaders -- until now they have been determined by birth. Korea needs guns -- who is it to give weapons to strangers? Korea needs money, for revolutions need supplies and those who sacrifice for a cause should not sacrifice more than their share

"Tomorrow we must separate. I cannot let you know where I am going. I can take risks for myself, but not for others.

"'Troubles are the seeds of joy.'" He muttered the old Korean proverb without conviction and gave a mock salute.

They regained the road one last time the next day and separated with the customary Korean exchange of salutations. Hobson placed several Mex coins into the drover's hands.

The pines and junipers arched over the road and the maples were starting to lose their leaves.

*****

Sadness and resolution hung in the air like the advent of winter. An unusual number of families with all their possessions were trudging northward on the long road to Manchuria. Extensive property holdings were posted with the signs of the Oriental Investment Company. OIC was a Japanese colonial exploitation company that put money into the Japanese government's coffers. Everywhere there were old people; rarely did he see young men between the ages of twenty and thirty-five. Several churches and mission schools had an abandoned look to them. Periodically he would run across road crews and railway crews that bore an uncanny resemblance to chain gangs. He took time to sleep, some Manchuria-bound families, however, labored on through the night taking turns sleeping atop their rickety carts. To Hobson, it brought to mind church school recollections of the Book of Exodus.

Eventually he arrived in the chain of villages he had known as a youth in southern Cholla province and took the ferry to an island known as Chindo. He went to the Christians about *Jade Rooster*. He sensed the villagers knew something, but they would not talk to him.

As he passed the totems at the entrance of a second village, the spirit poles reminded him of something. In the second village, he sought out the local mudang, the shaman.

Around the communal well there were several women pounding their wash. Several men examined an ox.

He would ask politely and then be handed off to someone who would act uncomfortable. Nonetheless, he persisted, he would be politely handed off to someone else. No one ever said "no," but no one

126

wanted to make the introduction to the mudang. He must have been passed among a dozen people who smiled painfully, but seemed incredibly vague. Then he was left standing against a wall and told to wait. Four hours passed and he knew this was a good test for a foreigner, since no foreigner could wait like a Korean. He waited with the patience of a foreigner who was almost Korean.

Then an old woman walked straight out of a paddy headed directly to him. The round-faced, high-cheekboned woman must have been very beautiful once and she now held herself as erect as a queen. The epicanthic fold in her eyelids made her eyes look as if they were shut and she was sleeping. Hobson sensed a very strong personality. The culture attempted to push strong women into the background. Woman mudang were like salmon swimming against the current. She would be impulsive and intuitive, and have the gift of what Koreans called nunchi, eye-measure.

She was taken aback by the fact he could speak Korean so well. Then she scolded him for a dozen small things in quick succession as if he were a schoolboy and tapped the chige at his feet with her foot. She held both his hands, then asked him if part of his heart was in Korea. He thought for a moment, then said, "yes."

"What is your name?"

"Hobson."

"No, that is not your real name, is it?"

"Does it matter? No, it is just a name. Like Korean people, and unlike Yankees, I do not mouth my name freely."

"Your ancestors rest here in Korea?"

Hobson paused, startled, "I don't know, but I think so."

She never once asked him what he was seeking.

She looked him straight in the eye and said he could attend the ceremony to be held that evening. She turned around and walked purposefully straight back across the paddy. Behind the paddy was a wildly wooded mountain.

*****

That evening, a fisherman led him up a mountain encased in an ancient stand of trees which swirled menacingly around them. The night was moonless and the stars of the Big Dipper, Chilsong or Stepping-Stones as the constellation was known in Korea, shown brightly. Just below the crest in a stand of ancient forest was an immense White Birch with colored ribbons tied in its branches. Somehow, the stand had survived the depredations of the charcoal burners and the Japanese lumber companies. On one side was a cleared grassy hollow and it was filled with villagers and a brightly dressed old woman, the mudang. This must be the "front" of the hollow.

The fisherman pointed to the great White Birch and repeated "sonang namu," which meant the sacred, cosmic tree. It was a tree that served as a ladder between the worlds of the living, the dead, and the gods. He then pointed to the mudang and said, "sanshin," meaning she was the shaman of a thousand spirits. The birch was as big around as the core of a gun turret and it held Hobson's attention.

Hobson knew these ceremonies were infrequent, lasted a long time -- sometimes days -- and that he had been lucky to find one.

The mudang was holding several knives that she was sharpening to a fine edge. She used them to cut several stakes and prepare a spear.

The mudang began the ceremony and balanced a pig upon the spear. The villagers took this as a good omen. She changed her clothes and her voice and bearing changed. She changed her clothes a second time and her voice and bearing changed once more. It was a strange forceful voice. She was preparing to make a trip down the cosmic ladder into the underworld and she was polling the spirits for a guide, with each change a different spirit took control of her body. The forceful voice was that of a long-forgotten hero and the long-forgotten hero was trying to raise the spirit of the sea dragon

In the ceremony, the mudang, controlled by the spirit of the long-forgotten hero, called upon the sea dragon and there was an answer. The mudang emitted a very strange deep and bubbly sound. Contact had been established with the sea dragon. The mudang spoke as if the long-forgotten hero was conducting a conversation with the sea dragon that only the hero could hear. She then changed her clothes once more to those of a general-at-sea. The sea dragon had designated General-at-sea or Admiral Yi Sun Shin as the guide to the underworld for the ceremony.

The crowd whispered excitedly among themselves. Several needed desperately to make contact with departed spirits.

Her voice was now rough and manly and the voice recounted the pedigree and many accomplishments of the Korean sea hero. It was all a matter of form since the lowliest Korean schoolboy knew the story of Admiral Yi Sun Shin. He was a particular favorite this evening because he had repelled the two Japanese invasions centuries ago. It would seem that he needed no introduction, but he, in recounting of the successful actions of his Korean turtle ships against the Japanese galleys, struck a responsive cord with the assembled villagers. Several called out in praise.

The mudang chanted and danced for a while and the dance simulated a long journey. Hobson saw a series of long knives staked parallel, cutting edge upward near the middle of the grassy hollow.

Finally the mudang and the spirit of Admiral Yi Sun Shin -- in one body -- walked across the edge of the knives, not once but several times.

They had crossed the bridge into the underworld. It was a bridge as fine and delicate and dangerous as the edge of a knife.

The Admiral seemed to speak to several persons and get answers that, at different times, pleased, amused, and sometimes sent particular villagers into depressed and horrified swoons. Many were there to resolve spiritual problems. They were invited by the mudang's assistant to ask their questions of Admiral Yi. Sometimes Admiral Yi answered the questions, and sometimes other spirits stepped forward. Coins were dropped into a basket or goods came forward as barter payment.

At the approach of dawn the Admiral turned to Hobson and for a short moment changed back into the mudang.

"Traveler, you are both of the land of our people, the people who dress in white, and yet not of this land. You are equally from the land of the great rice paddies and not of that land either. You search for a resolution of unhappinesses. I can only see the path to one resolution, the lesser one."

For just a moment, she was the mudang, and then she changed to Yi again. Yi said a man had drowned aboard a great foreign junk named for a bird, *Jade Rooster*. Yi pronounced it awkwardly, and then the mudang's posture changed so she seemed taller and she became that person and cried out in anguish. Hobson found himself talking to a ghost, the ghost of still another Asian.

Hobson asked if the ghost could describe where *Jade Rooster* sank. The dead man's ghost described his last visual recollection. The man was tied to a mast. Directly ahead of him about a li, he could see a small island and directly off his right shoulder he could see two immense rocks. A kingfisher skittered about searching for fish. The tide was low and he could see broad tidal flats over his left shoulder. He knew it was low tide because there was nearly thirty feet in range between the present tide level and the dark green line of slime on the island's shingle and on the two rocks which marked the tidal crest. Near one rock was a gourd buoy painted red.

Hobson asked where the sun was and the mudang described its position. He asked if the man could see smoke anywhere on the horizon and the man said no.

He asked who the dead man was, but the spirit would not reply.

Secrecy even after death, Hobson thought.

There was great anger in the drowning man's voice…and then the voice ceased as if it was cut off, as if the dead man had been pulled back. Then there was a new voice that was even angrier. The voice changed, then changed again, there were several that seemed to be jamming through the mudang at once. It was several people. The ancestors, some recently departed, were extremely angry. The dead man was clearly not among friends this night.

The word "mansei" was repeated over and over again. They foretold of great massacres of Koreans being burned in buildings, executions, the forbidden use of family names, and desecration of honored symbols. Koreans would be forced to dishonor and deny their ancestors. The voices changed more quickly now and they became louder. Then there was a hush. It was the Admiral speaking now, Admiral Yi Sun Shin who had protected Korean against the two Japanese invasions. His voice was cold and controlled, yet the loudest and angriest. He said there would be terrible vengeance against the island invaders, more terrible than any Korean could ever guess. This was a time of great darkness, but retribution would come in a great flash of light and heat. Nothing could stand before the great retribution and the ancestors would again be honored and could rest in peace again. The voice of Admiral Yi wavered and warned that Koreans would not be able to rest for many generations for the great retribution would be a long time coming.

Yi's spirit squared on Hobson and spoke gruffly as an admiral would have spoken to a lowly seaman of his Turtle Fleet, "You will be connected to the Great Retribution, both an honor and a terrible, terrible deed."

Then she was the mudang again and she was staggering toward the bridge of knives. She crossed the knives several times in her bare feet, then took a few steps and collapsed. Her assistants came to her aid, but she could not be revived and fell into a dead sleep.

Hobson dropped several Mex into the basket and waited.

*****

"You should come back after you have completed your search, there were other ghosts I saw on my journey when I went looking for the ship." She attempted to pronounce "*Jade Rooster*", but could not. The mudang said those few brief words and then turned her attention to the villagers. She was totally feminine and an old woman once again.

She seemed totally refreshed and at ease.

The villagers watched him. Some warily and others with curiosity. Hobson did not know what to make of it all, but sensed that he was in great danger. He had been a spiritual witness to foul play. That knowledge, however ethereal, could have consequences for someone. He left the village and for several days carefully retraced his circuitous route from Chemulp'o. There were checkpoints to be avoided and travelers to be watched. Falling in among a group of silent monks with bamboo lanterns, he trudged half-asleep by recumbent sentries. Days later, Hobson returned hungry, footsore, and in need of a bath. He slept through the next day.

Witches and seances? Was it anything to trust? Could *Jade Rooster* be found if she was underwater? Was this enough to work with? What

about the masts, would they still be visible? Had they been cut down?
Was the depth great enough to submerge a barque with masts erect, so
close to shore? Hobson didn't think so, since in the mudang's
description there were mud flats nearby. There were few places near the
Korean coast in the West Sea that could swallow 80 vertical feet of
barque at a minimum. The masts had been chopped down and hidden.
A barque's draft would be somewhere between 12 and 15 feet. The
coast was visible from the west and there were twin rocks, mud flats and
an island visible at low tide. *Jade Rooster* was not taken for herself he felt,
but for her cargo.

Who was the man and why had he died a slow death to the incoming
tide?

It all seemed as substantial as a morning fog, yet it was his only lead.
A strangely detailed lead.

CHAPTER SIXTEEN

With Hobson's new lead, Sabatelli fell into his element, organizing and salvaging. He was somewhat skeptical of information derived from a medium, but at least the information suggested an approach and he was sophisticated enough not to look too closely at the source, especially considering the detailed nature of the information. Each mudang was close to those matters that troubled her village, he could understand that. In a mudang's capacity as a seeker of spiritual assistance she heard and saw many things...

Hobson, the product of a missionary background, could not accept shamanism on a spiritual basis, but he sensed a rational basis for its results. A mudang learned much from her clientele and could extrapolate from that knowledge. A mudang could be an insightful advisor who used ancient time-accepted trappings to legitimize her points.

With Sabatelli, Hobson gathered a collection of coastal charts and Sailing Directions -- though portions of the coast were uncharted. The weary Hobson had Sabatelli telegraph for the draft and freeboard of *Jade Rooster*. He added six feet to that figure for the depth required to drown an upright man tied to a mast. That would be the approximate minimum depth at low tide. Sabatelli questioned fishermen about snagged nets and collected homemade charts from pilots. He went to Major Koizumi and requested permission to charter a steam cutter to search for *Jade Rooster* off the coast of Cholla province. Koizumi, his glasses on the tip of his nose, questioned Sabatelli condescendingly.

"Do you have new information about *Jade Rooster* barque?

Koizumi had a photograph in his hand and Sabatelli realized it was a copy of the heads-in-baskets photograph. Their interest was serious and it continued.

"No, just a hunch. Accounts describe a network of islands, and the drifting boat had been found in the southern West Sea. The returned crewmen say they were returned on a course pretty near 'due Northwest' to Chefoo. Korea's on the reciprocal of that course. There's some talk of Mokp'o."

Hobson remained silent and assumed his usual station one step back, and to Sabatelli's right.

"Has some one talked to you about *Jade Rooster*? I think this is a matter for the police to handle. It is an American ship, true, but its cargo must be secured. These Koreans are thieves, all of them. It's their nature, but that will be corrected in time."

"No one has mentioned *Jade Rooster* to us." Hobson said to Koizumi.

Was a ghost no one? Was a woman shaman speaking the words of a ghost no one? The mudang had not directly mentioned "the loss of *Jade Rooster*. In any event, Hobson was not ready to share the fine points with a Japanese officer until he had some indication those fine points would be reciprocated.

It took quite a while to get the approvals from the Japanese authorities, but at last they came. Koizumi informed them that a military police noncommissioned officer named Matsuda, would accompany the steam cutter. Hobson smiled inwardly upon hearing the name of their assigned police shadow. How many Japanese military policemen spoke English?

*****

135

It was a gasping, wheezing old Japanese steam cutter manned by three Korean crewmen, which throbbed along at a respectable 6 to 8 knots. A beamy 40' bathtub, its well-maintained white hull and cabin wrapped around a boiler that took a dominating position about a third of the way back from the bow. In its cindered splendor, it could beat the four-knots currents that plagued the Korean coast. Hobson would have preferred sail, but this was the most efficient way to check the ten or so possible sites. She did have a sooty steadying sail, which made her ride easier and another sail just forward of the cabin. Together, the sails offered marginal help heading downwind. She also had a steam windlass that would make kedging easier. She had exaggerated bilge keels so she could sit easily in the mud when the tide went out. Neither Sabatelli nor Hobson had any illusions about a slow examination of Cholla's West Coast. With a 30-foot tidal range, they anticipated finding themselves mudbound frequently.

The steam cutter had served as a pilot boat and never operated outside of Chemulp'o harbor so Sabatelli set about outfitting her for coastal work. The cutter had not been configured for berthing; they would have to pitch tents and sleep ashore. There might be a benefit there. It might allow Hobson to take side excursions. Sabatelli bought anchors, a compass, lead line, tide books, coastal charts, and a Ross glass. Her decks were covered with baskets full of coal, tins of food, a shepherd's stove, and tent bags.

"Lighthouse is never going to accept this expense. How am I going to explain going on a coastal picnic... er, expedition based on native superstition and hocus-pocus. Believe the word of a some Korean gypsy medium? They'll think I've gone Asiatic. Sabatelli said with skepticism, but surprisingly did not offer much resistance.

"Different ships, different long splices. This is Korea and answers will come in their own way," Sabatelli said with finality and a hint of desperation.

So Sabatelli, Hobson, Matsuda, and the steam cutter's crew cruised down Korea's rugged West Coast under a dark cloud of their own making...across the West Sea which billowed gently like blue silk.

*****

The steam cutter trailed an ancient, once-painted sampan. Hobson had tried to find a Whitehall, but none of the Western merchant ships would sell or lend him one. He'd put three rowlocks on the sampan, two on the gunwales, and one in the middle of the transom. Two oars for rowing and a longer one for sculling. Oddly, Hobson knew the Chinese name for the sculling oar, yuloh, but not the Korean word. His strange interest in rowing was known. Foreign naval sailors – an acknowledged strange breed -- had rowing competitions. The new interest in exercise had not yet caught on in Korea. Physical exertion was physical labor, and physical labor was confined to the lower classes. And no one in his right mind did physical labor without compensation. Even among the Europeans, the merchant marine sailors suspected that betting heightened the average matelote's interest more than the prospect of good clean exercise.

Rowing was done seated. Sculling with a long oar could be done standing in the Korean manner. Standing you could peer down into the depths and not go very fast. In some ways, the sampan was a better choice than a Whitehall. The name "sampan" meant "three boards" and the boat was simply constructed, about three planks wide, and no one gave a second thought to anyone – even a Westerner sculling a sampan.

As far as the crew knew, they were cruising along the coast looking for a wreck broken on the rocks. So many rocks, Hobson knew, that spiked skyward like turrets, spires, and pillars. Another prospect was the barque had become a drifting derelict. The story was they were cruising the coast without a specific itinerary, but Hobson had a dozen sites he wanted to inspect. His "recreational" rowing would obscure the true intent of these special excursions.

*****

The cutter was uncomfortable at first, not physically uncomfortable, but culturally uncomfortable. The Koreans were constantly in motion, the massive Japanese military policeman had assumed an "official" posture, and the two Americans thrashed about with charts and navigational instruments. They shared no common language. Matsuda spoke some English and some Korean, the Koreans spoke some Japanese, and Sabatelli spoke only English. Hobson was the common link. He spoke Korean, but would not let on to the crew or Matsuda that he also spoke Japanese. He spoke Pidgin English or Korean to Matsuda, but never Japanese.

Matsuda and Sabatelli were very conscious of their positions. The Koreans stoked coal and did heavy lifting, Hobson noted with irony, even though both Matsuda and Sabatelli dwarfed the largest men in the Korean crew. Boredom set in and when it became clear that the launch leaked badly, they each took turns at the pumps, each in their shirtsleeves and gallowses. With a chill in the air, they too puffed forth a stream of steam.

Hobson helped to pitch the tents, took the wheel, cast the lead line, and helped kedge the cutter out of trouble when the cutter invariably got caught in the mud during a rapidly falling tide. Hobson lost track of the hours they spent carving mud with their keel.

At each village they drew fresh water for the boiler, and Hobson discreetly eyed the local baskets.

*****

It was culinary preferences that eventually eroded the barriers of class and culture. Matsuda regarded Sabatelli's tinned American food with repugnance. The Koreans trailed fishing lines and began pulling fish aboard. They hadn't asked if they could do it, it seemed to natural to them. Why ask permission to breathe? Matsuda's eyes were large with interest.

Hobson soon found himself trying to identify the fish for Matsuda, pollock, cod, and snapper. No long thereafter, Matsuda was participating in the fishing with the crew. Hobson and Sabatelli preferred fresh fish, however unidentifiable, to corned beef hash, too.

From time to time, fishing boats would approach like bumboats with their wares. Hobson was surprised how many Japanese fishing vessels now prowled the Korea coast. Hobson eyed their baskets, too.

Italian, Japanese, and Korean cuisine gradually merged into a one pot and pan culinary muddle. Apart from his need for coffee, Sabatelli was happy to go with anything else grown or caught locally. The crew watched Sabatelli manipulate his coffee grinder with amusement. With fresh water from the boiler, there was no lack of fresh coffee.

Not long after Matsuda was discussing beisu-boru with Sabatelli. And Sabatelli, who showed a talent for cards, began to give instruction in western card games to Matsuda and the crew.

******

"We are not going to find anything." Hobson remarked, as he looked out at mudflats that seemed to stretch out forever.

"So why did you have me charter to steam cutter?" Sabatelli snorted.

"I mean, even if we find something. We are not going to find anything." Hobson responded unfazed and looking over his shoulder. There was no one within hearing.

"Look, the U. S. Navy is pretty skittish about the Japanese, and I am, too. This Japanese noncommissioned officer seems to be okay, but he is here to spy on us. I met him briefly in Seoul and now I get the feeling that one contact may be an embarrassment for him. Now there's a distance, where we'd been pretty chummy. There's some other factor here. The Japanese have an interest in all this somehow."

Sabatelli shook his head.

"Not that concerned." Hobson added. "He's not a sailor, knows nothing about coastal chartwork, and his English is not that good. I suspect he can't even swim.

"The Japanese military police, or the Kempeitai either, for that matter, don't know we have a set of sites to my way of figuring. We're going to every possible site and act as if we had discovered nothing. In fact every day I am just going to do some leisurely rowing and come back pleasantly refreshed, my daily constitutional. At least until I can figure out how the Japanese fit into all this."

"Just so Lighthouse Insurance gets that barque back." Sabatelli said in a way that indicated that his professional survival depended on it.

*****

It was part of the daily routine. They had several canvas tents with stoves which they pitched ashore.

One day was particularly mild. Just as the sun was setting, the Korean crew built a bonfire on the beach as the tide went out. On the horizon were rocks and islands strewn like twisted chess pieces from an overturned board. The flickering light from the fire played on the rocks while the setting sun glowed behind them with a cold raspberry hue. The pines, weathered by wind and saltwater, were twisted and picturesque.

"Elysian, positively Elysian." Sabatelli observed.

Something tugged at his subconscious, and Hobson, though touched by the beauty of the location, was not sure why he felt uneasy. It had that picturesque aesthetic quality reserved for Korean gravesites. There were posts strewn about and partially caved in holes that seemed in a sort of circle. Often mountainsides were chosen for graves and special ceremonies, but not always.

The Korean crew, feeling playful, had built the fire far greater than needed. Once the sun had set the beach took on an eerie aspect. Somewhere beyond the light cast by the fire were watchers...the Kempeitai, the New Hwarang, the otherworldly? He could not tell. He simply had the feeling that there was a presence that lurked beyond the light of the fire.

Hobson's mind returned to the mudang and to the heads. Spirits, spirits, every religion he knew believed in spirits in one form or another. If there were such things as spirits, where did they reside? Were certain places more prone to spiritual infestation than others? Who decided where spirits resided? Did they pick places that displeased, or places that pleased? Did the spirits decide themselves or were there some rules or a formula for linkage? Or did they not pick at all, but remain where they had fallen? If choice were a factor, this cove would be haunted.

What kept spirits from piling up? How many Koreans had lived and died since the first descendant of Hwan Ung had issued from the she-bear turned into a woman? Perhaps all these places with appropriate yin and yang were simply view ports, no more. As he thought about it, he realized that the shaman had to cross a bridge to contact the spirits and Christianity sent the spirits to a mansion. It was better for spirits to have their own place where the living could get on with their own lives.

He tossed several logs on the fire. Something primeval told him that light and fire kept evil away. Rational Hobson chuckled, but intuitive Hobson was not about to pass judgment.

That night he dreamed of drowning men and women. He was consumed by swirling currents and cold, cold water that grew ever darker as he descended into a mighty, all-encompassing maelstrom. He could not see their faces though he tried desperately to seize the pale bodies as they drifted past. He searched their blank faces trying to identify a lay missionary and his wife. He would reach for the bodies and they would come apart in his hands. He found himself entangled in the clothing discarded by disintegrating bodies and screaming soundlessly.

In the morning he awoke and rubbed the tattoos of a pig and a rooster on his ankles that assured a sailor that he would never die a watery death.

*****

Behind a heavy steel door purchased from Wells Fargo, Stuyvesant Draper studied the framed portrait of Lefcadio Hearn with disgust, pecked at his typewriter, and laughed. His laugh had a hollow echo because he was alone and the room was airtight.

Because of Hearn and his ilk, Draper was probably the only librarian he knew who risked an anonymous death. East was East and West was West and those who attempted to get the twain to meet rated a knife between the ribs. The naval militia officer took his bolo knife and tossed it at the photo and continued to sip his tepid saki. He was surprised to see the knife stick point first slightly to the right and about neck level with the great scholar of things Japanese.

He reshuffled the papers and re-arranged the files, "Construction of Capital Ships," "Battle Cruiser Design," "Kongo," "Fuel Estimates," "Eight-eight Fleet," "Transcripts of Diet Discussion of Naval budget," "Navy General Staff," and "Sato Tetsutaro." Next he would arrange the charts, sailing directions and personal diaries. He was not sure how to handle patents and industrial processes.

Scion of a distinguished New York family, Stuyvesant Draper had shown a talent for dead languages, had become a rising authority on ancient Greece, and had developed as a much-sought-after lecturer on the Peloponnesian Wars. As a graduate student, he had been honored to serve as a backup guest lecturer on the Peloponnesian Wars at the Naval War College in Newport. No great commitment, just a fill in when the professor, a guest lecturer only, could not make the lecture. A first rate scholar, he had chosen Japanese as his modern language for no other reason than he had enjoyed Gilbert & Sullivan's Mikado, preferred Japanese silk for ties, and found paper parasols delightful. He found his visits to Newport enjoyable. During those visits, he came to realize that he had missed something, the benefits of an adventurous, misspent youth. He had had no youth. He had squandered it soaking up languages and winning prizes.

The answer to the sudden call for adventure had been a sharp white uniform with a high white collar. The Great White Fleet had left a strong national imprint, particularly on young minds, and at his university in the Empire State, membership in an organization that had mobilized during the Spanish-American War, the New York Naval Militia, had gained currency. The militia members spent their time learning semaphore, handling rifles, pushing around field pieces, marching in parades, and, from time to time, cruising the Hudson or Long Island Sound in antiquated naval vessels or aboard yacht-like steam launches. This was camaraderie and the prospect of naval adventure in bite size portions.

Meanwhile Draper became involved with a comely, but married, Japanese woman, the wife of an instructor at the same upper West Side university. This, however, set the stage when on one of his visiting lecturer jaunts, a War College student and naval officer, learned that Draper had studied Japanese and was in the naval militia. The naval officer asked Draper if he would be interested in traveling to further his linguistic studies. Often, the students wore civilian clothes, so he had no idea to whom he was speaking. It turned out that he had talked to a senior officer with the Office of Naval Intelligence, not that the man wearing a uniform would have told him that.

It had all boiled down to a hunt for a more fulfilling love life, having tasted the fruits however briefly.

His university gave him a sabbatical with surprising alacrity and the next thing he knew he was on his way from the Empire State to the Island Empire.

His duties consisted of monitoring Japanese naval and military affairs and collecting all the navigational information he could about Japan and its possessions. Sometimes he interviewed returning merchant skippers and sometimes he sent junior officers off on cross-country leave. The U. S. Navy and the Imperial Japanese Navy recognized each other as potential adversaries, some considering a clash as inevitable. All high-level planning on either side of the Pacific took cognizance of the possibility.

Occasionally, his skills had been diverted to other locales. He had spent some time with the marines in the Philippines, but his knowledge of Tagalog was minimal and the undertakings unsubtle. Always, he looked for signs of Japanese intervention.

He was involved in the height of ungentlemanly conduct, espionage. His fellow college lecturers at the New York university would not have approved.

Not that they would have been the only ones. Within the Navy there was doubt with regard to the utility of the Office of Naval Intelligence. A Navy won by virtue of the caliber of its guns, the seamanship of its officers, and the courage of its men. Backdoor eavesdropping was ungentlemanly and ineffectual.

If they only knew. In essence, he saw himself as a librarian. He gathered books and publications and indexed them. He transcribed reports. He synopsized documents. He had even developed a cross-referencing system. He published a monthly classified report that was distributed to dozens of naval commands.

Several of his counterparts at other embassies had from, time to time, simply disappeared. Japan was in the throes of a military power struggle and he realized that he ran the risk of clandestine elimination, an option so simple to bring to fruition as to be laughable. The great strategist of Asia, Sun Tzu, had laid out the necessity for intelligence services and clandestine operations with greater success than any Western strategist ever had.

He, Stuyvesant Draper, could disappear in the blink of an eye for the crime of describing Japanese ship construction too well. Yet in many naval circles he and his duties were viewed with distaste.

To date, he met only one woman who had shown an interest in him and she had been Portuguese. On the other hand, the level of intrigue had cured him of that desire for adventure for some time to come.

He looked at the portrait of Lefcadio Hearn and laughed. His laugh echoed back.

*****

Korean and Japanese fishing junks laced lazily through the coastal islands. Unlike his family's sleek, old Yankee schooner, their junks were heavy-timbered and angular. The larger boats were under sail, while the smaller boats were rowed only. Sometimes, when they came close to shore or an island, Sabatelli would notice women swimming with small net bags with gourd buoys. They whistled and then would sink below the surface.

"Hae nyo, women of the sea." Hobson offered. "They're divers. They swim off the coast and harvest octopus, shellfish, just about anything edible. Sometimes, a boat takes them out. Most of the time they just swim off the beach. I used to try to keep up with them when I was a youngster. Couldn't do it, by a far sight. They could swim farther and dive deeper than I ever could. Deeper and farther than most men. They had a reputation for toughness that was out of keeping with the general Western impression of Asian women. "

"No Madame Butterflies, eh?"

Sabatelli explained the new opera to Hobson.

Hobson guffawed.

*****

The list of villages, the groundings, and Hobson's rowing melded into a blur. Hobson visited site after site without success. Sabatelli and Hobson began to doubt the wisdom of crediting a witch's vision. In the villages, from time to time, Hobson thought he saw men and women he had known from his parents' missionary work, but held his tongue. Matsuda's presence, either personally or as a Japanese soldier, had a chilling effect on their contacts on the Korean villagers and until he

146

understood the full extent of why, he was not going to draw attention to anyone or show. It might jeopardize them. It might jeopardize him.

Aboard the steam cutter, there was a great deal of mystery about his ability to speak Korean. The crew regarded him with consternation. Even Matsuda asked him several times where he had learned to speak Korean so well and wondered why he had taken the effort to learn. Hobson had rehearsed his story. He had been stationed at Pearl Harbor and there he had amused himself by learning the language from an immigrant cane-cutting family. Matsuda shrugged, he had learned Korean because it was his job. Sailors were a strange and eccentric lot the world over.

Several evenings, Hobson lit his corncob with his back to the wind and watched the reflected sunlight dance on the surface of the West Sea and remembered when he had seen these waters last. He scratched his head under his watch cap and turned up his collar to the growing chill.

The approaches to Mokp'o were a sailor's nightmare, a maze of islands, contorted rock formations, and leeshore dead-ends. One morning, a Korean fishing boat with a rich harvest of octopus and eels approached them just southwest of Mokpo.

Just starboard of the fishing boat's tiller Hobson spotted it. One weathered flat basket with a double interwoven blue reed.

*****

They put in to the nearest village for water and Hobson realized it was a mistake, a terrible mistake. Why had he ever returned? What difference did one barque make? The dead were dead.

It was a village he knew all too well, one of the largest on this stretch of coast. Memories cascaded over him. Its market was a chaotic maze of dangling drying fish, fresh vegetables, woven mats, some ceramics, and bustling, aggressive Cholla Koreans.

"It is you, isn't it."

Hobson recognized the voice immediately, turned, and knew the moment had come. He was in dungarees, a watch sweater and a peacoat. Who would recognize him, it had been years. But he knew. She would not have recognized him at a distance, but he had not kept his distance.

It was Eun, as lovely as he had remembered her, her hair in braids coiled behind her ears. She must be a schoolmarm now, he thought. Married, too, for she wore the hanbok of a married woman. He looked cautiously around for Matsuda, but Matsuda was off examining fish, well behind him deep in the marketplace.

"No one knows me here," he said hoping she would take his full meaning. "My name is Hobson…now.

"I see."

How could she "see?" He was returning with a different name and in strange clothes like a thief or a spy.

"You know your parents are dead. Yes, you'd know that."

She grabbed him by the wrist and pulled him through a gate into a courtyard, then stared him into a wall. The courtyard wall was eight feet tall. They were out of sight, out of Matsuda's sight.

It was such a sudden rush of emotion that he felt the muscles in his face tightening up and he had difficulty maintaining his balance. It was unfair, incredibly unfair. Their deaths and seeing her now. He must regain control, he was a sailor now, a hard bitten "seen-everything" old salt.

"I knew they had died, but there was never any explanation. I suppose I guessed why." The words sounded strange to him. He realized he had never said them to anyone.

It was her turn to look furtive.

"Umyong."

It was the Korean word for fate, fortune, and destiny.

The compound was large, it was the home of a yangban, an aristocrat. The girls who came to the missionary schools were often from the yangban class.

"Umyong. Poor Chosun, a shrimp among hungry whales. Your parents came to us with generous hearts and they have suffered for those generous hearts. The countries around us are so great and there is not one to help us. I sometimes think to be Korean is to be born under a unlucky cloud."

He remembered when they were playmates and she was a tomboy in a culture that kept its women behind walls when it could. Now she was still small, but rounded in every aspect. Somehow the missionaries had overcome the Korean tendency to shelter and protectiveness women by using the Koreans' own love of scholarship. Her hair was black silk woven into braids, in a manner more fascinating to him than any coxcombing a sailor could weave. She stood with an air he could not put his finger on. Pride? Defiance?

"Much has changed since you left. We are heavily taxed and many have had their lands seized by the Japanese. Our men are conscripted into labor gangs. I must teach a school curriculum that is strictly controlled by the Japanese.

"People are taken away in the night." She looked up and blinked rapidly.

"Several from our mission, your parents' mission, became part of the Sinminhoe, the New People's Society, a Korean political party. It was your father and mother's doing…indirectly. They taught us about government and ways of making laws and about what they thought human beings should be able to expect in life. They helped us start a newspaper. Your parents were proud of those who joined the Sinminhoe. They told us how change came about in democratic countries."

Korea had needed change desperately to survive and his parents had realized it.

"But this is not a democratic country. We organized politically to resist Japanese colonialism and absolutely nothing happened. The Japanese laughed at us, and slowly took over the schools and conscripted the politically active into their military and into civil construction battalions. Part of Sinminhoe went underground and sought the overthrow of the Japanese by... by force of arms. They went out of the country for military training in China, Hawaii, and Nebraska. They called themselves the New Hwarang."

Hobson could only think of those dark brown eyes. Those dark brown eyes were blinking rapidly now, trying to hold back tears. What was it they talked about back at Sangley Point, oriental inscrutability? It was only relative and merely a matter of degree.

He had to focus. The hwarang were elite warriors with a chivalrous code from Korea's distant past, too distant for him now. She was agitated and kept pulling at the fabric on one elbow.

"Your father was torn. He knew you needed certain laws for democracies to operate and here those laws did not exist. Perhaps he read our men too much Thomas Paine, Patrick Henry, and others."

She had always paid better attention in school. Hobson could imagine his father teaching civics to students hungry for answers.

"He gave them advice; I am not sure what it was. All I know was the Japanese kept getting worse. The military police in Korea have the ability to enforce what they call "summary convictions". Many of the western missionaries and newspapermen have been deported or executed or disappeared."

"Eventually some of our people felt they had no choice, they attacked police stations. You heard of that American, Stevens, who was assassinated by Chon Myong-un and Chang In-hwan in San Francisco. He had helped to set up the Japanese Resident-General's government in Korea."

Her English with its musical inflection made her all more dear. They had grown up together speaking Korean and yet now she spoke English to him. The courtyard wall and the use of a foreign language were protection against spies and collaborators.

Hobson had been in San Francisco when it happened, not long after the earthquake.

"They assassinated the Resident General when he visited Harbin in China. Some set up revolutionary governments in exile. The disbanded Korean Army has formed the Righteous Army and fights in the mountains or from Manchuria or Siberia. We get pamphlets from them regularly. There is a group that started here…"

"There's fighting, really? You're not involved, are you? Is there any hope? How do they survive?" Hobson had to break the spell and think.

She lowered her voice.

"The new Hwarang, the New Flower Youth, the warriors."

He simply wanted to look at her, but her words had his senses reeling. Hwarang were warriors, the Korean equivalent of samurai.

"Your parents helped, in their way. We were their adopted people. I do not know how to say this. I think the Japanese used "summary conviction." They executed them. They were missionaries, westerners, and extremely dangerous because they had ties to the outside world. They might be able to mobilize opinion. Remember how dangerous Americans were. The Japanese won a war against the Russians and took territory from the Russians and Teddy Roosevelt made them give it back."

His parents had come to show Cholla province a better way and there were those…who had not approved of that way. Deep down, he had expected as much.

"My husband was a member of the New Hwarang. They came for him one night. I am in mourning."

How could he have missed it? She was dressed in hemp and wore straw shoes.

He felt his heart swell to reach out, some way, some how, but his brain could not see a way. And it was her he longed for, now even more.

What was his future? He was a low-caste sailor leading a profession that destroyed the families of its most loyal. She was an educated woman from a yangban family and dedicated to her country. He could not return, the Japanese would not permit him, permit him to act freely and openly. Japan was taking control and symbols of alternatives would disappear or become dormant.

"The Japanese came one night and they disappeared. The schooner was gone, too, and we never heard from them again. Eventually someone wrote back to the stateside mission. There was no replacement."

That was what he had suspected. He had seen the letter. There were rumors of a new Japanese iron hand and he knew his parents were stiff-necked Yankees. He knew there was no use coming back and yet he had changed his name in the off chance he might have to come back. That name was on a Kempeitai list somewhere. He had no clout in America, and no one would listen to a young American in Korea. And what would he have to say? Anything different from what a Korean his own age might say? And he would stand out just enough to make life difficult for all around him. He was a foreign influence just like the

Japanese. Was any foreign influence better than any other foreign influence?

CHAPTER SEVENTEEN

Her tears trickled quietly and she sniffled bravely. He told her about himself, what he had done for the past few years. Her eyes lit up. She too had grown up in two cultures. Travel, adventure, she could identify with, at least intellectually.

She was married, children, established, settled. She ran a church-related school. On the other hand, he realized that although he could transit two very different worlds, he was not really established in either.

"Have you seen this?"

For some forlorn reason he showed her the Sabatelli's photograph. For no reason he could think of, but he had to. He felt so lost and without hope, perhaps it was simply to bring things to "now" as opposed to "then."

She shook herself and the tears stopped.

"This one I know." She tapped Sato's head. "Moon. He came around from another district in Cholla. At least that is what we heard. A real firebrand with the New Hwarang. At the time I figured he would go overseas and help with building an army. In the end, I believe it is the only way we will make the Japanese leave, by force of arms. I was wrong about him. The word since, has been that he was an agent provocateur."

It was a strange foreign phrase he had heard in San Francisco. Men seeded into union situations to turn things violent and to make overreaction easy. Her husband had been an insurrectionist – that was what they were called in the Philippines. It was a phrase associated with political tension and treachery. How different their lives were now. Had life passed him by?

Sato was Moon or Moon was Sato. What did it mean? Why had the Kims called him Sato?

*****

She ushered him out the gate and disappeared behind the wall. It had been a fleeting meeting and awkward. It would not be seemly for her to be seen with foreign men and there was no way she could explain his link to the village without jeopardizing Hobson, herself, and perhaps the village itself.

He felt a strong desire to sleep in the village on ondul heated floors again under an ibul quilt. He missed the smell of charcoal and that solid, low-lying warmth. His world had changed now, he slept in the floating netherworld of a "dream sack," a naval hammock. The village seemed very close to home. No, he could not sleep here in the village without arousing Matsuda's curiosity.

For some reason, Hobson felt – more than ever -- that he alone could unravel the skein of *Jade Rooster*. He felt compelled to do so. The dark presence that had brought death to his parents and Eun's husband was somehow linked its disappearance. He stomached his anger...for the time being, he had to.

He had nowhere to direct it.

CHAPTER EIGHTEEN

The baskets with the double blue reed had served as a beacon. He knew what he would find the next day.

They anchored near one of the probable sites and Hobson went rowing, the usual practice by now. A light snow began to fall without accumulation on the twisted, wind-swept pines and junipers.

The last man to stand on *Jade Rooster*'s decks was near.

As he approached he heard hae nyo whistling as they breached. The water was still warm enough for those hardened by habit and as he rounded a twin rocks, he saw two women with white headwraps swimming. An island was in the distance and a large expanse of mudflat. In one swimmer's gourd-buoyed basket were several abalone, an octopus, and a single-fold block. It comprised her catch for the day, mostly edible and in this last instance, useable. She had to have salvaged the block that day from a western ship, a barque he was sure.

He tried to recall the mudang's words, the words of the angry drowning man.

He sculled along containing his excitement and then he saw it -- barely awash -- a mast stump breaking the surface from time to time. The mast stump was wrapped in manila line in an unseamanlike manner and a sack of what looked like clothing was all that remained of Saito or Moon or whatever his name had been. It must have been difficult to cut the mast off that high above the deck.

Below Hobson was an oblong black shadow with its standing rigging flapping in the current like a witch's shawl. Its main deck was ten feet below the surface at its lowest point. The hae nyo slipped away, ignoring him.

He had to be sure. He stripped down to his woolen underwear and dove in. The murky water was warmer than the air, but it still caused him to suck in his breath. He tied the sampan to the wreck's rigging, then he worked his way along the gunwales with his hands. It was a western vessel, wood, not steel. The woodwork was right and from time to time he felt a belaying pin or block. He recovered a block with the words "Lunenberg, N.S." on it.

The hull was tilted to port and down at the bow. He found the second mast stump in deeper water. He dove again and worked his way to the bowsprit. He had to be careful or he might get caught under the network and standing rigging. Each time he surfaced more quickly. The cold and depth were taking their toll. He found the dolphin strikers and worked his way back. He could see nothing; he did all his identification by feel. He surfaced and dove again ignoring the cold that seemed to be attacking his ears and eyes. Then he found it, a bit of shipwright's vanity carved below the bowsprit, less than half a fathom in length. He felt it completely and surfaced. Submerging again, he felt it completely again and scratched it to be sure. When he surfaced, he looked under his fingernails. Pale green paint. Paint the color of jade. The figurehead had been carved in the upright shape of a strutting and defiant bird -- one with a great arched, flowing tail.

He climbed back into the sampan as the snow began to fall more heavily. The tide had just begun to flood.

*****

As he returned to the steam cutter and peeled off his wet woolen underwear, the wind was raising and he began to shiver uncontrollably.

Hobson looked back. Somewhere deep in that black hull was the answer to a puzzle that had tallied four heads and that was linked to a country in mourning. The revelation should not have been that startling, but he was breathing heavily and felt a constriction in his chest. Was it the exertion or something else?

The wreck's heavily tarred and now chaffing standing rigging had flapped like a witch's shawl. That image and the sudden encounter with Eun had brought back his personal ghosts. Witches and ghosts. How that imagery had flowed through the trans-Pacific trade in ship names like Sea Witch and Halloween. Cutty's Sark was Gaelic for a witch's shirt. Was a mudang a medium or a witch or simply a guide to the other side? Was he slipping in and out of the rational? Witches, death, and darkness.

More disturbing still, the silhouette of the hull of a barque was not unlike the silhouette of a schooner. He realized this above all this was the thing he dreaded most. More than anything, he dreaded the thought of finding a schooner, a particular schooner.

And then he was at the steam cutter. He had taken a long time sculling back and his woolen underwear was dry. One of the Korean crewmen offered him some of Sabatelli's coffee. He found himself gazing at Sabatelli's coffee grinder and the yin and yang pattern of the cast iron arches on its wheels.

"Did you find anything?" Sabatelli asked as he had done so many times before.

"No, not yet."

It was growing colder, he thought with a frisson. It was cold, cold…as a witch's caress.

*****

The steam cutter puffed eastward for several days beyond Mokp'o and then began its return trip to Chemulp'o without retracing its steps. The strong currents and far-ranging tides made its progress appear halting and undecided, and Hobson thought that in a way, the cutter reflected the malaise of its passengers. Sabatelli did not know he had found the barque and felt he had wasted his time and money. Hobson had held back with a sailor's circumspection, and mistrust of those outside the chain of command. Hobson was in the throes of indecision. Why had he allowed himself to come back to Korea? Should he do something? What could he do?

At cove, they had anchored out, and Hobson made several trips to ferry in Matsuda and the crew. Proceeding up the shingle from his beached sampan, Hobson found himself eye level with the barrels of two well-oiled Nambu pistols. Two bodies lay in the road behind the Japanese military policemen that held the pistols. One body had a puddle below its head that Hobson assumed was blood. He could smell gunsmoke and there was that eerie silence which follows a loud report. Hobson could hear women shrieking and crying, but, true to Confucian custom, they did so behind closed doors. The mixed odor of burning charcoal, garlic, and night soil seemed particularly pungent. The two Japanese military policemen seemed edgy and both Hobson and Sabatelli made sure to assume cooperative postures.

Beyond the two, several other military policemen were herding young men into a wagon and a platoon of foot-weary soldiers formed a loose circle around the entire evolution. Most Korean houses had perimeter walls that sealed their homes off from the street and it was difficult to see where the young men were coming from. It was clear, the Japanese were not being very selective, any able-bodied candidate would do. Hobson realized that he did not look very official in his dungarees and peajacket. A westerner, perhaps a missionary, was an unwelcome complication that could be easily resolved. Interference by foreigners might mean reports and embarrassment. Dead foreigners required an apology, at most.

Matsuda came around the corner, sized up the situation, and began barking orders. The Korean men were hustled off and the handguns returned to their holsters.

Matsuda offered no words of explanation.

*****

Deeper in the village they came upon another westerner.

He was a big blond man who by appearance would have made a better Viking than a clergyman, Hobson thought when he saw him swinging back and forth the gate of a house with a thatched roof. Hobson readily identified the props; he carried a Bible in one hand and he wore Korean rubber slippers. Hobson's father had always carried a Bible, not that it was so necessary, just to symbolize his purpose. Some faiths wore clerical collars, others wore crucifixes, and the variations were endless. He wore a heavy frock coat, a shirt and tie, and carried a western newsboy's hat with its brim in his hand. He seemed to work the gate back and forth on its hinge distractedly.

He continued to swing the gate. The missionary did not want to have anything to do with Hobson or Sabatelli. He had seen them with Matsuda and assumed they were somehow working with the Japanese Resident-General. Hobson sensed this and began talking to the blond man in Korean. Hobson realized it was the first time he had ever talked to a Caucasian in Korean.

"What's going on?" Hobson questioned. "Has someone read the riot act? Why are the Japanese rounding up Korean men? I saw two men dead in the street. What's this all about, forced conscription? Surely the locals after enjoying the benefits of a superior Nipponese culture here and colonial paternalism, can't be shirking?"

The words were not that important, it was the use of the language. You cannot learn a language without coming to some understanding of the people who speak it. An American who had gone through what it required to have that level of proficiency in Korean might be worthy of a minor degree of trust. Any missionary knew no one who spoke Korean could be ignorant of Korea's unhappy circumstances.

The response came in English. "You sir, may choose to be flippant, but those two young men were students of mine and died because of their attitude toward their Nipponese overlords. And I am afraid that the attitude which bought them their deaths may have been my doing."

Hobson thought the man wobbled slightly. He opened his handkerchief and wiped his forehead in a very awkward way.

" So, if you are going to be sarcastic, even at the expense of the sons of Nippon, kindly do so with someone who is presently more emotionally disposed to see mirth or irony in this situation."

"Sorry."

Hobson realized the Viking was tense and drunk. His breathing was shallow, marked by faint tendrils of steam.

"Eight men, either Righteous Army or Young Hwarang sympathizers were beheaded on a hilltop to the east of here. Several months back, another four were beheaded on a mountain crest not too far south of here.

Hobson felt in his pocket for the photograph.

"We knew they might come. Most of the other villages have been raided. They are engaging a double effort, these days. Interrogating for 'bandits' and conscripting labor for railroad work. Several Koreans die for every mile of track. They need to constantly replenish their labor supply. And there is a lot of mining that is going to have to be done if the Nippon's military machine is going to match world power standards."

"I'm with the U. S Navy…my people were missionaries here once. We're trying to find a barque. It seems beheadings are pretty common around here. Have you seen this?"

"Oh,"

He seemed to have a thought on the U. S. Navy, but could not get it to form words. "Well damn them when ready Gridley and let drift the torpedoes. Well, my advice to you is to remember that under the regime Japanaise, improper political behavior, let alone overt guerrilla activity, will buy you 'summary conviction.'"

"Yes, we have heard about summary conviction."

The blonde man examined the photograph slowly. "That's Moon and that's Hoyt. I have not made the acquaintance of the others, not likely to either. Moon was a turncoat and Hoyt was a bloodsucker. He was Navy, too, you know."

The missionary eyed Hobson closely.

"Perhaps you should be more selective. He used to work in Pusan in some capacity. Got out of the Navy, I'm told. Only fellow I know who took the effort to learn the language, but then couldn't bother to sympathize with the people. Learned it from his mistress, his pillow dictionary, I'm told. Tried to get as much money as he could out of the New Hwarang. The basket and the… er, heads, are in a boat. This has to do with that ship, *Jade Rooster*, doesn't it? Those are the words on the sides of the boat in the picture. They were supposed to bring us…"

Matsuda burst out from behind a building and gestured emphatically for Hobson and Sabatelli to follow. Hobson watched the Viking whose attention was on a treeline that bordered a rice paddy at a distance. Hobson caught the brief glimmering reflection of steel.

In that moment, Hobson was forced to reverse his assessment of the Viking. The edge of the missionary's coat fluttered for just a moment and he thought he saw the scroll-like curve of a derringer fastened to one of the blond man's gallowses. The Viking had removed his hat to be more identifiable at a distance.

"Name's Iversen and yours?

"Hobson."

"The Hobson…of the Navy. Cuba Hobson?"

"No, that's another fellow."

"Headed to Seoul or Pyongyang?" The blond missionary's tone grew in intensity.

"Chemulp'o."

"Maybe I'll see you there. There's…."

Sabatelli and Hobson were led around a corner and Iversen was gone. If Hobson had a clear sense of the significance of that glint of steel in the tree line that the platoon of Japanese soldiers and smattering of military police were not going to live out the day. The missionary, drunk as he might be, was where he was for a purpose. The missionary was pursuing a very Old Testament course of action. There were insurrectionists in the tree lines and behind the dikes in the rice paddy.

Matsuda was preoccupied with getting Sabatelli and Hobson out of the area. Matsuda heard an exchange of shots, fanned Hobson and Sabatelli forward, and assumed -- perhaps erroneously -- that everything was under control.

CHAPTER NINETEEN

On another mountain several prisoners were shackled with their wrists bound behind them to waist-high posts. There were twice as many this time and again sacks had been placed over their heads. Several slumped over in pain hoping for death. Others had only been rounded up in the villages that night.

Koizumi took his uniform blouse off and drew his sword from his scabbard. His kendo was rusty and he knew it. Stationed in this godforsaken land among little more than savages there was little opportunity to refine his skills. He made a few practice swings.

"Mansei!" cried a woman who had been tortured terribly, but held up well. He cut the cry off abruptly.

In the shadows just beyond the circle of lantern light, Atticaris checked his list. All the victims he had recommended were there. He had run a taut division when he had been in the Navy. No Irish pennants – improperly secured or stowed loose ends -- tolerated. Irish pennants were untidy, unseamanlike. This exercise was like pruning; the organism had to be cut back periodically to bear the best fruit. He could draw a good deal of money out of all this, if he cultivated it properly. Encouraging the insurrectionists to buy guns and then selling the insurrectionists to the Kempeitai, would not last forever, he sighed. But if carefully manipulated his project, it would produce several lucrative harvests.

He knew filibusterers who had assembled armed adventurers and marched through countries like conquistadors. Most died poor and poorly with a bullet for their efforts. No, money had to be earned progressively. The single big score was the dream of wastrels. Money had to be harvested over and over again. The greedy seeking a single prize never prospered.

Koizumi had welcomed Atticaris' idea for the executions. He had practiced kendo for years, but could never really know how it felt to separate a man from his life with a thin sliver of steel.

"Mansei!"

He took the cries as challenges and responded resolutely.

"Mansei!"

He particularly liked it when two challenged at once and he was forced to cover ground quickly before either could take a breath to repeat the cry. The Koreans did not know that he had turned it into a sort of game. They knew they were being executed and this gesture of defiance came instinctively.

"Mansei," the chant was getting weaker as one by one the voices were stopped.

"Man…"

The last voice was that of a schoolmarm from a village on the coast, an attractive young woman named Eun.

*****

Matsuda placed the heads on the posts that guarded the approaches to their respective villages.

CHAPTER TWENTY

Hobson wanted to tell Sabatelli that he had discovered *Jade Rooster*, but something told him to hold off. There was too much Hobson did not know, and too much he did not understand. Sabatelli's interest seemed far too persistent for just one fairly insignificant vessel lost at sea with a nondescript cargo list. Whatever Atticaris had been smuggling, if Sabatelli knew what it was, he was not to be trusted. And if it was a routine voyage why was he so zealous?

Hobson would tell him later, after he talked with Mr. Draper.

****

They brought the cutter back to Chemulp'o and paid off the crew. The weekly steamboat from Chemulp'o back to Kobe and Yokohama was several days off.

A typhoon kept him indoors for several days. The winds tore at the roof of his inn and the rain dripped into his room through several parts of the ceiling. Then the weather cleared and he decided to take the sampan out to Wolmido, a small island in the harbor. He fought the incredible currents, beached until he could catch his breath, and then headed back.

The sun had just set when he returned to the dock. Several small sampans followed him in. There were more silhouettes around than usual, but Hobson was not surprised. The typhoon had driven everyone indoors and now it seemed normal for the inhabitants of the harbor to surge forth with a collective sigh of survival.

The dock was a narrow one and Hobson noticed two large men talking and positioned in a manner that blocked his way up the ramp. He looked behind him and two husky fisherman had just landed and were walking shoulder to shoulder directly toward him. He could see the steam from their breaths and he looked into their eyes, but there was no eye contact. They looked right through him as if he was not there.

Serving with the fleet was an education in waterfront survival and all Hobson's senses were alert.

To a ship approaching land, that zone that included the water's edge, the rocks and shoals, offered the greatest dangers. The farther a ship went out to sea, the safer it was. That zone which divided land from water was a source of constant danger for ships. The same applied to a ship's crew on the waterfront -- with its human rocks and shoals -- it was the most dangerous area for sailors. The farther inland a sailor ashore went, the safer he was. The waterfront, approached from either land or sea, was fraught with peril.

In the last few decades, there had been riots in South American countries where American sailors on liberty had been set upon and killed by mobs. The fleet had been dispatched and war only narrowly averted. Sailors were easily identified foreigners and were too frequently the targets of criminal or political intrigue. On a large scale, Maine had been sunk not that far from the pier. On a smaller scale, a significant portion of the sailors listed as deserters were disappearances, victims of foul play.

Some sailors carried brass knuckles, blackjacks, or socks filled with sand in the pockets of their peacoats. A stack of coins rolled in the back of a neckerchief was an old standby in the summer. Waterfront treachery was one reason boxing champs were popular on liberty. Gunnarson might occasionally come back to the launch alone, but, Hobson guessed, he never went on liberty alone.

Hobson did not like the feel of this and turned and walked toward the fishermen. They accelerated toward him. Without a word, he grabbed one and threw him headlong into a boat. The other, he took over his shoulder with a judo throw. The two by the ramp had turned and were not talking anymore, they were moving in his direction. One dove at him and he sidestepped. The other tried to tag him with some sort of threshing tool. He grabbed the wrist, extended the arm, and snapped it with an armbar.

Out of the corner of his eye, he noticed the form of a Japanese military policeman floating face down just beyond a fishing boat. It was drifting with the tide.

Four additional fishermen had landed on the far end of the dock. The dock was long and narrow and icy. The attacks could only take place from two directions and only by a few at a time. Hobson reminded himself that, above all, he had to stay on his feet. Once down, he was through.

He overheard them saying "yusool." It was the word for an early Korean form of judo. They had identified their quarry's tactics and were making adjustments.

This time they rushed him from both sides. None of the men was taller than he was, but they were strong and heavily built. One pinned Hobson's hands against his sides. Another, using a Ssirum – Korean folk wrestling -- hip technique lifted both Hobson's feet of the dock. Another placed a thick canvas bag over his head blinding him. Suddenly he found himself inverted and head down in a basket of sea urchins. Urchin spines laced his shoulders, neck and back, but the bag protected his eyes. The pain was excruciating. Then they carried him stomach down holding him like a battering ram.

The men talked among themselves in Korean. There had to be a dozen of them. The fact that they spoke Korean was no help to Hobson. They could be Kempeitai Koreans or New Hwarang Koreans or any of a dozen other factions that any unhappy, unsettled situation generated. The men were moving very rapidly and changing direction constantly, jostling him ungently. They were not pleased with Hobson whom they spoke of as the "nuisance meegook," the nuisance American. Two punches to the kidneys, punctuated with the word "yusool," emphasized that all physical skills had their limitations.

*****

He was drawn from the basket and set on the floor, but not gently. Hands began to pull the sea urchins spines from his neck. Wherever he was, it was unheated and he began to shiver. He had not worn much, expecting his rowing to keep him warm. Occasionally, a point of light glimmered through the sack.

A voice spoke in cultured Korean. Japanese and Korean had different social levels of speech. A farmer and an emperor used completely different forms of speech and employed different degrees of politeness. The relative social standing of the addressee determined the manner of speech and address, not the absolute social class of the speaker. A yangban, an aristocrat, Hobson judged.

The floor sounded wet and gritty and Hobson could smell fish.

"The sea urchins were not our idea, they were an improvised solution. Such is guerrilla warfare"

Guerrilla warfare. He had heard the term, but it was not a common one.

The hands were gentle and scented. Women, two women, perhaps.

"You know that you are watched, watched constantly, Mr. Hobson." Another voice, this time speaking English with a Midwestern accent. Iverson.

"Just Hobson, thanks. I know who you are."

"Doesn't matter, young man, I am on my way out of here, exiting unceremoniously with too many other western missionaries."

169

"How did it turn out, that set-to with the Japanese military police and the conscripts? Settle their hash?" Hobson was whistling in the dark.

"Not all knowledge is beneficial. Better you did not know. The sons of Nippon have murdered too many of my flock. I am not comfortable with inciting retribution, it is not my vocation, but there comes a point."

Some of the sea urchin spines were coming out, some were breaking off. He was going to be a sight in the morning.

The yangban spoke in English. "Well, Hobson, it is good there was a scuffle. The Japanese would not approve of your getting friendly with us... insurrectionists. Now Hobson, you work for your country's government. I think you are more important than you appreciate."

Hobson resisted the urge to guffaw. His English had a Hawaiian shortness to its delivery.

"Only so much as I have to."

"Your country signed a treaty in 1882 with Korea to protect it from aggressors."

Hobson did not know if that was true, and kept quiet.

"The Japanese are grinding us under their heels. We are their very first colony and they plan to do it right. Shortly we will be another Japan, new language, new names and total serfs, " the yangban said. "America is just standing by."

He paused. "I am Kim."

He said, "I am Kim" as if it should have some significance to Hobson. He used the forms in Korean that indicated he was the Kim.

Hobson talked through the canvas bag. "Kim? There are thousands of Kims, more Kims than Carter's got pills, more than all the Smiths and Joneses in America combined. What's that suppose t'mean?"

"You spoke to my wife in Chinatown, in Yokohama...and to another Korean man."

"Yes, Mr. Kim."

"No, not Mr. Kim, just another man, a man who had recently escaped from a Japanese jail and who had been smuggled out of the country. I swapped places with him on *Jade Rooster*. I came in from Hawaii where we are training more New Hwarang. I needed to be smuggled in and he needed to be smuggled out. Our group was the group buying products from Mr. Hoyt. Shortly after our boats came to *Jade Rooster* we made the switch.

The scented hands were rubbing the sea urchin punctures with a liquid that stung and smelled like urine.

"Hoyt was selling you guns?"

There was a long pause.

Iverson spoke with discomfort, "And if he was?"

"Well, for one, it wasn't Hoyt that was selling. It was a fellow higher up named Atticaris. Atticaris is the prime bad egg. Chock full of filibustardy."

There was silence.

"Little matter, I think. We knew then, and know better now, that we were dealing with the devil. We had little choice. We have little choice."

"Well, it is a big matter because Atticaris distances himself from the peddling. I think he adds to his take by betraying his buyers in small installments. You're not his only customer."

Another long pause, there was a whispered consultation. "Betrayals in installments?"

"Probably does double duty. It fixes to keep the business from being traced back to him, and it keeps you insurrectionists sprightly developin' new leaders who in turn find new sources of greenbacks or Mex. New greenbacks or Mex mean continued purchases."

Kim laughed dryly. "Ah, yes, Hobson, Hobson of the Navy," he seemed to enjoy that manner of address. Perhaps it made him feel as if he was talking to someone who mattered. "It was so very practical."

" Very business like. Our purchases will soon come to a close in any event, I think unless we get help from the outside. Rebellions need money. No one supplies guns for free. Where are we to get the money? We raised money to buy certain weapons from Hoyt and he nearly tricked us out of our money.

"Our people are taxed to excess by the Japanese and must only sell to the Japanese at prices they dictate. A rebel government can impose taxes too, but our people can't pay them. We can rob the Japanese from time to time to raise money – the Oriental Investment Company is bleeding the currency and valuable metals out of Korea -- but Japan's new colony is very heavily garrisoned and not adverse to taking reprisals against anyone or any village that might support us. We mount a raid and they conscript a nearby village for forced railroad labor in retaliation. Lately, it has been more theatrical. Prisoners have been taken, some beheaded and their heads placed where they can achieve the most dramatic effect. Many, too many, of our people are fleeing to Manchuria. I fear that they will get little rest there. I think Manchuria will be next.

"We missed our chance. We could have allied quickly with the West like Japan and Siam and survived. Unfortunately we have always had to watch China, Japan and Russia. We threw our lot in with China to play off the others and now China is a sick and ineffectual empire. Japan has brushed China aside effortlessly in the past, and it recently sank the Russian Fleet. No country in Asia can stand against it.

"We need guns, we need money. Americans have both and I know from my time in Hawaii that Americans do not trust the Japanese. Tell your officers we need help. Tell your leaders they must abide by the treaty. Not you personally, but surely every Navy has an intelligence service."

Hobson did not respond. International demands voiced through a third class petty officer, had about a snowball's chance in hell. Surely they knew that, but he realized they were desperate and any possibility was worth pursuing. He thought of explaining where he stood in the naval pecking order and mentally fished for the Korean word for pawn. He exhaled audibly.

"You have a yarn to share 'bout *Jade Rooster*?" Hobson felt could only begin to understand all this if he could understand the portion he had come to resolve.

CHAPTER TWENTY-ONE

"There was to be a swap in addition to the purchase of arms. Captain Brewer did not know about the swap, nor did his second mate. Hoyt, or as you say, Atticaris, had built up our trust. A pattern developed of small sales for US greenbacks or Mexican silver. Not arm's length after a while, we'd show up and buy things as if we were going to the store."

Mexican silver dollars were the universal currency of the Far East.

"This was a bigger sale than usual and we knew the shipment would be on *Jade Rooster*. I booked passage on *Jade Rooster* with my wife. I needed to get in unnoticed and there was a teacher who was too active, too well known, and too wanted by the Kempeitai to be allowed to stay in Korea.

"While the weapons were changing hands, we would swap places. The crew had little to do with us and wouldn't notice any difference between two Koreans of roughly the same size. For the most part they would watch the woman. It seems strange to know this, but I took comfort in knowing they would watch my wife"

Hobson felt himself drifting into shock. Forty or fifty urchin spines were the equivalent of several dozen wasp stings.

"I was out of sight when *Jade Rooster* anchored and a few of our men came aboard. Hoyt and the captain and second mate pulled revolvers and took the money they had brought with them. They were in the process of disarming our men and I had no idea what was intended.

"Everything was going wrong and I had only seconds to consider. I had a pistol and shot Hoyt and the captain outright. A gunfight ensued and Hoyt's group was wiped out. The rest of the crew was not involved and we either set them adrift or had them move *Jade Rooster* eastward toward to Mokp'o. Eventually we set them free in Chefoo."

Hobson was not sure whether the pain of the urchin stings was making his wits sharper or duller.

"Hold now, you said you shot Brewer and Hoyt. They were beheaded."

"Well, Hobson of the Navy..."

There was that grand title again.

"...they were long dead by then. Your mention of deaths by installment is ironic. Yes, we were greatly disturbed by the recent beheading of four of our rebels and we decided to send a message. An eye for an eye. There have been several beheadings since, and we have retaliated. I suppose death is death. Death by bullet or death by beheading has the same result in the long run. We, however, do not truly engage in beheading of prisoners. We attempt to stay as civilized as guerrilla war will let us. An unattainable hope of virtue, I suspect."

Kim sniffed. Hobson thought he it was an unconscious self-critical gesture.

" In this case, we went among the enemy dead, selected those heads that were unmarked and arranged them 'for presentation.' Severed heads are eerie, unnatural. The Japanese know it, we know it. The world over, whatever your religion or background, bodies without heads make people uneasy."

"Well, mind, don't use that particular style of basket again." Hobson told him why. "Now here's a thought to give your consideration, Mr. Kim. What would a fellow do if he wanted to contact you in the future."

"A fellow couldn't. You couldn't. If people can contact me, they can kill me and there is a reward for me."

"Well, I'll put my noggin to it. There must be a way."

The voice remained still for several minutes. Talking blindfolded was a new experience, Hobson found it aided his concentration. He seemed more sensitive to pauses and changes in breathing. Perhaps he had always been sensitive to these secondary indications of mood and stress, at a subconscious level.

"They put the heads on the posts outside villages," was Kim's response.

Hobson had not known that.

"You mean the totem posts." Grisly business, this matching of carvings, Hobson thought to himself.

"Yes, they don't stay up long. The families take them down. The mudangs say that is making the spirits uneasy. All this decapitation is very bad business. The totems are to keep away bad spirits, not to herald wandering, unhappy spirits."

Hobson did not like the reference to lost wandering spirits.

The voice continued, "You have a message for me, give it to a mudang. They know everyone and everything that goes on in Cholla province. The Japanese have nothing but contempt for the shamanists. Japan is, after all, bringing civilization to this backward corner of the world."

Hobson noted that dark tone of cynicism again.

"Our superstitious beliefs only serve to convince our island cousins of their spiritual superiority. You, of course, realize that they recognize their emperor who walks the earth."

"What about the fellow who went by 'Moon?'"

Iverson cleared his throat and excused himself. His footsteps trailed off into a gritty, distant shuffle and then the room was quiet.

"Mr. Iverson is a morally sensitive man, " Kim confided. "Moon? Or maybe Sato. He traveled under the Japanese name. There is great pressure to adopt Japanese names, to become Japanese in form. I think of him as Sato. He was nowhere to be seen at the time."

Another pause, the breathing restricted.

"Sato was an embarrassment. He was supposed to serve as a bodyguard for my wife and I, and then return to Hawaii to help train other Koreans. He was a fundraiser. He helped raise money and develop contacts with the Korean expatriate community. To our consternation, we found some of our major financial supporters began to simply disappear and we found ourselves constantly looking for new sources of funds.

"I didn't really catch on until I heard him talking to Hoyt. He was very close to Hoyt throughout the voyage. When Hoyt turned on us, I went looking for 'Moon.' Some of my men searched 'Moon's' stateroom and then we had a 'talk' with him.

"Moon, or perhaps more correctly Sato, was a Japanese agent provocateur. He was assigned to encourage us to do rash things, if he could, and to identify our operations and supporters in America.

"I said we try to stay as civilized…as guerrilla warfare will permit us. Sato was a spy for the Japanese. His business was pure treachery. I will never know if he was Japanese or Korean. His Korean was flawless. Regrettably, with him we were not so civilized.

"We scuttled *Jade Rooster* to hide her, then tied Sato to the mast and let the tide come in. We removed his head after he'd drowned.

"We had entertained other more distasteful options, but this end seemed fitting. Like a drowning rat, if I may use a Western simile. In the East we hold rats in much higher esteem than we do men such as Sato."

Hobson thought he detected another change in Kim's breathing.

"I was a man of moral sensitivity once."

"What about the ordnance?" Hobson asked.

"It was all very rushed and distressing. We could never find the goods. A quick search of the holds revealed only barrels of a very smelly waxy substance. Some sort of fish oil product, I think.

"We were stuck with a vessel that might have the goods we wished to buy and we had to hide it quickly. It was a vessel that we were not capable of sailing, only sinking. We scuttled it and hoped the hae nyo might find the secret. The hae nyo however would not swim into the holds of the vessel though she was in shallow water. Diving underwater is one thing, diving underwater into a contained space with obstruction over one's head – between one and the surface – is still another. While we have been struggling to come up with an answer to our predicament, our members continue to be rounded up and the Japanese continue their raids.

"I put this to you, Hobson of the Navy. You are looking for *Jade Rooster*. We care nothing for her or her routine cargo. If you find her, is there any need to turn any of her unusual contents over to our island cousins?"

CHAPTER TWENTY-TWO

They placed him again headfirst into a large basket - without urchins this time - and left him in front of a police box.

The local police brought him to the headquarters building. Koizumi seemed amused. "So you have been visiting with the local banditry."

Hobson was in agony.

"It has not been an easy job, bringing civilization to this country. There are not enough jails to hold those who do not acknowledge the benefits of the Emperor's leadership. There is much work to be done and we throw some into the labor battalions." Koizumi seemed preoccupied.

"It will take years to bring this country to a level satisfactory to Japan. I suppose they threatened you or gave you some sad story of oppression."

This was a different Koizumi, gone was the bon vivant of Japan.

"They told me not to look for *Jade Rooster*..." Hobson lied. "And asked why the U.S. had abandoned them."

Matsuda poured Hobson a teacup of makkolli, from a teapot. The room started to reel.

"Abandoned them? Abandon them? What does America care about Asian affairs? These people are only a step or two only above savages, in their one-room huts. Why deny Japan its destiny? Korea has been a weak and foolish country, a tributary country of China. China is sick and weak. It's been corrupt and undisciplined for a long time. Its end is near. The Western countries are dissecting its carcass. Korea is an orphan now; it needs a sempai, a big brother to make its decisions for it.

The makkolli laced through Hobson and warmed him. He felt a rising sense of well-being and a strange martial kinship with Koizumi and Matsuda.

"We know what Korea needs. We have risen from feudalism to a modern sensation in a matter of decades. We have discipline; we have done the impossible. We were a backward country and now we are a country that has fought a Western country and prevailed. Korea needs that discipline and we are the ones to impart a discipline that Asians can understand."

Hobson sat attentively, but his silence seemed to incite Koizumi to a new level of justification.

"We are new to colonialism that's true, but we'll do it better than the British and the others. They do it for economic gain only, rarely superimposing their cultural system on their colonies. We will make Korea a true part of Japan in every way. In a few years, Koreans will speak Japanese, have Japanese names, do those things that Japanese do, and perhaps at some point be indistinguishable from Japanese. What greater gift could we give them, we will make them nearly Japanese?"

Hobson found it took every last bit of concentration to talk. "I may be feelin' sort of all-overish, but it seems they're not wanting the 'gift."

Koizumi exhaled slowly.

"You've heard of Darwin and survival of the fittest. You're in the Navy; navies understand what survival of the fittest means. Korea was vulnerable to attack by China, Russia, or Japan. If we didn't step in someone else would have. Japan is strong. Korea is weak. They need what we have to offer. To a lesser extent we need what they have...minerals, lumber, and labor. Until we came, Korea was unfit to survive."

Hobson nodded and his head flopped drowsily.

"Your country's got a few colonies now, Hawaii and Samoa and Cuba and Guam and the Philippines." Koizumi smiled.

"How are you going to handle them? The how do you call it, 'Philippine Insurrection' shows that all do not enjoy the guiding touch of the American paternal hand. No, you have your hands occupied for the time being, I think. You tell that to Mr. Draper."

"Who'd that be?"

"You know, the intelligence officer with the Office of Naval Intelligence."

"Oh, I'm only a collier sailor."

Koizumi slapped Hobson condescendingly on the back and chuckled as he had in Japan. The pain nearly made him pass out.

*****

Two days later, the Mitsubishi steamship left Chemulp'o for Kobe with Sabatelli and Hobson. From Kobe, Hobson took another steamship to Yokohama and then went to look for Mr. Draper in Tokio. It was nearly the Christmas leave period. After he reported to Draper, he would catch a steamer to Shanghai. He marveled at the amount of non-participatory steaming he was enjoying.

The office was unchanged. Hobson noted that although Draper always looked disheveled, every book, chart and photograph had a certain order. A portly man in a striped suit with heavy glasses also waited in the office. Hobson was expected.

"Mr. Smith here from the Embassy is also interested in hearing your report. You can speak freely. Don't give me just the facts, I want to hear your thoughts and er, insights."

Hobson felt uncomfortable. Lately people seemed to be overestimating his significance in the great cosmic scheme. What was so wrong with being a third class quartermaster aboard a collier?

"The whole system they - the Nip Army and the Kempeitai -- have put in place is as cold as...as..."

Hobson realized the witch analogy, "a witch's heart," which he had intended, had too emotional a grip on him. He fell into a more naval one.

"...as a pawnbroker's heart."

He reviewed his log using it to prompt a string of observations that ran the entirety of the afternoon. He gave a day-by-day account of his search for *Jade Rooster*, starting with the day he'd left Shanghai.

"You saw the boat? How deep is it? Not like a pearl diver job, is it? Hard to get into tight spaces and dark?" Draper asked.

Hobson shrugged his shoulders. "*Jade Rooster* was scuttled. Looked like they punched a couple holes just above the waterline and then shifted the ballast. Not too big a job to raise the whole barque, I figure. Take longer to raise the whole vessel with getting everything in place and all. Harder to retrieve the ordnance by itself, but faster."

"So Major Koizumi thinks I work for the Office of Naval Intelligence? Heck, I am the Office of Naval Intelligence out here. All of it. Not many Japanese language scholars around. Heck, and there's just a few in the Navy Department interested in Japan or intelligence at all."

"Mr. Smith" asked several questions about Kim and the New Hwarang and Iversen. He seemed very interested in the man Hobson had never actually seen.

"Watch the woman," Mr. Smith repeated with a wry look of appreciation.

Hobson rubbed his neck and could still feel the damage from the sea urchin spines. It would be a week before he could sleep right.

"Is it true? Have we failed to honor our treaty? Or was that bunkum."

Draper looked perplexed and Hobson thought of Koizumi.

"Well, there are a couple ways of looking at our involvement here in the Far East.

"First thing, who is Kim? Is he an elected official or a head of state? Did the Korean head of state ever ask for our help under the treaty? The Japanese finessed the matter very efficiently. Where they didn't the Koreans blundered in time with the music. The Japanese intimidated the Korean Emperor and made him sign papers and treaties that eventually lent the appearance of legitimacy to the Japanese's Annexation of Korea. The appearance of legitimacy is often enough for political purposes."

"Did the Korean people rise in arms as a group? No, not at first, not for a while. They were in the bad habit of going the way their emperor declared and with fellows like emperors there is no loyal opposition. After the Korean Emperor abdicated, the prince was placed essentially under house arrest; there was a vacuum that did not fill quickly. There was no readily available spokesman for the Koreans, no rallying point.

"Yes, there was a treaty. Unfortunately, the Japanese did not take power with an overt show of arms. No, they just employed a finely orchestrated series of palace shenanigans.

"Now, we had a choice and I can't really say why we elected to stand aside and let it happen. It might have been one reason and it might have been many. We're a democracy and why we do things in often a stew of many people's thoughts and impressions.

"Sure there is some self-interest going on here. The Philippines are something of a headache for us. If we interfere in someone else's insurrection problem, well, they can feel free to interfere in ours. Trouble is, the U.S. is thousands of miles away and Japan is right here. It is a great strain to have any sort of presence out here. The Nips have what the strategists back in Newport call "interior lines of communications " and everything we do takes months to accomplish and a fortune to support.

" We're not even sure how involved we want to get in Pacific affairs. Deep down inside, most of us think we backed into colonialism -- almost by accident -- and our style of administration will be benign, even costly. The Japanese, on the other hand, will make Korea pay for the great Japanese Imperial adventure."

Draper picked up a report several inches thick and fanned its pages.

"There's cynicism on our part, too. If Japan doesn't take Korea someone else will. Some think it is better that Japan takes Korea because they are Asians and may be more sympathetic. I don't think so. The Japanese aren't long on empathy beyond the shores of their own islands. They are too wrapped up in being a child prodigy nation."

Draper thought a minute about these words, and then stood up. His sleepy demeanor had disappeared.

"See that pile of documents over there? That's what occupies me most of my time. It's the Imperial Japanese Naval Budget. Right now we Americans are on a collision course with Japan. All their documents assume we will be their next naval opponent, we are known as the "hypothetical enemy." Budget expenditures are put together to make the Imperial Japanese Navy seventy percent the size of the United States Navy. The United States Navy that has to cover two oceans, and is half the world away. The Japanese are discussing procuring eight battleships and eight cruisers on the floors of the Diet. That's our immediate concern, not injustice on the Asian mainland."

Hobson could see bits and pieces of ships blueprints. They were not American ships.

"Mr. Kim talks about the U.S. coming to the aid of Korea. Couldn't be fleet help. Everyone saw the trouble the Russians had getting their fleet to Japanese home waters, and how easy it was for the Japanese to defeat them in those same home waters. No, Korea's troubles are Japanese and our troubles will be Japanese someday. We are not ready for that...yet."

Draper made an expansive gesture.

"Funny thing is, I like these people. The culture's rich and fascinating and the people can be sensitive and kind. When they get derailed, however, it's a real train wreck. Right now the U.S. and Japan are on the same rail headed in opposite directions."

Draper and "Mr. Smith" wandered off into discussion of details of the Japanese order of battle and suddenly remembered that Hobson was still there.

"Now, what's your reading on *Jade Rooster*?"

Hobson asked if he could smoke his pipe and Draper assented. "Mr. Smith" drew a Meerschaum from his vest pocket and offered Hobson tobacco, dark Korean tobacco. He set the pouch down by an art deco desk lamp.

"Well, sirs, as my chief would say, the whole story has got considerable more curves than a barrel of fishhooks... considerable so. I figure Atticaris meant to sell the pneumatic dynamite gun and the Gatling guns to the highest bidder. He promised them to the Koreans, then got a higher bid from the Moros."

Hobson thought it all fairly obvious, but then he had come face to face with all the participants.

"The pneumatic dynamite gun and the Gatling guns could be sold double, once to the Koreans and once to the Filipino rebels, because Atticaris would never have to deliver to the Koreans. Any deals with the Koreans weren't worth beans. When the Koreans met *Jade Rooster*, he had Hoyt act in his stead as he always did, just like he had that handle-barred ex-marine, O'Hare, in Mindanao. Hoyt was going to rob Koreans, get rid of their bodies and sell the Gatling guns and pneumatic dynamite gun and whatever else they had bought a second time to the Moros. Captain Brewer would back him up. Later, maybe they'd come back peddling to the Koreans. Start the gunrunning all over again."

Hobson turned the subject to the New Hwarang. He told of his conversations with the drover, Eun, and Kim.

"The problem was the New Hwarang did not know about Atticaris and it seemed Hoyt was in charge of the peddling. Brewer and Hoyt led the bullyboys and their apparent leadership cost them their heads. Sato's double-dealing cost him his.

"The whole consarned design, I guess, went wrong sudden like and the Koreans got the drop on Brewer and the part of his crew working with the gunrunners. The first Mr. Kim who sailed aboard *Jade Rooster* was not the same Mr. Kim who boarded the boat that night. The first Mr. Kim was a big kahuna from the New Hwarang's Hawaii organization. The second "Mr. Kim" was on the lam from a Japanese jail. The New Hwarang were smuggling the second Kim out of the country. One was already on the way in; he was swapped for one who was on the way out of the country. The insurrectionist leaders knew about the barque and the gunrunning so they piggybacked the swap on the gun exchange. The Hwarang flimflam swap fouled the Atticaris flimflam robbery. The Kims had figured out that Sato was a spy sent into Cholla province by the Kempeitai to smoke out troublemakers. Atticaris was working the other end with the Kempeitai, too, getting head money for most of the same people that he had sold guns to. Head money, funny."

They could hear other people moving about the building. The room was getting stuffy. Hobson noticed that the oak-trimmed transom was closed.

"The heads were just 'make-see pidgin' to the Kempeitai mirroring an equally grisly message the Kempeitai was sending to them. They thought they'd killed the heart of the treachery, the headmen."

"Mr. Smith" smiled at Hobson's unconscious second play on words.

Draper nodded. "So where do you think the ordnance is now and do you think it will ever get into the hands of the Moros?"

Hobson tapped his pipe against his brogan. "Sir, you said we are the 'hypothetical enemy. Maybe we ought to climb this rope ladder one more rung. We've taken to thinking Atticaris' only profit in this was a double sale and head money. What'f the Japanese are paying him to run guns to the Moros to start America down the road of the death by a thousand cuts? Those guns could be just another thorn in our side and another way to divert our attention. Money paid to support the Army in the Philippines, money to the Marines in the Philippines - there's only so much money for things - is money that's not going to support a stronger fleet.

"I don't think the New Hwarang have the guns. They may be there, but they couldn't find them in the short time before they had to shift the ballast and scuttle the barque. If they'd found the guns they would have just set the barque adrift. As for Atticaris' plans, well, remember the dry goods store in Manila? Remember we learned Atticaris had purchased some long handle woolies and a giant coffee grinder?

"Ever see a Morse hand-operated air pump for hardhat divers?"

Draper wore a naval uniform, but his duties did not involve him in the more mundane naval matters.

Draper looked puzzled, "No."

"They have one at Cavite. It looks like a giant coffee grinder. Atticaris is going to attempt to salvage that ordnance. I think Korea is a touch hot for sales right now. He'll sell them to the Moros just as he'd planned. Cocksure as Billy-be-damned, figure for all we know, he's sold that ordnance maybe five times over."

Hobson put out his pipe.

"Sir, I guess that's about it for me."

Draper smiled. "Not quite. You will get new orders at Shanghai. You'll be heading back to Korea. I figure you have ten days there, no more."

Hobson did some mental arithmetic and released a sigh of resignation. "Well, sir, that'll give me just enough time to settle some accounts with respect to my own jade rooster."

"What are we going to tell Mr. Sabatelli?" Hobson asked.

Draper seemed uninterested.

"I will think of something."

CHAPTER TWENTY-THREE

At quarters, three nights before the race, Lieutenant Commander Wheelwright assembled the crew on the fantail under a large canvas awning.

"Our cutter crew has got a race the day after tomorrow with *Baltimore*. *Baltimore* says we don't have 'the warrior spirit.'" The look on his face made clear the magnitude of this insult.

There were yells and catcalls. *Baltimore*'s failings were described in detail. The cruiser was a symbol, both hated and admired. The crew's blood was up and no one was safe. Certain cutter oarsmen heard their character flaws made public...at length.

Wheelwright paused patiently, and then raised his hand. "Now up my way the best oarsmen eat oysters. I believe the great Ned Hanlon and that Australian, Trickett, ate oysters."

He spoke of professional oarsmen. Rowing was the first international professional sport.

Pluto's crew wondered where this was going. Naval messes did not serve oysters in the Asiatic Fleet. Even "the Quality," with their white ties and boiled shirts and shorthaired girlfriends in the rarefied confines of the Carleton in Shanghai, rarely enjoyed oysters.

A storekeeper rolled out a handtruck with a case of tins. One of the crew reached for a tin. A petty officer read the label aloud, "Oysters, tinned bluepoint oysters."

In the front rank, the cutter's crew puffed up to full height. They were practicing twice a day now and slept fitfully, first the blankets on, then the blankets off. Their metabolisms were surging, racing up and down like the turns of a ship's screw in high seas. Every muscular cord in their necks was clearly defined. Now, they were going on the diet regimen of champions and they had become a caste unto themselves.

Their captain had such faith in them that he had spent a fortune getting them oysters from stateside. Everyone knew that was what the professionals ate. The skipper had said so.

*****

The two ships were moored in parallel and the fleet spectators were gathering. Hobson had returned to Shanghai from Korea and his visit with Draper in Japan. The quartermaster could not find Tiger or the Oyster Pirate.

There was an offshore breeze. Shanghai did not have a dominant scent, it was too big to have a single characteristic scent, Hobson thought. Of course, there was the smell of incense. Everywhere there were people there was the smell of burning incense and in Shanghai there were people everywhere. Shanghai was one of the most populous cities in the world. Incense did not count, somehow, it was too conscious an effort.

Lieutenant Commander Wheelwright had come up with canned oysters and guaranteed they were the secret to success on the East Coast where all great oarsmen came from, except that fellow from Canada and that other fellow from Australia.

The race was a test of rowing ability and seamanship. That was how the Admiral described it. The course was four miles long; it had a down current leg and an up current leg. The race was starting at three hours after high tide. The current would combine the river current with the maximum flow of an ebbing tide.

Baltimore had her cutter in the water in no time. Hobson could not find Tiger or the Oyster Pirate. Lieutenant Commander Wheelwright looked impatient, so Hobson had the remainder of the crew lower the cutter.

*****

Tiger and the Oyster Pirate came whistling down the manropes. Hobson couldn't put his finger on it but they looked...wet.

There was too much going on. So Hobson let it slide, but in the back of his mind it bothered him.

Despite the cold, *Pluto*'s cutter crew was wearing shorts fashioned from dungaree trousers and long underwear shirts with the sleeves shortened. The Oyster Pirate had pulled out his sewing machine and appliqued the name *Pluto* on the back of each shirt. *Baltimore*'s cutter crew wore the same skullcaps, fancy blue striped shirts, and knit shorts that the oarsmen in the newspaper etchings wore.

There was a warm up period. The Oyster Pirate still seemed reluctant to function as stroke, but Hobson knew he was the one for the job. Tiger seemed out of breath for once, but slowly came up to form.

*****

The Admiral reiterated his "rowing and seamanship" speech as the flag lieutenant supervised the laying of course buoys. Tendrils of steam accompanied his words. He was tall, dignified, lean, and every inch an admiral. China's future was swirling like a kaleidoscope and he enjoyed this diversion. Keeping an eye on the Great Powers and the warlords was an exhausting pursuit.

Hobson could see Gunnarson ready at his oar with several other oarsmen of equal bulk in *Baltimore*'s cutter. Each boat had to round the yellow buoy to port and the finish line would be an imaginary line between the jackstaffs of *Baltimore* and *Pluto*. The flag lieutenant would sight the line and declare the winner. There would be absolutely no contact between the boats or the race would be re-run. The Oyster

Pirate groaned and his hands began flapping dramatically, "Th-th-that means in an out and back race, don't win by too much or the losing cutter will try to ram the leading returning cutter. Just cross over, sheer off a few oars, and take its chances at a second race."

Perhaps anticipating this, the Admiral added through his speaking trumpet, "Any crew deliberately making contact with the other crew will automatically be declared the loser."

The Oyster Pirate hummed with approval, "Jus' goes to show, ossifers, the ones that rate flags, ain't totally adrift in their cranial faculties."

Hobson noticed that for once he spoke without a stoppage.

*****

"She handles funny today," Tiger said absent-mindedly. Hobson, not wanting any feeling that this was a hoodoo boat to set them off on a bad foot, quickly interjected, "Shanghai currents, it doesn't mean nothin'."

Tiger thought for a moment, and seemed satisfied.

*****

An ancient swivel gun with a blank charge unearthed from some deep recess in *Baltimore*'s magazine started the race. The swivel gun's charge predated smokeless powder. It went off and the boats seemed to hesitate, then burst out of the rolling cloud of smoke like barshot. *Baltimore*'s cutter surged ahead and positioned itself in a line with the shortest course to the yellow buoy. They had power, exceptional power.

Hobson noticed their coxswain had a tendency to fishtail, which was inefficient, but this failing also presented problems for any overtaking boat.

They started with short strokes and as they gained momentum, lengthened their strokes. Soon both boats were skimming along like multi-winged, low-flying birds. Chins in, backs straight, feet braced against the stretchers, and the power came from their backs rather than their arms.

"O-o-oysters!" The Oyster Pirate yelled with each stroke and the crew smiled with clinched teeth.

"Oysters!" They chimed in.

"Minstrels! Sleeves!" Someone from *Baltimore* had raised the cry and Hobson wondered if it was Gunnarson. Steam cascaded from their mouths with each stroke. It may have inspired *Baltimore*'s oarsmen to greater efforts; cruiser sailors could not go down to grimy coalpassers.

It incensed *Pluto*'s crew who started chanting, "Oysters!" with the full venom of a battle cry.

Halfway to the yellow buoy, *Pluto*'s cutter was nearly even with *Baltimore*'s. Pass on the inside or on the outside?

"Pass-pass-pass on the outside," yelled the Oyster Pirate. It seemed to make sense, so Hobson nodded to Tiger as coxswain.

The crews began to exchange raw language and Hobson realized that his crew had better wind, better endurance. *Pluto*'s insults came faster.

A junk came out of nowhere and began to lumber across the course.

Hobson gauged the junk's progress. "She's broadside to the current, she probably won't get in our way."

Tiger said nothing.

Hobson thought a minute. Why was the junk there at all? "Cox, we can win this. It's gonna be heavy weather, but we can win this. If that junk belongs to someone you know, like Madame Kwan, have her heave to or turn down current a midge."

Tiger gave Hobson a look of supreme innocence that was a dead give away.

Tiger began yelling in Cantonese and the junk suddenly turned shoreward.

The cursing from *Baltimore*'s crew grew more sporadic.

As they approached the yellow buoy, Tiger yelled, "Can't round close. Too little room, we hit, we have a do over."

Baltimore's cutter had the inside position, but *Pluto*'s cutter had half a boat length.

The turn had a whiplash feel to it. They were suddenly rowing not with the current, but against it.

*****

No one talked now. It was simply wheeze, pull, and sweat, wheeze, pull, and sweat. Both crews were soaked with perspiration, red-faced, and miserable. Their lungs ached. Wheeze, pull, and sweat.

"No rudder, no rudder." Tiger's cry was at the very top of his register. He held the rudder up in his hands. The rudder was there, what was he talking about? It would work if he reshipped it. It was intact, but with hand motions he indicated the gudgeon that secured the rudder to the keel was no longer there. The cutter turned broadside to the course and nearly struck *Baltimore*'s cutter.

"We're taking water." The oarsman all the way aft on the port side was looking down between his legs.

"Emergency steering gear. Cox, use the extra oar."

There were two extra oars. An oar could be used as a rudder. A knife appeared from nowhere and a length of painter was cut to jury-rig a rowlock. Ancient ships had once used oars to steer before rudders had been invented, before Noah had sewn on his crow.

"The hull's parted, back by the gudgeon."

Hobson knew they were going to lose. "Nothing we can do, just keep rowing, y'r able, y'r Oysters. They've got nothin'."

"Oysters! You go fast. You go faster." Tiger had now shipped the oar in place of the useless rudder and struggled to put the cutter back on course. The portside was stronger and he wrestled to keep the cutter headed toward the finish line as they sloughed back and forth. So now they had assumed the name and battle cry of "oysters," a creature that went nowhere and was a bottomfeeder.

Surprisingly *Baltimore*'s cutter had come even with *Pluto*'s cutter, but could not seem to pass. They were yelling a good deal about minstrels and coalpassers, but were looking spent and gasping to get the words out. They knew that they still had the advantage of raw power and began to dig more deeply with their oars.

The two cutters swerved toward each other. "Trail oars", echoed from both excited coxswains. Trailing oars narrowed each boat's spread or coverage and lessened the possibility of contact and a repeat race. The two cutters slowly drew apart.

Their oars resumed their hypnotic wing-like sweeps.

Pluto's cutter began to gain again. Three quarters of the way back it had regained its half a boat lead on *Baltimore*'s cutter.

"Hey-hey-hey rumdum, bully beef, man-'o-war sailor-men, whoo-hoo fatboys," the Oyster Pirate jeered. It was a weak jibe, and his arms were occupied so it had come without the usual preliminary semaphore of hand gestures. Nothing really, but the timing was right and *Baltimore*'s cutter caught a crab. Two men were knocked off their thwarts. They unraveled like an old watch sweater.

Pluto's cutter crabbed sideways between the two anchored ships with a full-length advantage and everyone with wet ankles.

*****

It was a raucous scene on *Pluto*. The cutter's crewmembers started throwing each other over the side. Tiger and the Oyster Pirate were among the first. The entire ship's crew got into the act and everyone above decks was fair game. Non-swimmers went rushing for the sanctuary of sickbay. The two ships were only a couple dozen yards apart and *Baltimore*'s cutter crew was yelling accusations among themselves, while the balance of their ship's crew was registering disapproval. The two ships were as close to utter chaos as naval sensibilities in the Asiatic Fleet would permit.

The Admiral seemed pleased, but discreetly retired to a stateroom on *Baltimore*. Lieutenant Commander Wheelwright allowed his executive officer to toss him off the bridge wing after prudently handing his hat to a steward.

The boatswain's mates lowered the Jacob's ladder to retrieve *Pluto*'s new crop of pilot fish in dungaree shorts and appliqued shirts.

Hobson watched Tiger and the Oyster Pirate swim around to the other side of *Pluto* and thought nothing of it. Several crewmembers dressed as characters from Neptune's Court had seized a firehose and were using it to repel boarders, the men overboard. The occasion was festive and the costumes had been resurrected from the Crossing the Line ceremony.

As he climbed the Jacob's ladder through the firehose stream and climbed onto the deck, he noticed one of the boatswain's mates hoisting a peculiar dark gray canvas bucket on deck. Its handle had a swivel shackle on it and above the swivel shackle was a "C" clamp with an augur-like screw. He noticed a very large grommet had been sewn in the bottom of the canvas. Behind him, there was increased pressure for him to scale the ladder. The water was extremely cold and someone had spotted several drowned rats in their Shanghai open-air natatorium.

Hobson quickly turned to the Bridge. Crottle was staring at the bucket, too, with an incredulous look.

CHAPTER TWENTY-FOUR

Hobson shivered uncontrollably and staggered to the boat falls. Lieutenant Commander Wheelwright, now in a dry uniform, inspected the bottom of the cutter with Hobson. Warrant Officer Crottle approached with genuine interest.

Wheelwright began thinking aloud. "Looks like someone drilled a hole horizontally through the keel. Why do that in the first place? Then later when the whole strip ripped away, the gudgeon went with it."

Crottle looked at it. "What if someone tied on a bucket as a sea anchor using the hole?"

A sea anchor was a drogue used by ships to keep them heading into the wind. A large one could bring a moving boat to a near standstill. A small one? A small one would exert drag. Sea anchors were sewn out of canvas. Most shipboard buckets were sewn out of canvas and nearly the same shape.

"Wouldn't exert too much drag down current, but up current it ripped the last foot of our keel clean off. Whoever did it, overdid it." Hobson speculated. He could not be upset, they'd won.

"Hey, Boats, where's that bucket I just saw come aboard?" Crottle stood right in front of the boatswain's mate whom Hobson hadn't noticed before.

The boatswain's mate looked sheepish and dragged the soggy mess out from under behind a coalscuttle.

"Why's it gray? Is that mildew? Look's like someone sewed a hole in the bottom, Boats," Crottle was asking, but seemed to know the answers already. Buckets were sewn from sail canvas and were normally off-white in color.

"Don't know, sir. Tiger and the Oyster Pirate just asked me to hoist it up."

Crottle gave a knowing smile. "I'd say, so it couldn't be seen in Shanghai harbor soup."

"Betting against their own crew?"

Hobson knew he had to step in. "No, couldn't be." Hobson remembered the look on Tiger's face when he held the rudder up. The Oyster Pirate wouldn't have risked the anger of his crew. He knew there had been heavy betting by the crew.

Hobson thought of *Baltimore*'s crew sweating the upcurrent leg. "No they did unto others as they ended up having done unto themselves."

Hobson was surprised to hear himself sounding Biblical. It reminded him of his father.

"There were two drogues in the race. Each was secured by one ship's crew to the other's cutter. Ours worked, the one using a "C" clamp, and it disappeared after the race. Theirs required drilling a hole right through the keel and tore off our rudder mounting, then ceased to have any effect at all."

Crottle remained silent for a while and then laughed. Hobson had never seen him laugh. It was a heavy unpleasant, rumbling laugh.

"What we got here is drogue rogues."

"It was to be a test of rowing. and seamanship. Well, the best right sleeve seamanship prevailed," Wheelwright said enigmatically and turned to head up to the bridge.

"Oysters in the mess again for anyone who wants them." He called back over his shoulder.

*****

Wheelwright sent Mr. Crottle and Cabin Cook Second Class Cheng over to the Admiral aboard *Baltimore* in their dress blues. Every member of the crew inspected them and picked imaginary lint off their uniforms. The launch crew shifted into dress blues of their own volition and had to fight off volunteers to take their places as boat crew. Each was required to down an oyster before they could descend the ladder. Crottle carried a half-filled coal shuttle in his left hand. The launch crew discharged their duties like powerful steam-driven machines of nautical perfection. Each took the measure of every man on *Baltimore*'s rail.

As Cheng and Crottle crossed the quarterdeck, *Baltimore*'s officer of the deck eyed the coal shuttle suspiciously.

Some of *Pluto*'s crew questioned the captain's choice of emissaries to *Baltimore*. Why only a Chinaman and a hard case? Why not the whole cutter crew and the captain?

Crottle returned with the shuttle and waved it as he climbed so the crew of *Baltimore* could take one last look. The corners of his mouth were slightly upturned and Hobson wondered if he was smiling.

The trophy was jammed into the coal of the coal shuttle like a bottle of champagne into an ice bucket.

*****

"Is that true about oysters being what the professional oarsman thrive on?" the executive officer asked Lieutenant Commander Wheelwright.

"Could be. I don't really know, but there were some for sale on the pier and I thought it might give them an edge. Never ate an oyster in my life. I'm from Vermont. Darned expensive cuisine around here."

"Might have helped," Wheelright added. "Anyway, what we ate wasn't so important, just so long as *Baltimore*'s skipper eating crow."

200

Pluto's executive officer had, more than once during the cruise, observed that Wheelwright's shirt advertisement etching good looks and Sunday school demeanor could be deceiving.

Part III

The Sailor Considered

Every man thinks meanly of himself for not having been a soldier or not having been to sea...

They are happy as brutes happy with a piece of fresh meat, with the grossest sensuality. But, Sir, the profession of soldiers and sailors has the dignity of danger. Mankind reverence those who have got over fear....

-Dr. Samuel Johnson

CHAPTER TWENTY-FIVE

The Navy -- and the Asiatic Fleet for that matter - have their ways, tried, true, and tested by time. Instructions and notices determined how things must be achieved and heaven help the junior officer who did not heed their cautionary advice. The instructions were often thorough, frequently voluminous, sometimes comprehensible, and always in writing. These instructions were at their best addressing problems that had been addressed before. Unfortunately, recovering ordnance in someone else's oyster bed had not been addressed before in the Realm of the Golden Dragon.

In the navy or military, generalists handle matters that are out of the ordinary. That is the derivation of the title general officer or general. A general officer addresses problems of general concern to his organization. The naval equivalent of a general is an admiral. In fact, admirals were once called generals-at-sea.

The Admiral was wary of operational requests from a Naval Militia lieutenant junior grade from the Office of Naval Intelligence, which was under the Bureau of Navigation the repository of "all things irregular." He was not sure how this undertaking could help him; he could guess how it might hurt him. This was the selective salvage of an American merchant ship in what were now Japanese waters and involved instruments of war.

Lieutenant Junior Grade Draper pointed out that the Japanese had already given permission for Lighthouse Insurance and one Petty Officer Hobson to search for *Jade Rooster* off the coast of Korea and that search had not been completed.

The plan entailed a tired old British steam tug with fore and aft sails, which had been given a hurried white paint job that had been paid for out of a fleet account titled "bronze fittings." It had a small crane capable of lifting a few hundred pounds. It now had a diving manual, an air pump, navy diving dress, diving ladder, a diving lamp, and a diving telephone among its gear.

Its boiler was old and patched. It would not be capable of any forced draft cruising, but it could get by as a diving platform. The new diving manual implied that just about anything afloat with moderate freeboard would support diving operations and the tug did fall into the category of "anything afloat."

What the tug did not have was a crew or a diving team.

*****

The Admiral fingered a piece of jade artwork he had purchased for his wife. He was concerned by China's instability. He worried about the ships he had far up the Yangtze. "Hobson goes for sure. I'm not sure I want a commissioned officer aboard. That has the odor of official action.

"Of course, you'll need a diver, some sort of officer, maybe a warrant, good with machinery. Diving, is that more like shipfitting or more like engine mechanics? Does it center on questions of plumbing, or matters dealing with gases under pressure? I'll get the flag lieutenant to trace out someone suitable. Not diplomatic types, if this turns into an incident, let's make it look like a total mistake. Small crew, the smaller the better. Pull them of the two ships that are in, good warrior spirit, what were their names? *Baltimore* and that godforsaken collier...oh, yes...*Pluto*. The one that pulls tricks. This should be right up their alley."

*****

204

Crottle ran the tug by the book. With just a seven-man crew he ran inspections and followed ship's routine right down to cutlass drills. Twice a day they ran out small arms.

The diver was a gunner's mate; divers were largely gunner's mates. Then there were two coalpassers from *Pluto*, two deck seaman, and a cook from *Baltimore*, and of course, a quartermaster named Hobson to handle the navigation. There should have been a tender and a diving officer for the diver, but the Admiral had scratched that. There should have been two or three divers, but the Admiral had scratched that, too. Sailors could learn. Some sailors could and would learn fast.

"Time is of the essence," were the Admiral's final words to the flag lieutenant on the matter.

*****

In the second dogwatch, the flag lieutenant and the Oyster Pirate proceeded down opposite ladders on very different ships. In keeping with tradition, the flag lieutenant proceeded down the officers' ladder on the starboard side of palatial *Pittsburgh* and the Oyster Pirate struggled down the crew's ladder on the port side of utilitarian *Pluto*.

The flag lieutenant was alone. He was making an appearance at a reception at the Shanghai Carleton on the Admiral's behalf, one of many functions the Admiral was invited to but could not attend. The Oyster Pirate had two shipmates with him because he was carrying a sewing machine and it was never a good idea to walk a tough waterfront alone with your hands full. A sailor alone with his hands full was an easy mark. Shanghai's waterfront was as tough as any in the world.

The Admiral's barge was a steam launch and the liberty launch for *Pluto* was, too. The sun was down, but Shanghai was a bustling city and the coxswains had little difficulty coming into their landings as long as they did not look directly into the lights.

The flag lieutenant in his boat cloak, a cape-like affair, made for the Shanghai Carleton and the Oyster Pirate and his comrades in their peacoats made for Limehouse Lou's Pawnshop.

The flag lieutenant hailed a hackney cab and waved away the ginricksha coolies. He was never sure why, but he did not think big Americans should be seen being pulled around by the smaller, leaner Asians. Somehow it did not look right, it did not look democratic somehow.

The Oyster Pirate and his comrades waved off the ginricksha coolies, too and resorted to shank's mare. The Oyster Pirate was on a tight budget.

*****

The flag lieutenant was well received at the Carleton. He was well known there and popular. There were statesmen from several countries present and military attachés from an equal number. After the Chinese guests, the largest number of guests was British, followed by French, Portuguese, Japanese, and German. The British were old hands at this colonial routine and seemed most comfortable. The Americans, Japanese, and Germans seemed less at home with their Chinese presence.

The receiving line was standard, and the flag lieutenant, whose duties included receiving high-ranking guests, remembered most of their names and titles and foibles. It was his job to do so. He danced several dances with the wives of the more notable dignities, because they enjoyed it, because he was a good dancer, and because he believed it to be part of his job. He had been selected for the job because he was perceived as an up-and-coming naval officer, spoke several languages, came from a socially pre-eminent Eastern family, and danced well. He made apologies for the Admiral and pressed the attack at being polite, charming, and sociable.

Two hours into the reception he believed he had satisfied his professional responsibilities and decided to attend to his own personal interests. He had spotted a shapely brunette who could have been a Gibson girl model, standing with a much older man. The older man seemed consumed in a conversation with several other men of equal age and he was not paying much attention to her. He caught her eye and glided in to make the rescue.

"More carats per acre here than any three farms in Pennsylvania."

Her eyebrows lifted. Was there a look there of jaded experience in one so young?

"Could say the same about manure and corn as well," she deadpanned.

"From here, or passing through?"

"Passing through, but you could get me a punch and convince me to stay longer."

He introduced himself and retrieved the punch. The punch at the Carleton was notorious, alleged to have provided the impetus for more than one indiscretion. Though many of the men wore white tie, some were wearing the new tuxedos.

"You're not the Senator's daughter?"

"Yup, that's me. The wayward, headstrong one. I suppose you've heard that I play poker and smoke cigars. And get back at all hours."

The flag lieutenant, who had been doing the social circuit for some time now, and with Shanghai training there was nothing that made him bat an eye.

"Fast motorcars and fast boats and slow horses are your byword."

"Ah, my reputation precedes me. I like to watch the people, don't you?"

The flag lieutenant said he did, too. It was, however, one of the underscored rules of his post that he never commented in public on anything or anyone he observed.

"See the Limey over there? The Coldstream Guard light colonel with the handkerchief in his sleeve? He's been in a duel, an actual duel. Illegal as all hell, but the other man's dead. They had to hustle him out of Paris."

A German naval officer knocked over a table with Chinese porcelain.

This one's someone to watch, thought the flag lieutenant, she has an appetite for strong language and strong liquor. Tough, world weary, or simply too adventurous for a lady? The flag lieutenant rubbed his finger absent-mindedly on his wrist for he too had a handkerchief up his sleeve.

"The Frenchman over there has something to do with a revival of those Greek games, what do you call them?"

She flickered a bejeweled hand that could feed all Shantung Province for three rotations of the watch. The rings and bracelets were worn over the gloves.

"The Olympics?"

"Yes, do you know if they make all the athletes run around naked like they did in ancient Greece. I'd be interested in knowing."

The flag lieutenant wondered if she was putting him on. What other strong appetites did she have?

"See that man behind you, the leonine man that holds himself so very stiff and upright. He's got a reserved table at Delmonico's just like Gould or Fiske or Morgan..."

"New York or San Francisco? How can you be sure?"

"... Don't really know. Anyway, that's Atticaris, the filibusterer."

208

"Really? A filibusterer, are you sure?" The flag lieutenant turned very slowly.

He was a tall man with his mass concentrated in his head, neck, and shoulders. Atticaris gave the woman a wave.

"Well, maybe not a filibusterer, but he's involved in something on the shadowy edge. He took me to the Turf Club the other day. My travelling companion, Mrs. Halloran, doesn't care much for him, but I think he's very interesting. I am not sure whether he's more interested in me or my father."

The flag lieutenant appraised her diamond necklace. "A man about town, or a man of the world? Not sure you can be both."

"Oh, he travels that's for sure. Hawaii, Philippines, Japan, Chinese interior, Korea..."

"Well, occasional trips might not qualify..."

"Oh no, he travels to all of those places quite regularly. Why he's headed to Korea the day after tomorrow or something like that."

"Well, bully for him. I've been there once or twice. Sort of sad and poor since the Japanese took over." The flag lieutenant tapped a pillar with his fingertips.

She made a half whirl that lifted the bottom of her skirt to reveal expensive high-button shoes. "From what I can tell, the Japanese are tough on everyone. The Chinese sure don't like them much. My daddy says we'll have to watch them or they'll take California away from us."

The flag lieutenant watched Atticaris in a mirror. Atticaris was wearing a tuxedo. Near him on his left, also in a tuxedo, was a man in an auburn beard who looked acutely uncomfortable. On Atticaris' right was a severe-looking Chinese military officer. The flag lieutenant could not identify the uniform or insignia. A warlord from the interior.

"How's this Atticaris-man-of-the-world getting around on his globetrotting jaunts?"

"Well he talks about going to Korea frequently and there are several men going with him. Big, loud, rough men. How's he get there? He doesn't tell me. Probably in something more stylish than one of those smudgy steel boats of yours with all those flags and hustle and bustle and those steel pipes sticking out of them."

"Steel pipes?"

"That's what they look like to me. Oh, guns or rifles or whatever you Naval people call them."

"Guns, miss, rifled guns. Rifled 14-inch guns."

She seemed impatient and the flag lieutenant decided he had done his duty. Now he would look out for personal interests. One hand for the ship and one hand for yourself

"Where's Mrs. Halloran tonight?"

"Sick, the poor dear." The brunette said looking upward out of the corners of her eyes.

He escorted her to the dance floor with a good idea how the evening would turn out. The flag lieutenant was a very good dancer. The Admiral kept a room in the Carleton, which in his privileged position as flag lieutenant, he knew the Admiral had no intention of using.

He wondered if she did play poker and smoke cigars and vowed to find out.

CHAPTER TWENTY-SIX

Like most port cities in Asia, sleep was for the lazy or the dead. The Oyster Pirate knew the pawnshop would be open. Lou, Limehouse Lou, did some of his best business between supper and midnight. By rights, the Oyster Pirate should not have needed a loan. His earnings from the cutter race exceeded several months' pay. Even beyond that, his savings and what he made playing ace-deucey it was still not enough. He was shipping a crate full of fans, paper parasols, carved and inlaid chests, daggers, and Chinese porcelain back to his cousin in San Francisco for his shop. Chinese notions. He needed just a bit more money to cover the cost of shipping. So in the end he decided to hock his sewing machine. The scuttlebutt was *Pluto* would not head back to the Philippines before the next payday, so he felt reasonably safe.

"No, naw really worth much, lad. I can only give you 20% of that piece's value."

"Oh, w-w-who do you think you're t-t-t-talking to? That's a Singer and it's first rate. Touched up some of the best tailor-mades in the fleet with that sewing machine. And I'm coming back for it."

Limehouse Lou was a portly British expatriate, with a worn out look, who never smiled.

"Right you are, my fine matelote, you'll be back for it. Like the sailor who left that ukulele, and the one who left me wit' that Brownie camera. And the bloke what left that railroad pocket watch. And I'm in line to be a Lord o' Admiralty 'cuz my cousin's political."

The other two sailors with the Oyster Pirate looked bored, but said nothing because the Oyster Pirate had said he'd stand them beers and a meat pie once their escort service was over. Some sailors were riding the civilian steamboats up the Yangtze as escorts. This was easier. One eyed the railroad pocket watch with interest.

The Oyster Pirate and Limehouse Lou engaged in a verbal tug of war for another ten minutes until they were both a bit red in the face and it was clear that they had the elements of a deal.

The Oyster Pirate went to where the crate was stored to make the last payment on the crate and its contents. Four coolie stevedores manhandled the crate on trucks to the cargo net on the dock. Then, the bills of lading and money were exchanged. The Oyster Pirate did not pay for insurance since, to him, it seemed to defy Providence. If Providence wanted the sea to swallow up you or your ship and your cargo, so be it. To attempt to profit through disaster was to spit in the eye of Providence. That Flying Dutchman had tried something like that. Well disaster...that was the way it was. Insurance seemed a slightly illegal way of avoiding destiny and defying the judgment of Providence.

Once the crate was aboard the 'Frisco-bound freighter, the Oyster Pirate felt a great weight lift from his shoulders and he jumped and yelled out several times. His escort gave him a sidelong look, but they were patient.

As they strutted along the dock the Oyster Pirate looked out beyond the string of tied-up boats. He thought more about insurance and wondered if it could ever be morally justifiable.

*****

A half dozen brawny men came up the alley from the opposite direction. The Oyster Pirate tensed, but then realized that he'd paid out almost all of his money already and they would not get much from him. The men walked down the cobblestones right by him and his escort. These men were carrying seabags. They were talking, and to the Oyster Pirate they looked and sounded like sailors. Not merchant sailors, at least not men who had always been merchant sailors. These were warship sailors and had been so recently. They wore no uniforms, but he was a sailor and he could tell. Naval sailors were used to working in divisions, in larger groups, and as a consequence they could move about comfortably in groups of a half dozen or a dozen and be casual about it. These men moved at a fast pace. Merchant crews were smaller and merchant seamen chummed around and traveled ashore in only two's or three's.

Then he saw him, the man in the straw boater. The man from Manila. He was wearing a sealskin coat this time over a real fancy set of black togs with a white shirt with jeweled studs. He was with a Chinese bullethead in some type of army uniform. Hobson had chased him once and *Pluto* had intercepted a shipment of guns. The Oyster Pirate could see where a benefit might come from this.

The group of sailors in civilian clothes and the man in the straw boater met and then they walked up an alley in the opposite direction, paralleling the water. The Oyster Pirate wanted to follow them, but his escort was now impatient for its fee. He jingled some Mex into their hands -- which they happily accepted -- and then they parted ways. They for Madame Kwan's and the Oyster Pirate for parts unknown. He was not going to rely on any hayseed from the Governor's office to help him now. As he followed them he realized that this was China and not the Philippines. The gunrunner or filibusterer or whatever he was, was beyond U.S. jurisdiction.

He took a couple deep breaths, realized that he had done what he'd set out to do that night, that he had no money left, and following the man seemed like something he ought to do. He had nothing better to do.

*****

213

A half-mile up river they stopped at an isolated pier and a rundown godown. As he followed them, he realized that as a group they composed an unusually large number for random circumstance, and wondered what the common denominator was. They stacked their dunnage and began to haul cargo or equipment out of the godown. In the distant shadows, he thought he detected another group of men also pulling gear out of the godown.

The Oyster Pirate saw the glint of brass on some long cylindrical items. Crew-served guns. Then he saw the helmet. The classic three-ported helmet. They were sailors and they were of above average size. Deep-sea divers. Divers wore 200 lbs. of gear, helmet, breastplate, lead belt, and lead shoes. You did not have to be any particular size - there were small divers -- but it helped to be sturdily built. These men were ruggedly constructed. This was some sort of salvage operation.

The largest bit of equipment they hauled aboard was an odd contraption, thought the Oyster Pirate.

It resembled a coffee grinder.

*****

Tiger Cheng waited for the Oyster Pirate at Madam Kwan's. The Oyster Pirate did not know it. Cheng had finished other business and thought he'd wait for his friend. When the escort came in without him, Cabin Cook Second Class and Cutter Coxswain Cheng, on impulse, went looking for his stroke oarsman.

Taking up the directions from the escort sailors, he wended his way up the docks toward the river.

*****

The Oyster Pirate watched the men load the yacht and settle in. He became bored and decided to examine the godown. He began his approach when he felt a tug on his sleeve. He turned with a start to see Tiger.

"This is not a good place, what are you doing?"

A whispered exchange followed. The godown was dark and some distance from the pier and the yacht lay nestled in an impossible maze of alleys and ramshackle walls.

Tiger thought he heard voices.

"Not good, let's get out of here."

They turned to backtrack when five Chinese men with lathi, bamboo staves, loomed out of the darkness.

"Hey, you sailorboys!" came the cry and the lathi began to swirl even as the words came out. Tiger and the Oyster made sweeping motions with their arms to brush away the lathi and they began to run.

They did a hundred yards before one of their assailants tripped the Oyster Pirate with his lathi. He stumbled and they began to swing down at him like lumberjacks sectioning up a log. Tiger doubled back and waded into the swinging lathi. He kicked one of the five hard in the groin, disarmed him, struck another in the head with his captured lathi and it suddenly became quiet. The Oyster Pirate groaned and struggled to his feet.

One of lathi men sneered, "You go away from this place. No women, no liquor here. You come back we..." He drew his hand across his throat. "Go away, you savvy?"

Tiger and the Oyster Pirate limped away watchfully sidelong.

*****

215

The flag lieutenant left the Shanghai Carleton after the Senator's daughter, at the end of the midwatch, and headed back to the Admiral's barge. He was somewhat embarrassed to note a spring in his step so late in the evening or rather so early in the morning.

In the corner of his eye, he caught two uniformed sailors staggering toward the fleet landing. Staggering sailors were nothing out of the ordinary in the Shanghai, but the flag lieutenant was feeling friendly and decided to walk with them at a discreet distance. He hoped they were "happy" drunks and not "mean" drunks. He noticed two shore patrolmen in the shadows sharing a smoke and took comfort in their watchful dereliction.

As he approached, he realized they were not staggering, as drunks should stagger, not staggering with a fluid looping sort of movement. This was staggering that involved effort for every movement.

"Shore patrol, shore patrol, here." He yelled with sudden realization. "Help! Bear a hand."

Tiger and the Oyster Pirate collapsed as the flag lieutenant and the shore patrol came running.

"Here, take them to the Carleton. They'll be a doctor there." The flag lieutenant was angry.

*****

The doorman at the Shanghai Carleton was a huge Sikh. Common sailors were not allowed within the hotel under normal circumstances, but the doorman did not hold the position he did, because he could not distinguish normal circumstances from abnormal circumstances. The fire in the flag lieutenant's eye was enough to tell him to keep clear, and to keep quiet.

A doctor was summoned and the shore patrol stripped off Tiger and the Oyster Pirate's jumpers. They had lost their flat hats and several buttons had disappeared from their peacoats. The faces of both sailors were blotched the color of eggplant.

The Oyster Pirate flapped his arm to show his lone tattoo and to build up momentum to speak. "Every sailor should get stenciled," he said through a mouth full of blood. "Seems those Shanghai goons were trying to go us one up, and emboss us."

The bluish tattoo was swollen and hard to distinguish among the welts.

"Last time I'm a-going to a Shanghai harvest time threshing bee."

*****

The flag lieutenant went to the Admiral with the story an hour later and in two hours the Shanghai Municipal Police raided the godown. There, they found a warehouse full of ownerless munitions. A group of surly Chinese watched them, but quietly kept their distance.

An aggressive young policeman named Fairbairn, who was gaining a reputation for skill in close-quarters situations, led the Shanghai policemen. They searched the area thoroughly.

"That group over there is associated in some way with an upcountry warlord, " said Fairbairn.

The yacht, however, was gone.

*****

The flag lieutenant laid out the story on flagship. The Admiral grumbled because he wanted to focus on China. The Chief Staff

Officer shifted in his chair uncomfortably experiencing digestive problems again.

"You say the girl says Atticaris is headed to Korea. Is there any reason for him to tell her anything? Can we trust her?" The Admiral asked.

The question was rhetorical and the flag lieutenant's habit of discretion inclined him to keep quiet.

"We know he's just left a warehouse full of munitions with a half dozen hooligans. We know he's been doing business in the Philippines," the flag lieutenant explained.

"Korea isn't my lookout, the Philippines is.

"But we just sent a tired old tug to Korea," the flag lieutenant interposed.

"Not officially."

"Get the skipper from *Baltimore* over here."

"Orders?" The Chief Staff Officer responded.

"Orders to take up station off Mindanao. And better send that sorry collier with them, they're going to be there for a while," the Admiral grumbled.

Had the Admiral been more attentive, he would have seen the faintest shaking of the flag lieutenant's head.

And so it came to pass that the Oyster Pirate in doing his duty caused the collier, *Pluto*, to sortie prematurely.

He never saw his sewing machine again.

*****

Two men turned the wheels on the air pump in a bobbing manner that reminded observers of workmen pumping railroad handcars. Another man, the quartermaster Hobson, tended the airhose, lifeline, and communications line. Gunnarson glowered at Hobson through his faceplate. Hobson reminded himself to never give Gunnarson an opportunity to even the score. He could expect no mercy and he should not expect a frontal attack.

Gunnarson was rightly incensed. He was the only diver. This was wreck diving and wreck diving required two divers down minimum, in addition to a standby diver and they did not have one of those either. One diver was used on the bottom to penetrate the hull and the other to handle the airhose, lifeline, and communications line and keep them clear. And extricate the first diver if he got stuck. Diving was like walking around with a barrel over your head. It was awkward and wrecks were tangles of diver-snaggers. If your airhose snagged or tore, you drowned. If you jammed in a tight spot, you died there. If your suit ripped or your belt ripped off... The possibilities for a watery grave were infinite, and in this project, he was alone. One suit, one diver. A normal dive team required two tenders, not one, and was usually comprised of six trained men. Crottle would have none of it. They had been given a job and nothing was harder than being a member of the black gang, so this was gravy.

Gunnarson is his diving dress, laden with heavy weighted shoes, a massive breast plate with 15 bolts, an extremely heavy helmet with three-porthole like openings threaded into a massive breast plate, lead weights around his waist, climbed awkwardly down the ladder and then slid down one of several descending lines to *Jade Rooster* as if he were made of lead himself. Underneath he wore two or three pair of wool long underwear and wool socks. He took extreme care not to rip his puffed-up, canvas-coated rubber suit.

Gunnarson started with a survey of the barque.

"On the bottom to the surface, the barque hums like she's still alive. It's the current, I figure. Still some bouyancy in the ol' wreck," he grumbled into the telephone.

He crawled around everything dragging his airhose and the lamp with him.

"On the bottom to the surface, I positively hate going it horizontal in this damn suit. The water trickles in."

The cargo had shifted and it had been packed tight. His great fear was getting his helmet wedged into a tight spot. He had no good words about the hold. The cargo for the most part was coopered in barrels. That made it a little easier. It was unlikely, but not impossible that the weapons were in the barrels. He found some ammunition crates which they brought up. There were crates marked "naval stores." He broke them up and concluded they were indeed naval stores.

The underwater voice on the telephone became agitated when Gunnarson found a crate of dynamite. "Bottom to surface, hell, I've been ramming around with this pry bar breaking up crates. If I'd hit this one just right I'd be Gunnarson, gunner's mate on the heavenly Ark." He did not bring up the dynamite. There was a strong possibility the dynamite was no longer stable, so he dragged the dynamite crates away from the wreck and buried them in the mud in deeper water.

They found the pumps, compressors, and tanks that comprised the compressed-air paraphernalia required to operate the gun. By themselves, they hardly constituted contraband, but they were heavily greased and placed in oiled bags in classic smuggler style. Nearby, Gunnarson found two crates, one of sewing machines and the other of typewriters. Neither crate showed any sign of waterproofing. Then they found several wheels. Unlike their naval versions, the Army pneumatic gun and Gatlings were designed to be wheeled around on limbers or carriages.

Over the telephone, Gunnarson and Crottle eventually concluded the weapons were not in the holds, but somewhere else and well concealed. Hobson had heard no rumors of anyone ashore using a Gatling gun or a pneumatic dynamite gun. This had to mean the New Hwarang had not been able to find the guns either.

About halfway through the first day, the telephone broke down. No one could tell if it was the batteries or the line or the mechanism itself. Saltwater and electricity were always at war, like coal cinders and the decks. Communications would have to return to the ancient practice of signaling via tugs on the lifeline and communications line. Unfortunately, since this was a hull penetration, the lifeline and communications line worked around corners and over obstructions. Clean tugs on the line were only a hope.

Underwater, the visibility was minimal, only a few feet at best, and the daylight hours were short. If the lantern shorted out, salvage would be impossible.

The telephone came alive again. "Bottom to surface, I've worked aft and I think I'm in the officers' or passengers' quarters now."

Gunnarson went through the staterooms squatting to keep the top of his helmet clear. He kicked off both doors. The proportions of the last two staterooms seemed inconsistent with the others and he began opening drawers and doors. Eventually he found what he was looking for beneath the berths. The cabinet doors above did not open and as he worked at them he realized they were nailed shut. Behind the cabinet doors he found several tin crates in both Atticaris' and Hoyt's staterooms. Gunnarson had heard about the ordnance crates on the prau in the Philippines. These tin crates had been boarded into the stateroom like cabinetry. An elaborate bit of work, Atticaris must have had Captain Brewer's full cooperation. Gunnarson manhandled up a single tin crate to the deck. Then he had the tug lower a chain from the small crane.

On the deck of the tug the tin crate revealed a Gatling gun. The gun was immersed in oil like a tinned sardine.

Crottle had Gunnarson stop work and the crew slowly pulled him to the surface. Crottle had Gunnarson clean the gun up, and mount it, which he did after some grousing. Gunnarson had suggested Hobson ready the weapons, but Crottle pronounced that Gunner's Mates attended to ordnance as long as he Crottle was in charge.

"After you're through playin' with that over-fed brass pepperbox, you can tear apart that telephone for your re-cre-ation and I want every piece to sparkle like the fine crystal in your Grandma's parlor."

Gunnarson gave Crottle a veiled look that implied that events could always change the existing chain of command.

CHAPTER TWENTY-SEVEN

The next day things got complicated and it took all day just to bring up a second gun. It was a matter of keeping the airhose, lifeline and communications lines free and ensuring the diver had enough room to use his tools. Staterooms and passageways on sailing ships were tight to begin with. Gunnarson, in a diving suit, was larger than any sailor the shipwrights had anticipated would walk *Jade Rooster*'s decks. Dragging deadweight tins of guns up ladders and down passageways involved a network of rollers, parbuckles, and block and tackle even when they were lightened with buoys and secured to a chain fall from the crane.

Throughout, Hobson worked attentively to take up the slack in Gunnarson's airhose to keep it from snagging. The tug was secured with four anchors to ensure there would be no sudden strain on that airhose. If the tug moved while Gunnarson was held fast -- intertwined among the ladders and hatches -- in the wreck of *Jade Rooster*, something would have to give. The smart money was on the airhose parting.

They had found the Gatling guns, but not the pneumatic dynamite gun.

*****

Atticaris lit a cheroot and enjoyed the breeze in his face.

He had selected the crew, mostly former Royal Navy sailors from Hong Kong. The British were presently allies of the Japanese, so there was little problem with them heading to a Japanese controlled country.

Despite a few setbacks, his affairs were falling into place rather well. The big limey with the auburn beard was a seasoned diver of HMS Lion and no one wanted to get on his bad side.

The business organization was in place, the seeds planted. Right now he was barely in the black. There were expenses, bribes, the ordnance, upfront salaries, the premium costs of transportation, but shortly that would change. The Kempeitai owed him a great deal of money and he had to figure out how to get the money he had collected out of the Philippines. Filibustering might have been an option, but it required an objective and he knew of no great treasury in Asia he could take with a manageable group of freebooters. No, he viewed activities of that sort as reckless. One bullet and a skilled leader, such as himself, disappeared from the picture, regardless of his worth. Armed adventure had its attractions, but staying in the background until the last minute suited his tastes better. Though an arms merchant, Atticaris resented the underlying democratic effluence of his wares. The old saw, "God had made men; Sam Colt had made men equal," was not to his liking.

Below decks, he could hear the crew playing cards. He could hear ranting that sounded as if it could erupt any minute in a fight to the death, but he knew it would not. There were thumps and thuds. This was a physical bunch.

An equal shot at anything was a dream; it was leveler's nonsense. Be clever and have the right people like you -- that was the key. He had advantages. Why should he desire to be on an equal footing with the common herd? He was clever, educated, and would he be immodest in thinking, daring. He could get people to like him. He'd soon list a Senator's daughter among his "friends." Oh, it was so much easier to be charming when you did not care, and the trick here was to persist and be successful.

What was it that Frenchman had said, "Behind every great fortune was a great crime." Well, his father had started down the right course, but had not quite mastered the trick and had been forced to live out the remainder of his life in hiding. He had sailed with Farragut and written a book, but he never played it right. The insurance company had seen through the phony claim, but had not turned him over to the police. The great crime, he mused, was probably an accumulation of misfeasance culminating in one great wrong.

Atticaris played both sides and kept his nose deftly to the prevailing winds. A man had to be smart. He wondered how many times he could sell that pneumatic dynamite gun and avoid the crossfires. There was something exhilarating about being close to these life-and-death struggles and yet not participating.

His father had talked of a reserved private table at Delmonico's as the ultimate measure of success. It would not be long now. Soon, he could afford to erect more buffers between himself and the gritty misdeeds, and no one could touch him.

Occasional weeding made the harvest more bountiful and he had done his weeding artfully. There were very few left in Korea who could trace him to their woes. There might be some more weeding ahead. Korean expatriate money would again be drifting from America toward Korea.

And such great harvests to come!

The warlord in China was talking about purchases. He wondered if he should play him against some other faction. There had been personal contact between Atticaris and the warlord. For the sake of some conventional sales, he had altered his style. Out of habit, he had handled these sales in a sub rosa manner. Well, perhaps in Shanghai he could operate in a more conventional manner.

In the Philippines, the insurrectionists were financing themselves through piracy. There would be a good deal of hard cash there.

Atticaris foresaw great things for his resilient little business organization. Not that many aboard would live that long, but he prided himself that he selected his men for the traits of self-interest, aggressiveness, and resource. Traits he valued in himself.

He pictured a table at Delmonico's and smiled and puffed at the cheroot.

*****

"Can't we just cut a hole in the hull?" Gunnarson asked impatiently as the deck rates unscrewed the helmet and detached it from his diving dress. It had been a cold, cramped dive. Several layers of wool long underwear were soaked from the waist down. The lantern barely cast enough light for the job. Gunnarson resented those on the surface.

"Man alive, it's all slanticular and plumb ugly down there. And I think I can feel the barque move. Don't like it, don't damn well like it."

The tug was beginning to bob more and that put a strain on the diver and his tenders.

"I don't care beans what you like or don't like, just get it done. We ain't got a stage for you to work from and we're not supposed to break up the barque." Crottle was growing tired of Gunnarson. Crottle was bigger than Gunnarson, but older. "Direct orders: no significant damage to the barque, just get the ordnance."

"Check my hose. It's awful cold for diving, down there and up here too. Sometimes a diver's breath con-dens-ates in the hose. Builds up and next thing a chunk of ice seals it up tight. Then you got yourself a dead, cold blue diver."

Gunnarson struggled forward, muttering and punching the bulkhead.

*****

226

The sky had a peculiar look, a familiar look that he could not put his finger on. Hobson took it as a bad omen. He had a nagging, distant recollection of experiencing bad weather in this area. His more recent naval experience told him that this was very late in the year for a typhoon and too cold for such a storm to achieve maximum force.

Hobson asked the local fishermen and they each pointed south and declared a typhoon was coming. Hobson told Crottle. Crottle showed the closest thing to fear Hobson had seen, "We have to hurry up."

Crottle directed various members of the crew to prepare the tug for heavy weather and then turned to Gunnarson.

"Mount the second gun, Guns."

"After the storm, you can get this skinny quartermaster to do it. You're Moro happy, sir. Ain't no doped-up Moros 'round here. This ain't the Philippines."

Crottle worked his massive hands and his face turned totally expressionless. There were several moments of silence. "You're a gunner's mate. Mount the other gun."

"We're not at war with the Japanese or the Koreans. I know personal some Koreans who are engagin' in, what you might call, the opposite of war with me. Yeah, at very close proximity."

Gunnarson had found feminine companionship ashore and he was beginning to chafe at the intensity of the project. He was not happy. He was working for a half-officer off an auxiliary and that officer had him screwed into a schedule so tight he could not breathe. Some of Gunnarson's hostile energy was dissipated when Gunnarson discovered a skivvy house a few miles down the coast, but that too made his hunger for release. Gunnarson owed Hobson three hundred dollars and it was clear Gunnarson did not like the concept.

"Mount the goddam gun. These Japanese or Koreans, they look like us? They wear uniforms like this? As far as I can tell over here we're

227

potentially at war with everybody. And I like it that way, so mount the consarned gun. They're all the enemy until someone with braid or a brain tells me different. And you ain't got braid, and you ain't gotta brain. There's a cannonball there instead. If you had a brain you'd be a snipe."

His face was darkening and Hobson remembered that he had killed men.

"This tug is gonna be 'all oak and ironbound' and pretty as a flagship. As far as you an' Hobson and your differences, as long as I'm in charge and I don't see anybody whose gonna change that any time soon..." Crottle's face was still expressionless.

"...and you an' Hobson are going to be as close as two coats of paint." He grabbed the front of Gunnarson's peajacket and lifted him up on to his toes and slammed him into the steel bulkhead. The thurunk resounded through the boat.

"Logged and noted, Guns?"

"Logged and noted...sir." Gunnarson responded looking from side to side.

"Am I going to let the funnels go to war with the decks? Damn no. It's one boat and it's one crew and it's one mission and we are going to finish it as one."

He dropped Gunnarson who brushed off his peajacket with exaggerated arm movements.

*****

One of *Baltimore*'s seamen spotted it first a few hours after sunrise. A steam yacht longer than the tug and closing at a steady speed. It was threading through the islands, but its objective was clear. It flew no flags.

Crottle watched it close the distance.

"Get Gunnarson on the surface. Everyone else go to general quarters."

Gunnarson complained in the expected manner, but allowed himself to be hoisted up.

The Gatlings concentrated on the yacht, which was a dark, dark blue that at night would look black.

Hobson viewed it through his binoculars. There were forms under canvas covers that could have been Maxim or Hotchkiss or Gatling guns.

"Fire across their bow."

The coalpasser on one of the Gatlings fired the gun, producing a graceful set of geysers across the West Sea.

Crottle bellowed through a loud hailer, "United States Navy. We are conducting diving operations. Stand clear. Any approach will be considered hostile. Haven't blown a boat out of the water in a week, and I'd welcome the target practice."

It was unlikely that the yacht had heard Crottle over its own engine noises, but the yacht slowed to about two knots.

"Parley. Parley. May we approach in our dory?" yelled a man in earmuffs and an incongruous hard straw boater, also through a loud hailer.

"Stand off three thousand yards minimum. One man rowin', one man parleyin'. Rower's mitts never leave the oars, savvy?"

It took them some time to get the boat over. The yacht had a good-sized crew, each one solidly put together. The biggest one rowed.

"Looks like a well-fed Coxey's Army." Gunnarson commented

Hobson had no doubt it would be Atticaris, and it was. He wore a sealskin coat and a scarf. The straw boater was on a lanyard. The rower's peajacket had a British cut and he wore a Player's Cut beard.

"They armed a salvage tug, did they? What next? So you gentlemen are going to make it tough for us. We have a few more crew-served weapons than you do, but I suppose you could still exact a price. You have done your duty. Most assuredly you have done your duty."

He had the rower bring the dory in close to the tug where Crottle was standing with his arms crossed.

When they were only yards away, Atticaris lowered his voice so only Crottle, Hobson, and Gunnarson could hear.

"You got here and dove on *Jade Rooster* fine. You couldn't find anything and then a typhoon came up and you busted something critical. You fellows can figure out what, a pump a hose, a faceplate. A thousand dollars Mex to each of you. I'll be back after the storm passes through. You be gone.

"A thousand Mex?" Gunnarson eyes were bright.

Crottle waved him off. "That's for everyone of the crew, all fifteen of us?"

Gunnarson smiled.

"You can't have fifteen on here, twelve maybe."

"We got fifteen."

Atticaris voice faltered for a moment. "Okay, fifteen thousand Mex."

"Got it now? It's in God We Trust, all others pay cash," Crottle bantered. "You want cooperation, it's cash on the barrelhead."

Atticaris did not respond. "This bucket can't keep up steam in a typhoon or whatever we're gonna get. The barometer's dropping pretty bejeezus fast. We'll ride it out at anchor. That'll be one or two days from now." Crottle's face had turned dark and ominous again.

"You leave then, we'll pay you, provided you turn over any ordnance you've pulled up. Remember we have more guns and better guns than you and maybe a little range, so don't start thinking too much. The U.S. government hasn't got any official beef with me and I want to keep it that way if I can. You're in a part of the world that reveres harmony and I prefer economic resolutions."

"We keep these two Gatlings?"

"Oh, are those mine? Nice pieces. Personally I'd prefer a Lewis or a Hotchkiss, there a bit more advanced." The canvas cover was now off one of his guns on the yacht. "Okay by me."

Say, the Japanese going to let you parade around with that boat?"

"We have an understanding."

"Hmmm. Wouldn't think these pieces of hardware were for them. Don't they care?"

"That's my business."

"You got that much silver on that nice, gussied-up yard boat of yours? That -- what do they call 'em -- yacht?"

"What we don't have, we can get."

CHAPTER TWENTY-EIGHT

"We're going for it, right, Mr. Crottle?" Gunnarson leaned into Crottle as the dory withdrew.

"No."

"No, what are you afraid Hobson's not going to go along with the drill?"

Crottle looked around, collared Hobson and Gunnarson and shoved them into the pilothouse.

"Get this very straight, Gunnarson. I ain't afraid of nothin'." Only half Crottle's attention was on Gunnarson, he was considering his options. "Now I know what the Navy can do to you, Guns, for what you're thinking. Well, settle your agitated little mind. Don't worry 'bout the Navy, you just worry 'bout me."

"There's a chief tried to keep me from doing my duty back at Olongapo, an' he couldn't take a hint either. They still ain't found him yet."

Hobson remained quiet. He thought there was a dangerous glint in Gunnarson's eye.

"You think that guy can afford to pay fifteen thousand Mex for a bunch of guns? They may be worth it to him, but he doesn't have that much on him and I made him think about this coming storm. Maybe the storm'll put us on the rocks and do his work for him."

Gunnarson wore the surly look of a man cheated and defeated.

*****

Crottle was buying time. He had no idea how he was going to deal with Atticaris. Crottle sent Hobson and Gunnarson ashore in the tug's wherry. Crottle knew about Hobson's earlier expedition to Korea and about the New Hwarang. He sent Hobson, rowing, with orders to find the mudang at Chindo. Gunnarson he sent ashore with orders to keep his mouth shut, get drunk, and visit his lady friend. Perhaps there was a Korean solution to their problem.

Gunnarson grumbled, but did not argue. Crottle was very convincing and Crottle wanted Gunnarson nowhere near the rest of the crew, for the time being.

*****

The swell kept building.

After dropping Gunnarson off with the tug's wherry, Hobson labored at his oars most of the rest of the day and part of the night to Chindo. The contorted rock formations of the numerous small island presented obstacles and served as reference points. Hobson had never approached Chindo from seaward. He found the same villager and ended up waiting in the same field. A fisherman again led him up the mountain to the turret-girthed great White Birch, this time through a few inches of snow.

The wind had picked up, and the clouds were slashing at the moon.

The mudang approached him and again held both his hands. She looked particularly radiant and he wished he had known her when she was young.

"You are dressed like a foreigner now."

"Yes. I am a foreigner."

"No."

"I have a message for Mr. Kim."

"Mr. Kim?"

She laughed. "Maybe you are a foreigner. That's all you give me? No generational name, no first name, no province, no village, no age?"

233

"Mr. Kim of the New Hwarang."

Her mouth became a tight, grim line.

"I have never heard of this, this New Hwarang. The hwarang died out long ago, they are only ghosts, spirits, shadows of the Shilla Kingdom, now."

He studied her face for any trace of irony. Her veiled eyes revealed nothing.

"Time is very important. Tell him the meegook behind the beheadings is on a western steam boat, a blue-hulled yacht, somewhere in the islands west of Chindo or perhaps at Mokp'o. He wears a strange straw hat, earmuffs, and a sealskin coat."

It was a challenge to explain the concept of "earmuffs."

" Has the Oriental Investment Company established itself someplace around here? He may be picking up Mexican silver, it may come from them." Hobson said.

"They are in Mokp'o, I think. I would have heard about him if he were around Chindo. This man has caused a great deal of pain, a great deal of sadness, has he not?" The mudang said slowly.

"For money alone."

"Perhaps, it is not important that Mr. Kim receive this message."

Hobson did not know how to answer that.

"There are several men with him and they have weapons of the kind that an army would use."

"He has dishonored the totems. The kibun, the harmony has been broken."

He thought about the particular Korean verb she had used. It more properly translated as "desecrated" than "dishonored."

*****

234

On his return Hobson found that all had gone well, except that Gunnarson had followed orders with too singular a level of dedication. Bossed around by a half officer from an auxiliary, tired of a grinding schedule of cramped, cold, wet, dives into a wooden coffin, and tended by one of those officer kiss-up rates that should have been stitched on the left sleeve, Gunnarson kicked out the jams and inhaled makkolli, matching cups, patron by patron. He had done so, so thoroughly, that sometime after midnight he felt the urge to execute a near-perfect swan dive off the seawall in front of the skivvy house. The dive was into waters that were not quite deep enough and he did something to his collarbone. After that, he might be able to do some salvage diving, but he could not use tools.

*****

It was drizzling and Crottle towered above everyone in his oilskins and a foul mood. "Gunnarson we got anyone else aboard who can dive that diving dress now that you have crippled yourself up? You know the Navy owns that body and you have damaged it, neglee-gent-ly. I got a mind to put you on report."

The rest of the crew avoided all eye contact.

Before the question was out, Hobson knew the answer. He was next in seniority.

"Hey, sir, this Hobson's a real bright fellow. Speaks languages, wins races, fights fancy imported style. Picked up how to be the diver's tender job real quick. I can teach him. Hell, I'll teach him everything I know, an' just the way I learned it," he said ominously.

"Teach him everything you know. That'll take half a day."

Hobson, under other circumstances, might have seen humor in that exchange. Hobson's life was now in Gunnarson's hands and worth not an Indian head nickel. It was, in fact, worth a negative three hundred dollars to Gunnarson.

*****

They slapped on the weighted suit and boots and belt and Gunnarson ran through several weeks' training in a few minutes. He told about the airhose and the spitcock to keep the faceplate from fogging and the stage and about not hold your breath ascending. Crottle asked him questions until Crottle was satisfied. Hobson could have asked questions until doomsday and not been satisfied. It did not matter. He was doomed.

"Now remember on the telephone for you it's 'Surface, on the bottom,...' and then make your report. I don't want us getting confused with maybe someone else's down there on this wonder." Gunnarson waved at the telephone with his good arm and seemed grimly happy.

"Let's get the dynamite gun and the other Gatling guns." Impatience showed in Crottle's voice. He wiped his walrus' moustache with his sleeve.

As soon as the faceplate was below water, Hobson held his breath. It was instinctive. Despite a helmet full of air, something said save that last breath as you left the surface.

His life was in the hands of two men. One whom he had bested and who owed him money, and the other a thoroughly hard case capable of anything. The currents made him bob and wobble in the diving suit. His stomach seemed to float and wobble like a jellyfish along with it.

The light penetrated the water for a few feet and then the water became dark, darker than night, blacker than coal.

He could feel the sides of *Jade Rooster.* Gunnarson was right they seemed to hum. He turned on the underwater lantern. His mind started

236

playing tricks with him. He wasn't clambering about a barque; he was aboard a schooner, his parents' old schooner. No, that could not be. He found the forward hatch and descended its akimbo ladder holding tightly onto reality.

Something floated very closely by his faceplate as he turned on his lantern. He reached for it and it flittered away. Some sort of marine life. Everything seemed alien and slow moving. It was eerily quiet and all he could hear was the steady thump of the manual air pump, which he could have mistaken for his own heartbeat. He climbed down the after ladder. For a moment he thought he saw some white fabric in the top corner of his far right faceplate. A shroud? Then it was gone. Visibility was only a few feet. Objects came and disappeared from view rapidly. His mind was playing tricks.

He found Atticaris' stateroom. It was right across from Hoyt's, just like the sketch. There was a leather satchel and a double-breasted jacket on the deck. A shaving cup and an inkwell lay broken against the bulkhead among of flurry of celluloid collars, and an elaborate gimbaled lamp lay in pieces next to it. It was a tight squeeze in diving dress and then Hobson found it hard to breathe.

*****

And then Hobson found himself on the deck of the tug.

You pinched off the airhose, you worthless fid," Gunnarson looked disappointed, deeply disappointed. "Mr. Crottle figured something was wrong and we pulled you up. Me, I wouldn't have bothered. You sleeve, am I the only guy who can do anything right around here?"

"Okay, now take these. Were going to cut into this Mr. Sabatelli's precious barque and get the hell outta here. Them girls over t'house not withstanding."

Was Gunnarson disappointed that he was alive or that Crottle was untying the Gordian knot?

Hobson took the tools and the crew improvised a stage upon which they lowered him along side *Jade Rooster*'s hull. The stage allowed him to stand outside the hull. It could not be used to lower him to the wreck or raise him from the bottom.

Hobson pried away a plank and then sawed a large opening directly into the stateroom the next morning. The swells had risen to a point where, at several points, Hobson became seasick underwater. They would soon have to suspend diving operations.

They brought up the field gun and the remaining Gatling guns by noon. There were far more than they had expected. By then, Crottle had timed the maximum swing to the west and set out the second anchor for a storm they now knew was coming from the South.

"Pneumatic gun, we still haven't recovered the pneumatic gun." Crottle growled. "Got most of the pieces, but not the limber or barrel itself."

Hobson knew that to Crottle Hobson's personal welfare played a very small part in all this.

CHAPTER TWENTY-NINE

The barometer began to drop faster than irreplaceable fittings into the bilge. It was too late in the season for a full-blown typhoon, but the tug was in no condition to weather any storm.

Crottle was at a disadvantage. He had been seafaring for several decades, but the majority of those decades had been spent below. He had learned the general concept of cyclonic winds from chalkings on the back of a coal shovel, but could not read the skies.

He held a council of war with Gunnarson and Hobson. Gunnarson was surprisingly helpful and Hobson had local knowledge. Between the three of them they developed a plan.

In most cases, getting sea room would have been the preferred strategy. That, however, required that the screws be capable of turning continuously to maintain headway. The badly patched boiler made that a doubtful option. They decided to keep up steam, but just enough to operate the steam windlass.

Hobson watched the seas and the skies. The building swells had been a bad first indication. The clouds arrive thin, then began building in height. It continued to drizzle and the winds had picked up.

"It will all depend on whether we can guess the wind direction." Hobson said flatly to Crottle. The storm would hit like a runaway pinwheel. It would come from the south, but the winds themselves would box the compass. The right side of the storm approached with the speed of the storm plus the speed of its accompanying winds. Hobson did not want to be in the upper right quadrant of a rapidly approaching storm.

They anchored away from *Jade Rooster*, which might shift in the storm. Any idea of attempting to muscle it out with four anchors was discarded; it was better to flow with the forces of nature than to buck them outright. They dropped the hook on the eastern side of the lagoon, which appeared to have good holding ground, and paid out anchor cable. They needed scope. The weight and elasticity of the anchor rode evened out the ride. The winds would shift, if they shift too fast or came from the wrong direction, the tug on its long anchor rode would swing right into one of the surrounding rock islands and break up. No one had any illusions about surviving breaking up on the rocks in these icy seas. They would have to be alert to changes in the storm and address emergencies as they occurred.

The tug rode at anchor like a hobbyhorse. Crottle had the crew wear lifejackets, rig lifelines, and lash everything down. They had a second anchor and drogue ready if the boat began to drag. Many of the crew were making offerings to Neptune at the lee rail and looking about the color of the cresting seas. The coalpassers below were taking a beating and struggling hard not to tip into the boiler fire.

Hobson's assigned responsibility was to determine the height of the storm, when it reached its maximum intensity. At the vortex, the winds would reach maximum velocity, but they would also change direction rapidly. They began to drag anchor and that demanded his attention.

"We have to swing and drop the second anchor," Hobson bellowed over the winds. The tug was clanking and chiming like a tinker's wagon.

Crottle nodded with grim resolution. He feared no man, but acts of God were another matter.

A heavy green wave swept the length of the tug and the boat shook it off like a dog. Going forward to free the anchor would take steady footing, nerve, and timing. Crottle and one-armed Gunnarson both started working forward while Hobson struggled with the wheel. At anchor, without headway, controlling the rudder was like wrestling with an unhinged barn door in a windstorm.

240

The islands served as protection, breaking the waves and deflecting the winds, but also as toothy sites for destruction.

Hobson swung the wheel over so that the tug could set two anchors and be at the bottom of a "V" with its top opening into the wind. He realized that the swing, if uncontrolled, would bring them dangerously close to a noticeably rockbound island. Crottle shoved the second anchor out just as a second big green wave hit. The line paid out uncontrolled. Gunnarson and Crottle both tried to get it secured around a bitt, but by then they had swung back directly to leeward of the original anchor. They could not muscle it in, and took wraps around the steam windlass instead.

Crottle and Gunnarson staggered to the wheelhouse and collapsed in a heap. Two *Baltimore* seamen operated the windlass and the tug inched between the two anchors.

In the end, the tug dragged both anchors and had its pilothouse windows smashed in. Yet, in its patched teakettle fashion, the tired old boat survived. By mid-day on the next day, the sky had begun to clear.

For once, Crottle did not conduct drills.

*****

After supper, Hobson took the watch from Gunnarson who went ashore with half the crew. He handed over the cutlass, revolver, and binoculars. The binoculars, in particular, would prove worthless on this near-moonless evening. It was port and starboard for night watches. This evening he had the duty and Crottle was aboard. There was one seaman and one fireman and just a sliver of a crescent moon. Characteristically, Gunnarson regarded him with a look of barely controlled malevolence. In Gunnarson's eyes, Hobson brought with him one Jonah-like incident after another.

The seas had begun to subside and, with the two Gatling guns re-mounted after the typhoon, Hobson felt secure. The rock formations and numerous islands circled the boat protectively and it was quiet again. He searched the water for boats and there were no boats. Every hour he walked the perimeter of the tug and searched for boats. There were no boats. A few hours after midnight, he began to hear noises and sensed that all was not right, but he could not identify the origin. Then he leaned over the side and saw several baskets bumping against the hull. He was sick of baskets. These baskets were tarred on the outside as waterproofing. Hobson hurriedly looked for the seaman on watch and tripped over his body.

This was it, they had been boarded and he was alone.

He did not see or hear movement, he simply felt it. When the blow came, Hobson raised his cutlass to parry just as Crottle had drilled into him twice a week for months. He felt the blow jar his wrist and then looked up to see the top half of his cutlass blade cut clean off. The steel in a Samurai sword was so vastly superior to the standard U.S Navy cutlass. The arch of the stroke had just passed his head, but there would be a return stroke. He leveled the Navy Colt and fired.

There were half a dozen of them. They had swum out through the frigid waters pushing their weapons in front of them in floating baskets. They had watched for days and figured any direct assualt against the Gatling guns would have been suicidal. Matsuda led with the samurai sword, which had just rendered Hobson's cutlass useless. They were all wet and dressed in black, wearing heavy black sweaters, and moving almost soundlessly in tabi socks.

"Dotteppara ni kaza ana wo akeru kara oboete oke!" Hobson yelled in anger without thinking, in Japanese. The threat, spoken in Japanese, stunned Matsuda for the merest fraction of a second or perhaps it was simply the cold. Matsuda had a very rigid picture of the world and the enemy did not speak Japanese.

Matsuda's face showed surprise and resignation as the revolver went off. Hobson fired three more times. Matsuda hissed, "Banzai" and sagged to the deck. Koizumi came up right behind him. He, too, was holding a samurai sword, expertly, very expertly. Hobson desperately needed to buy distance and time to reload.

Crottle fired a Krag-Jorgensen and Koizumi looked disappointed. Hobson noticed that, for once, Koizumi was not wearing his glasses on the tip of his nose. He was not wearing them at all. The other four had revolvers that were no match in the long run against a Krag -- once the element of surprise had been lost. Hobson managed to unlatch the jams on one Gatling and then proceeded to grind up the remainder of the boarding party and large portions of the deck and the rail. The young fireman who was below decks, came up clutching a Krag and thoroughly shaken.

Hobson shook his head. It had taken some doing to swim out to the tug in these waters this time of year. Matsuda was a spiritual son of the Emperor and no amount of beisu-boru or judo soft-soaping was going to deter him from his duty. His duty was to expand the greater Japan prosperity sphere. He did not care for Koizumi, but Koizumi had not dictated that Korea would be Japan's, someone else had done that. The Emperor or someone the Emperor trusted had made that determination and that was good enough for Matsuda. It had not occurred to Hobson that Matsuda was Kempeitai, too, but how many military policemen spoke English, however halting, and French, too?

Hobson looked around him. Crottle and the young fireman still clutched their rifles with a wide-eyed quality. "Wide-eyed" was a phrase that normally denoted wonder, but this was different. He had heard about this strange look to the eyes from the battle veterans. It showed briefly in those moments of intense fear when all senses called for a forced draft to the boilers. Wide-eyed was the acute awareness of a kill-or-be-killed situation.

Several Nambu revolvers, Japanese guns modeled after the American Colt, littered the deck. The revolver, like the steamship, was one of the great American inventions. For all his Asian wrestling experience, Hobson knew he could never have taken Matsuda. For him, his Navy Colt had been, to recall the classic Colt advertising phrase, "the great equalizer." And that was how Jackson had described the Gatling guns, as "equalizers, jumbo style." It was ironic that Atticaris sold equality in the form of a handful of steel, and Atticaris was an evil man. The world was a confusing place, a confusing place indeed.

*****

They washed down the decks at sunrise and what did not dry, froze. The holes and splinters from the Gatling gun were the hardest to conceal.

"What'll we do with the bodies?" the young fireman asked. Crottle had Hobson go ashore and talk to the mudang. The bodies were not going to wash ashore and draw attention.

*****

Two crewmen manned the air pumps and Hobson submerged again.

Gunnarson had searched the entire ship. The Gatling guns had been divided between Atticaris' staterooms, but the pneumatic dynamite gun and its limber were still missing.

Hobson hit the spitcock with his cheek and cleared the condensation on his faceplate. He tried to recall the relationships. Four heads in four baskets. Royster Lines pressuring its skippers to turn profits, big profits.

"Surface, on the bottom, the barque's really vibrating. The current must be up. I'm going forward into the hold and then work my way aft again."

There was no answer. The telephone had failed again. He signaled "okay" with a tug on the lifeline. There was a responding tug.

He shuffled through the hole at Atticaris' stateroom and then forward to the hold. He saw nothing new.

He shuffled back and was knocked off his feet. The barque had shifted. He regained his feet and decided to test the tension to his hose and lifeline. There was something wrong. There was resistance.

He attempted to retrace his steps and came upon a ladder blocking his way. Ships were built to be tossed about. A ship's ladder should not have come loose. He examined the ladder. A pin and plate that anchored one side had rusted through and the ladder had torn away from its footing.

There was a tug from the surface, "okay?"

He responded with a tug, "okay."

The hose and lifeline could get around the ladder. He could not. He would have to double the hose and get to the surface some other way. They would not be able to haul him to the surface by his lifeline.

Where was the dynamite gun?

His breathing seemed labored. Was the airhose beginning to freeze shut?

He shuffled aft toward the captain's cabin. Captains, mates, and other ship's officers were traditionally berthed in the after section of the ship.

The after end of a sailing ship normally contained three things, the rudder and wheel, small-arms armory, and the ship's leadership. The combination was no accident; it was the time-honored combination for preventing or fighting mutinies. Often, the lines that controlled the wheel ran right through the captain's cabin. It allowed him to keep track of the ship's movement, but it also allowed the captain and a small band of loyal crewmen to control the heading of the ship.

Hobson held his electric lantern up and labored around a second ladder. The limited radius of its light shed a pasty white light. Gunnarson had torn the door off its hinges. Hobson swept the lantern across the cabin and saw nothing but furniture and what used to be charts and plotting equipment. He crouched to enter.

The Gatling guns had been concealed in opposite staterooms. Captain Brewer was sensitive to the distribution of his weighty cargo about the barque. The weapons were concealed relatively high and aft to keep them away from the crew. The crew slept forward and would be continually in and out of holds. Two Gatling guns could counterbalance each other. As far as he knew, he was looking for a single pneumatic dynamite gun.

It was hard to think and it was becoming hard to breathe.

Navy diving dress was massive and awkward. Hobson guessed that Gunnarson had not lingered. This cabin had a particularly cramped feel. The gun racks were intact. It would be difficult for free divers such as hae nyo to recover weapons in here. It was not that deep, but there was a deck, a hatch and a ladder between the cabin and the surface. And it was dark. Hae nyo did not carry lights. One benefit of tethered diving was the ability to move sideways, as well as up and down, and with an airhose you could always find your way back. The rack held a few Winchester repeating rifles, some Remington fowling pieces, and

246

assorted Colt revolvers. The barque's wheel was nearly directly above him. Where were the lines that ran back to the rudder?

There were no rudder lines. Hobson walked backward out of the captain's cabin and stood up.

Brewer had constructed an overhead void in his cabin. He dropped the ceiling or overhead and in doing so had concealed the rudder cables. The void also concealed the pneumatic dynamite gun that was mounted overhead above the keel. It was right where the whipstaff would have been on a ship in Columbus' time. Positioned as it was, it had the least effect on changing the barque's metacenter. It was not the perfect solution, but a good solution under the circumstances, and away from prying eyes.

As he studied the cabin a hand in white reached around him and touched his elbow.

*****

Hobson yelled and cursed and then yelled and cursed again.

Precious air, he was wasting precious air and he was having increasing difficulty breathing. His breathing was rapid and shallow and his nerves were raw. Diving was strain enough, but now he was not sure how he was going to get to the surface and now someone was down there with him.

He turned slowly to look into the sightless eyes of a hae nyo in her white garb. So one had found her way down the dark hatchway in the warmer months and lost her way to the surface. Brave woman, the stakes were high. Had she lost someone to summary execution? Was that what made the risk worthwhile? A life for guns?

She had been tangled above Gunnarson and him during their searches, all along, but the shifting of the wreck had finally freed her.

*****

He climbed the ladder. It required great effort to just think. He signaled for slack. Once on the deck of *Jade Rooster*, he looked up. It was murky and he thought he could make out the shadow of the tug just a fathom or tow above him. He coiled three fathoms of hose and lifeline at his feet. He tried to jump, and then to swim, but only tumbled back to the slanting deck of *Jade Rooster*.

Then he thought to open the control valve. The pressure built in his helmet until his eardrums seemed to be driven into his skull, his suit inflated, and his arms were forced out so he looked like up puffed-up gingerbread man. He began to rise and his ascent accelerated as he approached the surface.

He found himself bobbing on the surface looking at the sky. Out of a side faceplate he could see a boat being lowered from the tug.

*****

"No ice, you worthless fid, you just pinched off your hose again," Gunnarson pronounced. "We had to pull the whole hose back through the other way. Wasn't that hard with you not attached."

Hobson rubbed the tattoos on his ankles and was curiously glad to see him.

"You know these people, Hobson." Crottle scowled and pointed to the mainland. "No one's spoken for the Winchesters. Mr. Draper knows about the dynamite gun and the Gatlings. Sabatelli's got his cargo list and they aren't on it, not that the dynamite gun and Gatlings were. The cargo's still there as far as we know. Not deep enough to crush the barrels."

"Yes."

"These people, they produce somethin' valuable, something that turns into cash quick? What's that blue-green pottery stuff?" Crottle pounded the rail with his massive hand.

"Celadon?"

"Yeah that's it. They can pack it on a boat so it won't break?" Crottle looked at the greenish Gatling guns that they would soon stow below decks.

"They've been doing that for years." Hobson wondered where all this was going.

"Well, don't people in this part of the world give small gifts when people leave?" And don't people who leave sometimes give small gifts? Well, as I see it Hobson. You and me and the Gunboat we are going to steam out of here with the dynamite gun and the Gatlings just like we're suppose to. The Moros aren't going to get their hands on these. And Sabatelli he's going to come along in the spring and salvage *Jade Rooster* proper.

"And we can leave those Winchesters and they'll be like underwater corroding batteries. Maybe when Sabatelli gets here they'll be useless lumps of brass and steel - you know that electrolo-whatsis -- and then again..."

Had Crottle forgotten that Atticaris waterproof packaged his products?

"Maybe some of them nice diving ladies will find them, especially if we buoy them and we put them where they ain't too deep or too hard to get at."

Hobson thought of the drowned hae nyo.

" I don't want it to be said we gave anything to anybody directly that we shouldn't have.

"If they do, some bad people will die, and maybe some good people will die. As I figure it, it's just none of my business. Y'know, Hobson. There's no telling in this world just how things is gonna turn out."

Hobson agreed.

They waited a few days for the steam yacht to return, but it never did.

*****

In a coastal village east of Mokp'o and Chindo, Rev. Hezikiah Kaulbach rose early on Sunday morning for two reasons, to build a fire in the church's potbelly stove and to review his sermon and scriptural readings in his mind. At five, it was still extremely cold, very dark, and the winds off the West Sea whistled through the Spartan hall. He looked out the window past the police box at the Chinaman's Restaurant. The restaurant was long closed, but the lanterns in the back were on and fluttering. They were always on. The string of curtained stalls in the back made the Chinaman's a house of ill fame. Kaulbach did not like it. The establishment was too close for his liking. Hezikiah Kaulbach was no stranger to men's petty vices and he knew his parish. Dissolution and debauchery were not unknown to him; he had served in waterfront missions before coming to Korea. The Chinaman owned the restaurant, but a local Korean owned the "house". Confucian values were hard on women, especially surplus daughters, and the Asian attitude toward sexual relations was different. Sometimes the money the girls earned went toward their dowry and sometimes it did not. He was not sure how he felt about it all, but he was uncomfortable for the most part. The church windows were locked tight, but he thought he could hear yelling. Not angry or desperate yelling, just the rowdiness of liquor

250

and a very late Saturday night. There had been a loud American sailor in a few nights earlier and it had been like this, too.

A large blue yacht lay anchored a little way out. Kaulbach had only seen a few yachts in his life and never in Korea. It was like no boat he'd ever seen in Korea. It must account for the boisterousness at the Chinaman's.

*****

Jin walked away from the Chinaman's. Her work was done and she was headed home for a visit. As she walked up the snow-covered dirt road, she noticed no one was in the police box and no fire was issuing from its stovepipe. But at five o'clock on a Sunday morning it did not seem so unusual as it might have in broad daylight. Someone was asleep on watch or the wood had run out or the police were short-handed.

About a quarter of a mile up the road, she noticed an approaching band of men in military police uniforms walking briskly. This she took as an apparent answer. The police box was unmanned because the police were out on some pressing assignment. A dozen men marched by her without saying a word. This she found unusual since her profession was well known in a small fishing village like this one, and her profession was always a source of catcalls. The catcalls were more earthy than malicious. She did not recognize any of the policemen and there were others who must have been soldiers. She realized that this was more policeman and soldiers than she had ever seen in one place. She thought they looked more Korean than Japanese, but it was difficult to tell. There were Koreans among the police.

She stopped and watched them as they strutted away at a brisk march. They were armed with rifles, not just pistols. They carried their rifles in front of them, not slung over their shoulders. Two broke off

251

and pushed off in a rowboat toward a strange foreign-looking blue boat. The other ten went past the police box.

It was at that point that Jin decided to scream.

*****

A woman's scream is one of the universal alarms. Rarely, will a woman be punished for the act of screaming in the heat of a show of arms. It is a sort of universal rule. If grim deeds are to be done, they will be done regardless of the screaming and those taking part have already steeled themselves to their task and against this form of annoyance. It is without apparent consequence. If one woman screams, others will too, intuitively, and so the alarm is raised. It is a noise that is not heard on one side and heard with great meaning by the other side.

Several men -- Korean men -- at the Chinaman's reached for their trousers. Seeing a group of Japanese police and soldiers could only mean one of a few things and none of them good. They pulled aside the curtains, grabbed their footgear and bolted.

There were others, tired, sleepy, and boozy who felt no concern and remained where they lay under a quilt, perhaps with long black silky hair on one shoulder. One or two reached for their pistols because they were the bodyguards. Acting as one and on signal, all the girls rose from their mats and went into the restaurant and crouched low behind the stove.

*****

Rev. Kaulbach had forgotten all about his sermon and scriptural readings. A group of Japanese had swept into the village and that meant labor battalion conscription or summary executions. There would be no service today and he would be lucky if his parish survived. The bottom dropped out of his stomach. He had a strong affection for his adopted people. He did not want to look, but he found he had to.

Instead of fanning out and conducting a sweep of the village, the ten men went straight for the Chinaman's and took up stations. He heard loud reports. Shots. A very large man with a beard and a sailor's coat staggered out of the house wounded. He exchanged several shots with the men in uniform and collapsed in the snow.

Then the uniformed men were herding a group of Westerners out of the establishment. Some of the Westerners were only half dressed and some were fully dressed. Three of the uniformed men put a bag over the head of one of the Westerners, a big man in a sealskin coat with his weight in his head and shoulders. Behind the bag dangled a straw hat on a lanyard.

Kaulbach did not know what to make of it all.

*****

Jin froze. She was afraid they would come back they way they had come. She moved toward courtyard wall and held herself against it, willing herself into invisibility, hoping the darkness would conceal her, hoping the dawn would not come early.

Incredibly, the dawn flared up just as she was hoping it would not. Then she realized that dawn was coming from the wrong direction. Out there something in the water was burning and shooting off fireworks as if it was the lunar New Year. It was the strange blue boat and the policemen were rowing back from it with several large satchels.

*****

Rev. Kaulbach saw the boat begin to burn just as the rowboat and the Japanese soldiers left it.

The man with the straw boater was buttstroked with a rifle and his knees buckled. He was then bound. One of the men with him attempted to run and was shot.

It became increasingly confusing after that. Bodies were dragged from the road or the Chinaman's and dumped into the sea. The soldiers and policemen left with only the one man. They did not conscript anyone. They did not execute a single Korean.

Kaulbach wondered if what he had seen might qualify as a miracle in some circles.

*****

Jin was shaking; it was not the cold, but seeing the uniformed men walking rapidly toward her. They were not marching any more, but were half dragging the man with the straw hat up the road. Jin realized she could see some form of equipment further up the road. The Japanese would have come in a gasoline or steam-driven truck. This looked more like a handcart. There was something wrong here.

As they filled back, she looked at their uniforms. There was something odd about their uniforms. They did not fit well. The boat began to blaze like a bonfire. As she looked more carefully at them in the flickering light, she noticed they had several had neatly darned holes in their coats, primarily in the chest area. Some coats had small dark stains.

Two soldiers ran to join the men in the rowboat and picked up the satchels, which had to be heavy by the way the soldiers carried them. They laughed and as they past the Christian church, one of the men threw something over the gate and yelled something inaudible.

As the men in uniform walked past one of them, a student recently returned from Hawaii, called out in his best English.

"Hey, sugar, better skidoo."

*****

After sun up, Rev. Kaulbach walked out to the gate. There he found several silver coins in the snow, Mexican coins. He could figure no rational reason for their presence, but he could use the silver. There were several parish families now who would not need to struggle through the winter.

******

Once back in Japan, Hobson went to look for the ropewalk man, Talmadge. Talmadge, like Hobson, straddled two cultures, and he too had lived among men of action. Hobson liked him.

The son was there. He had an Excelsior motorcycle half-apart leaning against the ropewalk building. The son was storming around in the house and this time Hobson could hear the wife chastising the son, saying he "had no shame" in tearful Japanese.

Talmadge seemed intent on worming, parceling, and serving some standing rigging. He was only worming so far and did not seem in any rush to move along to the other processes, though Hobson could smell hot tar. Hobson wondered if someone else should be handling that task.

Hobson told him the story.

The ropewalk man turned the subject to comets, Aurora Australialis, the passage of Venus, and seemed to forget the whole *Jade Rooster* matter. He mused on how Teddy Roosevelt might be remembered by

255

history. "The Japanese don't know what a moose is. Don't like TR much either."

Talmadge examined the line he was using for worming.

"Sabatelli's been persistent, I observe. Commendably so, commendably so. You sure he wasn't in with that Atticaris fellow."

"Not as far as I can tell."

"Not in with Koizumi, maybe? Seems too dangerous a game for him to play, though. Not like Sabatelli to play a dangerous game, just one close to his chest."

Hobson thought a moment. "Can't quite see how."

"I hear Sabatelli got in trouble in Hawaii, woman trouble. That's why he's out here."

"I heard that too."

"Not the same level of trouble. Nope. No severed heads. No, if anything gets severed it's a might lower." Talmadge looked toward the house. "Sabatelli's got motivation. Wonder if he got into something in Hawaii?"

Hobson decided to ask his other question. "Sir, you know where I can buy a used sewing machine?"

"You going in for sailmaking? A heavy duty one?"

"No, a small one for sailor togs. One that can be stowed shipboard."

He had talked Draper into paying for it. The ship carrying the crate with the Oyster Pirate's Chinese notions had been lost at sea. It had never made it to San Francisco. There was talk of Algerines, Philippine pirates.

"I just might."

Talmadge walked over and looked into a pot of steaming tar.

"This son of mine, you think they'd take him in the Navy? He's big and speaks two languages."

"Otherwise I'm going to have to have him Shanghai-ed. Of course to some t'other destination. Shanghai's too darn close."

CHAPTER THIRTY

Sabatelli urged the master of the British tug on. Several master divers lounged against the lee rail. He had had a devil of a time rounding up divers. It seemed every diver in Asia was off on a project.

The tug had to get on station over *Jade Rooster* before anything could go wrong. Navy divers had been on the wreck a few weeks back and who knew what havoc they had played. Draper had cabled him the latitude and longitude of the location and lines of position that Hobson had held back on him. Deuce, the underwriters had not abandoned the cargo, how could the Navy do that to him? Did the Navy have the right to search the sunken vessel for arms? It would take a barge full of lawyers to sort things out if they damaged any of the cargo in doing so.

"Before we left, you wouldn't tell us what the cargo was. Now you tell me we're being paid bonuses to salvage a cargo of perfume?" A rugged, gray-haired fellow in oilskins said at Sabatelli's side.

"Not perfume, a valuable component of perfume. We're talking about ambergris, gray ambergris. A redundancy, my good man, since the word 'ambergris is French for 'gray amber." Sabatelli found himself getting grandiloquent just thinking about the extraordinary substance.

"And we're salvaging barrels of it. Worth more by weight than gold."

Sabatelli tilted his head as if he was sniffing the sweet odor of wealth.

"The stuff turns up in the tropics. Came upon it in Hawaii. It took a bit to gather some business partners and float a few notes. Great day in the morning, it's worth a king's ransom. The French use it for pills and candles and hair ointments. The Turks carry it to Mecca. The Chinese are paying top dollar and want it to make pomanders. Dash it, there's not a man on this ship, other than me, knows what a pomander is."

The master diver moved over to where the others were standing to be sure his company had been paid in advance, in Mexican silver.

"Never heard of this hamper-grease and I think this fellow drinks," he said with an air of confidentiality.

*****

A diminutive sampan bobbed in the waves drifting sideways to the icy wind, nearly broaching. A small, improvised pole with the pre-annexation flag of Korea heightened its visibility. The currents of the East Sea, as it was known locally, carried it through a light snow squall. The sampan was directly on the steamship route between Pusan and Kobe. In it were three very simple baskets devoid of fancy edging.

Nestled in each basket - and well preserved by the sub-freezing temperatures -- lay a cleanly severed, and very pale, human head. Two heads were Asian. One with a cauliflower ear, and the second - perhaps the object of some grisly humor - with a pair of ill-fitting glasses on the tip of its nose. The third head was Occidental, a gentleman of means, and though the others were expressionless, this one held an expression of deep surprise. The hat that belonged to the third head had blown off and rested in the bilges. It was a strawboater with a distinctive blue and red band.

A statement had been made. To some, a message in a bottle would have been the time-honored method for casting a communication adrift -- to be read by the random discoverer --but to the apparently cold-hearted originators a more dramatic form of message had seemed more appropriate. It was, after all, "make see pidgin."

POSTLUDE

Naval Constructor Richard Pearson Hobson, hero of the Spanish-American War, skippered the blockship *Merrimac* into Havana harbor, where he failed to block the channel, was captured, and then exchanged. He was considered one of the three great naval heroes of that war, but not by all. He later became a member of the House of Representatives unpopular for his stands on women's suffrage, alcohol, drugs, the black soldiers in the Brownsville riots, and ironically for predicting war with Japan. In 1933, he was awarded the Medal of Honor for his service aboard *Merrimac*. He was in no way related to the hero of *Jade Rooster* who borrowed the name at a recruiter's suggestion.

There was no collier, *Pluto*. There was a *Saturn* of similar size and history, but her crew was entirely merchant marine. The U. S. Navy authorized naval personnel to serve aboard colliers, but the Navy was short of officers and men during this period and chose to use naval personnel they had aboard the combatant ships. The Naval Collier Service became the Naval Auxiliary Service in 1912. Asian merchant sailors aboard colliers were paid half what their received during this period, but in fairness that pay rate was high by Asian standards.

Baltimore, veteran of the Battle of Manila Bay, had left the Pacific and was in reserve in the Atlantic by the time portrayed in the *Jade Rooster*. Several sailors recruited in China and serving in the United States Navy participated in the Battle of Manila Bay aboard various ships, but they could not apply for U.S. citizenship under the Chinese Exclusion Act of 1882. They had fought for the U. S. but could not hold its citizenship. Admiral Dewey was disturbed by this situation and wrote several letters to Congress, to no avail.

Exclusion was a concern to the Japanese as well and the source of tension between the U. S. and Japan. Exclusion of Japanese at the time of *Jade Rooster* was under the "Gentlemen's Agreement of 1908" which became Federal law under the Immigration Act of 1924.

Buck dancing was the predecessor of tap-dancing. Ragtime music has withstood the test of time and minstrel shows have not. Josephus Daniels did not eliminate liquor Navy-wide until 1914. The distinction between right and left sleeve rates was eliminated after World War II.

The Office of Naval Intelligence was the U. S. Navy's primary source of intelligence from its establishment in the late 19th Century until the establishment of the Central Intelligence Agency in 1947. Its contributions to naval successes in the Pacific during WWII were invaluable.

The New York Naval Militia is one of the oldest Naval Militias in the country. Its members served in the Spanish-American War and have served in every naval conflict since.

There was a Captain George M. Colvocoresses, graduate of Norwich Academy Class of '31, who wrote a book on his Antarctic explorations and sued Admiral Farragut over prize money earned at Mobile Bay. He was a Greek orphan adopted by an American naval family. He was allegedly murdered in Bridgeport, Connecticut under suspicious circumstance. A George P. Colvocoresses, also of Norwich University, Class of '66, is listed as a U. S. N. midshipman by the Norwich Academy webpage and I believe rose to the rank of Rear Admiral USN.

The state of Connecticut was the center of arms and sewing machine manufacture during most of the 19th and 20th Centuries. It was long known as the home of the insurance industry, an industry which originated around insuring cargoes. Health and life insurance came later.

The pneumatic dynamite gun aboard *Vesuvius* was one of the U.S. Navy's earliest procurement disasters. The weapon could only be trained by swinging the entire ship and the ship was a shiphandler's nightmare. The weapon was shortly overtaken by technology. Perhaps things would have gone better, some said, if she had been named after an American, rather than a foreign, volcano. Then again we were beginning to see ourselves as a global navy.

Shanghai fell to the Japanese in 1937 and then to the Communists in 1947. If it were not famous by the 1930's, Marlene Dietrich made it notorious. "It took the company of more than one man to earn me the name of 'Shanghai Lil.'" It is one of the world's largest cities and the only large city whose name is also a verb.

Educator Jigoro Kano, father of judo, was an educator and a member of the International Olympic Committee. He died in 1938 on a return voyage from an IOC meeting in Cairo. Judo became an Olympic sport in 1964.

From a world history standpoint, neither the Japanese nor the Koreans monopolized the practice of execution by beheading and it could be said the French improved upon it slightly by attaching the art of knitting to its ceremonial aspects. However at the turn of the last century, Gilbert & Sullivan's The Mikado had immortalized the practice as one peculiarly Eastern in Western minds. To the north, the practice left its mark on the Korean landscape at Chòltu-san (Chop Heads Mountain) where 8,000 Korean Christians were beheaded. The Middle Kingdom continued the practice with enthusiasm and the scrapbooks of Asiatic Fleet sailors of the 'Twenties and 'Thirties were replete with Chinese execution photos taken with Brownies. The captured Allied commandos who participated in the second raid on Singapore during WWII were beheaded. It has been argued that the Japanese considered this was an honored, warrior's death.

Ambergris is no longer used in perfumes.

The Japanese subjugation of Korea was, if anything, more brutal than portrayed. Missionary school educated Koreans have provided a disproportionate portion of Korea's leadership beginning in the Japanese period and since. The Republic of South Korea was one of the 20th Century's economic miracles. Ironically, a portion of this miracle was derived from the more positive aspects of the Japanese dark period.

In early May, 1883, Emily Warren Roebling was the first person to cross the completed Brooklyn Bridge. "...She and a coachman had crossed over from Brooklyn in a new Victoria, its varnish gleaming in the sunshine. She had taken a live rooster along with her, as a sign of victory, and from one end of the bridge to the other, the men had stopped their work to cheer and lift their hats as she came riding by." After 14 years and 27 deaths, the Brooklyn Bridge over the East River was open, connecting the cities of New York and Brooklyn.

Her husband, Washington Roebling, the driving force behind the construction of the bridge had been confined to a bed in a darkened room for the past eleven years. Her husband while establishing the footings for the bridge had unknowingly contracted caisson's disease, an ailment which would be more commonly known among divers as "the bends." After her husband became bedridden, Mrs. Roebling had served as his intermediary supervising the work and reporting to her husband and the bridge trustees. Thousands from Brooklyn and Manhattan Island attended the dedication ceremony with President Chester A. Arthur and New York Governor Grover Cleveland. Designed by her late father-in-law John A. Roebling, the Brooklyn Bridge was the largest suspension bridge of its age and was considered the foremost engineering project of the 19th Century. A freak accident during the planning of the bridge had destroyed his health, too, and quiclkly claimed his life.

A rooster was the well-known symbol of victory in the late 19th Century and the early 20th Century.

Printed in the United States
63351LVS00001B/1-99

9 780977 997701